BRIGHT BLUE SKY AND GRAY SILENCE

826NYC BOOKS
372 FIFTH AVENUE
BROOKLYN, NY 11215

First 826NYC edition 2016

Manufactured in the United States of Brooklyn America
978-1-934750-71-1

The writing in this book was produced in spring of 2016 during an 826NYC in-schools project at the High School of Fashion Industries. Ms. Rebecca Eisenberg and Rebecca Darugar led the project with the help of 826NYC volunteers and Columbia Artists and Teachers.

Designed by Sarah Azpeitia
Edited by Alli Dunn, Jill Fitterling, Erin Furlong, Lindsay Griffiths, Caroline Knecht, Nora Pelizzari, Lauren Rogers, and Rachel Spurrier
Printed by Bookmobile

This program is supported, in part, by public funds from the New York City Department of Cultural Affairs in partnership with the City Council and the New York State Council on the Arts with the support of Governor Andrew M. Cuomo and the New York State Legislature.

Thank you to AT&T and Amazon for supporting this program.

826NYC is a nonprofit organization dedicated to supporting students ages 6-18 with their creative and expository writing skills, and to helping teachers inspire their students to write. Our services are structured around our belief that great leaps in learning can happen with one-on-one attention and that strong writing skills are fundamental to future success.

826NYC
372 Fifth Avenue
Brooklyn, NY 11215
718.499.9884
WWW.826NYC.ORG

BRIGHT BLUE SKY AND GRAY SILENCE

Personal Narratives by the Students at the High School of Fashion Industries

CONTENTS

xiii   **Letter From The Editorial Board**

xv   **Foreword by Sheri Booker**

WHEN THE GOING GETS TOUGH, WE KEEP GOING

21   My Second Home, *Sebastian Aguilar*

23   The Death That Changed It All, *Isiah Branch-El*

25   Jonathan, *Icis Feldman*

27   Cherished Moments, *Oulimata Ba*

28   Remembering, *Jenna Suriel*

29   Adventures In The Dominican Republic, *Jailene Salazar*

30   Hugs & Kisses, *Kamila Akabirova*

32   I Prefer My Room to a Hospital, *Ezri Gorostiza*

34   Bulwer Place, *Ashley Lopez*

36   Smoky Halls, *Amaya Contreras*

38   Tears of Excitement and Sadness, *Kimberly Marquez*

39   The Biggest Surprise, *Jasirah Nur*

40   Four Years Under, *Diavion Benn*

42   Disney World, *Emmanuella Reina*

45   Aspiring Princess, *Hennessy Jimenez*

46   The Spotlight, *Yailin Gachuz*

48   Au Naturale, *Jarai Ross-Mackey*

51   Up at the Catch, *Marylou Andrades*

53   For Some, *Halei Aviles*

55   Self-Righteous, *Kayla Nelson*

57   Serving Hard Time, *Juan Guzman*

59 Nothing to Something, *Madison Hornbrook*

60 Moment of Life, *Shanya Weathers*

62 222, *Shaniya Martinez*

65 My Special Place, *Cindy Morocho*

68 Figment of my Imagination, *Tennille Chong*

WHERE WE'RE FROM AND WHO WE LOVE

73 $2.75, *Gladys Bles*

76 Brownstone, *Ashley Laird*

78 Popcorn Fields, *Dawelys Almonte*

81 Along the Avenue, *Lisseth Aguilar*

84 Brooklyn Trails, *Mushfika Chowdhury*

86 Jersey City, *Alexis Caban*

89 House of Beloved, *Isis Jannierre Bates*

91 Stolen Safety, *Chevanie Peter Cunningham*

94 My Escape, *Keyanna Spann*

96 The House Across the Street, *Rashail Shakil*

99 Basement Chronicles, *Lauryn Vincent*

101 The Comfort Inn, *Mercedez Tiburcio*

104 Five-Sided Wall, *Yoselin Sarita*

106 Mother Nature, My Friend; Father Technology, My Enemy, *Anita Briggs*

108 Utopian Getaway, *Elysse Babooram*

110 The Antique Shop, *Alice Sungurov*

112 The Holy Trinity, *Samantha Berger*

114 Through the Dark, *Gelia Brador*

116 What Time Is It?, *Bonnie Lynch*

118 My Twin, *Aaliyah Fairweather*

120 How to Survive a Hurricane, *Aria Faziha Khandaker*

123 Maybe, *Natalie Gay*

125 The Waiting Game, *Angelica Lora*

127 What an Awful Place, *Nicole Quach*

130 Finding Me, *Lizet Cielo Velazquez*

132 I Remember School: Middle and High, *Kassandra Hernandez*

136   The Gym, *Jasmine Brooks*

138   Bigger Than You Think, *Sharoya Bracey*

141   Losing Life's Grip, *Chelsea James*

143   Where the Memories Lie, *Jessenia Guzman*

145   Memories, *Ashley Javier*

147   Love and Growing Up, *Treysha Robinson*

152   The Boy in the Trails, *Tyler Roarty*

154   Cocoon, *Natalie Ulloa*

WHERE WE GO AND WHAT WE CARRY WITH US

159   Myself Again, *Iyanna Webster*

160   The Sunset Painting, *Nicole Cruz Aparicio*

162   Up, *Daniel Cruz*

164   Night Marmalade, *Paris Jerome*

165   The Highline, *Natasha Santiago*

166   Enjoy and Appreciate, *Stephanie Pujols*

168   The Island of Excitement, *Bianca Jackson*

170   Tropical Paradise of Nassau, *Alexandria Haughton*

172   First Time on the Road, *Maria Paz Guerron*

177   The Best Memory, *Aaliyah Castillo*

178   My Little Blue Beach, *Kelfri Bueno*

180   My Fire Escape, *Fiona Briseño Meyer*

182   Boardwalk, *Elizabeth Canela*

185   The Lost Sister, *Samantha Alvarado*

187   The 17th of January, *Claudibel Batista*

189   A Place I Used to Call Home, *Shania James*

193   Long-Lost Grandfather, *Fanta Kante*

195   Bonds, *Shaziah La Van-Small*

199   San Francisco, *Tammy Leong*

201   Going Bananas for Bananas, *Amencis Berquin*

203   The Day My World Stopped, *Emily Martinez*

206   Heroes and Happy Endings, *Jully Patel*

208   Do You Know What I Mean?, *Nathalie Rosario*

210   A Day in Times Square, *Tiara Morene*

212   The Hood Called School, *Celine Pichardo*

214 A Tragic Night on the "B" Train, *Jada Lebell*

216 The Angel, *Annie Dong*

221 Getaway, *Zuairah Islam*

223 Old San Juan, *Danielle Jean-Louis*

225 School, *Iynn Lee*

226 Removing My Appendix, *Carmen Salas*

228 August 5th, *Charlize Torres*

230 Overdramatic, *Kiara Husbands*

232 A Drastic Change, *Onjalik Rasuul*

SEEING OURSELVES ABOVE THE CLOUDS

237 Behind the Big Walls, *Keilyn Mercado*

239 Reconnection, *Kadeem Aaron Lamorell*

245 What Is No Longer Ours, *Kianni Bradshaw*

247 A Little Bench in the Big Apple, *Maya Della*

249 The Hallway, *Alejandra Deleon*

252 Memories Can Happen Anywhere, *Shaniqua Blackwell*

255 Sol, *Natalie Candelario Herrera*

257 My Personal Little Bubble, *Mileidys Mosquera*

259 Just Get Up and Go, *Paula Ferreira*

261 Lunchroom Best Friend to Everyday Sister, *Tenia Poole*

262 A Colombian-American Education, *Anyela Coronado*

269 Remember, *Ruth Cabrera*

271 The Struggles of Being Me: Overcoming Stage Fright, *Chastity Glasby*

272 When Mean Girls Attack, *Tammy Fong*

276 Invincible, *Brittney Idehen*

279 Memories from Granite Street, *Justine Cooper*

282 Memories in the Park, *Derek Ronda*

283 The Sunset, *Liu Ying*

285 Personal Narrative, *Jarlyn Alvarez*

286 My Island Experience, *Sagine Teerath*

287 My Epiphany, *Akacia Thomas*

289 Trading the City for a Moment of Bliss, *Ana Sanchez*

291   How to Hold Your Depression Just a Bit Too Close, *Spencer Ayvas*

296   Bethpage, *Camren Hernandez*

299   I Am Home, *Susana Delossantos*

301   Hurt, *Abigail Perez*

304   Dark and Light, *Neftalin Rodriguez*

WE CRAVE THE MAYHEM

309   Limitless, *Alexis Baez*

311   Knockout, *Erica Johnson*

313   Little Shop of Treasures, *Jah China DeLeon*

316   Cardboard Chronicles, *Brandy Sarabia*

320   Away, *Jah Meeka Taylor*

322   Home, *Andrea Aviles*

324   Home Is Where the Heart Is, *Diana Garcia Martinez*

326   Hospital Run!, *Hilary Leon*

327   Pickle, *Olivia Gigante*

329   A Valuable Lesson from Growing up in a Nursing Home, *Patricia Santana*

332   That Valentine's Day, *Felicity Goodman*

334   Grilled Cheese Sandwich, *Elizabeth Vanderhorst*

336   The Borderline, *Enyasha Harris*

339   Cucina, *Sephira Bryant*

341   Nirvana, *Nadine Roca*

342   Eating at Restaurants Alone, *Samantha Duer*

344   Experiences in 138, *Asatta Bradford*

346   Advice to a Younger Me, *Amaris Larose*

348   Speak Up! Let Your Thoughts Flow, *Arianna Alcide*

350   To Give Time to Animals and Get Annoyance Back, *David Morales*

354   Grace Beauty Salon Transformation, *Shaimelys Marcano Santos*

357   Tell the Heavens I am Done Waiting, *Fatha Alma*

358   White Noise, *Asia Reddish*

360   Middle School, *Shirley Rosemond*

362   An American in America, *Sukari Webb*

364   Home Sweet Home, *Jinet Almanzar*

365   Shamari, *Mariah Amador*

367   Money Given, *Akira Lewis*

368   Lunch, *Sophia Mohammed*

373   My Life Was a Stage: Survival Guide, *Audra Pryce*

376   Tranquility Calls, *Rachel Hocher*

383   **Meet The Authors**

461   **Acknowledgements**

463   **About 826NYC and Our Programs**

Dear Readers,

The personal narratives in this book will take you to some places you know and to others you've never been before. You'll step into the lives of New York City students who meet every day at the High School of Fashion Industries but who have different backgrounds, interests, and experiences. We are artists, trendsetters, and musicians. We are unique, confident, and ambitious. We are indefinable.

In Ms. Eisenberg's class in March and April of 2016 we had the opportunity to work with the staff and volunteers from 826NYC, as well as with Columbia Artists and Teachers on our personal narratives. Every Wednesday for six weeks we wrote independently, collaborated with our classmates, and crafted the pieces bound within this anthology.

There are themes and ideas within this book that you may relate to and others that may surprise you. Some stories take place in familiar places and others will take you beyond the boundaries of space.

We hope you enjoy.

Love,

Lisseth Aguilar
Annie Dong
Zuairah Islam
Tammy Leong
Jarai Ross-Mackey
Carmen Salas
Alice Sungurov
Sukari Webb

Foreword

by SHERI BOOKER

When I was first asked to write the foreword for this collection of essays, I jumped at the opportunity to read the works of the young writers at the High School of Fashion Industries for two reasons: first, there is a certain rawness that pours out of young minds when prompted to write, and second, I know the power of seeing your work in print at this age. I also know that having students write about place is a journey in itself. And who doesn't need a great escape every now and then?

There are many things that define us, but the places we go leave indelible footprints on the memories stored in our minds. As we create our internal roadmaps on this journey of life, it is the reminder of the people, the feelings, and the signature of time that pushes us forward or reminds us how to return home. Sometimes we are haunted. Other times we are healed.

Contrary to what some people may expect from a group of young writers, the pieces in this anthology are strong and at times brutally honest. These courageous authors have taken ownership of their narratives and committed to telling their truths. They have managed to dig deep inside themselves, pulling out the difficult details of life-changing events.

Even as high school students, they have found the beauty in life's challenges. They have given themselves permission to dream, feel, and remember. Some of their stories were downright funny. Others left me on the brink of tears. The depth of their writing inspired me. It takes heart to write like this—even in short pieces.

One of the greatest challenges for a writer is finding your own voice. However, every writer in this project has not only found their voice but also mastered it. Many of the pages read like poetry. The rich details jumped off the page, and I was often left wanting more.

As I read each piece, I couldn't help but to think of all the places that have shaped me over the years. I felt a wide range of emotions. I was saddened that the Baltimore that raised me is long and gone. I felt a sense of adventure when I thought back to my time living in the South African bush. I thought of the funeral home where I worked, the hospital room where my mother stayed, the classrooms where I went to college. I remembered the sights and sounds, but most of all I remembered the people connected to those places.

Strong writing connects readers to the most intimate parts of themselves. I have not written anything since my mother died two years ago. Maybe I was too afraid to return to the place where she left me. But the stories here have encouraged me to get ready to go there.

The essays in this book are a reminder that place has no boundaries. That it is real and imagined. That it is beautiful and heartbreaking. That we carry little pieces of the places that touch us inside and that they eventually shape us into the people we become. We can only hope that this is the beginning and that we will read more from these writers in the future. These stories will forever have a place in my heart.

BRIGHT BLUE SKY
AND GRAY SILENCE

WHEN THE GOING GETS TOUGH, WE KEEP GOING

My Second Home

by SEBASTIAN AGUILAR

It was a crisp, dull morning. My father woke me up from my very deep sleep and told me to get dressed. All I remember is getting into the car and my dad driving. It was endless; I felt like we were driving in a labyrinth. It felt as if something was off, the odd feeling you get when you are about to present in class. The feeling was also mixed with odd pain inside; I didn't know where. After many curves on a hill with very narrow roads, we stopped. The sky was so grey and cold that you could barely see anything in the mist-filled morning sky. My dad informed me that my grandfather was in a car accident, and I realized we were there to try and pick up the car that was dangling on the side of the hill. My grandfather was pushed off, which made his car tip and fall down the hill. I didn't really react; I was very young. I just stood there not really understanding the tragic event that happened to one of my favorite people in the world, not knowing my loving grandfather had passed away.

I stood there watching everything that was going on. It was as if it was all in slow motion. The sounds were not there; it was all silent. After that it was pretty much a blur. All I remember is his funeral. I remember the thousands and thousands of people that showed up to his funeral to say their goodbyes. I remember the sound of everyone crying and sobbing, not believing he passed away.

Whenever I go to Mexico, I will see it as the place I lost a person that I loved, but I will also see it as the place where I have family. The place I can go to seek comfort, where my uncles, aunts, and cousins live. I now see it as my second home, filled with childhood memories. I will always miss my grandfather, and whenever I visit Mexico, my family and I always try to visit him in the cemetery. Mexico will always be a place where I lost someone I loved but that is also my second home.

The Death That Changed It All

by ISIAH BRANCH-EL

Last words I heard you say were, "Come over this weekend. We're gonna work on your driving skills." Everything went wrong so fast…

Utica Avenue, busy as usual. Streets full of mean-mugged people trying to get to their destination. My cousin Say, Uncle Jay, friend Rico, and I were waiting for a taxi to stop for us. We were on our way to the Kings Plaza Mall to buy some new clothes. After about five taxis drove right past us, an all-black taxi with deep tinted windows and a gold license plate that read "86E0AL5" stopped in front of us. Before we could even settle down into the taxi, the driver began speeding to beat the red light. Only halfway to the mall, my uncle got a call from my grandmother. Even though she had a soft voice, I could hear tears coming from the other line. We all grew curious about why my grandma was so emotional.

I could hear her mutter softly, "Daz is dead. We need you guys to come back to the hospital!"

I could feel my heart being broken into a million pieces, a river of tears pouring down my face. I really couldn't believe it; the man who raised me like his own child was dead. I could feel my uncle grabbing my cousin and me closer to hug us. All I could do was cry. The driver stopped the car to give us some tissues to wipe the tears, every tissue drowned with tears just like the one before it. I could feel the sadness and guilt coming from the driver's face. We gave him the address and asked him to drive us back home. As we approached the house, I could see my aunt in her car trying to hold herself together. She told us she would drive us to the hospital. It was a long trip from Brooklyn to the hospital, all the way in New Jersey. Only a quarter of the way there, I could feel myself falling asleep from the smooth, quiet ride.

As I opened my eyes, I could see my family all together outside the car holding hands, crying with one another. I stayed in the car for a few minutes crying to myself, reminiscing on the memories I had shared with my Uncle Daz.

I thought to myself, "My family needs me. I have to be strong for them! Daz would have wanted me to be!" I stepped out of the car and could see nothing but emotional faces. One by one, I gave each person a tight hug and told them I love them and to stay strong. Head down, hands in my pocket, I could feel myself growing weaker with every step I took to the room. I was finally outside Daz's room.

I wiped my face clean of all my tears and finally walked in the room. I could see him connected to all these wires. I walked up to him and held his hand tightly and cried in his chest until I was dried of tears. As I took a step back, I looked at Daz one more time.

The last words I told him were, "I love you, Uncle Daz!"

Jonathan

by ICIS FELDMAN

Jonathan was my cousin. He was my favorite cousin; he made me feel safe and secure. When I was upset or wasn't talking to anyone, he would always cheer me up and make me laugh by tickling me and doing goofy things. He was always smiling and had a positive attitude, and everyone else around him did, too. His personality just had an impact on people's moods and energy so easily. I remember copying everything he did; I wanted to be just like him and make everyone smile and laugh.

The morning I found out he passed away, I felt the world stop. I remember that morning like it was yesterday. Even though I was eight in the fourth grade and am now fifteen in the tenth grade, that really is an unforgettable day for me. I was so confused and couldn't understand what was told to me. I woke up to my mom crying on the edge of my bed. She was on the phone talking to somebody. I remember being so curious to whom she was talking and why she was crying. Instead of asking, I waited patiently for her to get off the phone. I don't know why I waited patiently. I think it was that I was scared to ask because I just knew it was going to be bad news.

When she got off the phone, she looked at me. Her eyes were so watery and her nose was red. I stared into her eyes waiting for her to explain to me what happened. I was so nervous about the news I was about to receive that I began to tear before she even opened her mouth. When she saw me start to tear, she wiped her tears away and tried to pull herself together, to be strong enough to tell me such terrible news.

She took a deep breath and told me, "I just got off the phone with your Aunt Melissa." She took a long pause…then continued, "She told me that Jonathan passed last night." It took me a while. I just sat up and sat there. I felt stuck.

Then when I finally processed what she told me, I burst out in tears. I was young and a little child; it was so hard for me, the pain was unbearable. I understood that people don't live forever, and I understood that eventually people I really love are going to pass away, but I thought that those people would leave after you grew old with them. I was hurt that he was young. Jonathan was sixteen. That killed me inside; I didn't know young people die. As dumb as that sounds, that's what I thought when I was eight. I continued to cry and scream. As I did so, I tried to ask my mom many questions. The first question I asked was, "Will I ever see him again?"

She answered by saying, "He will always be with you, and one day when it's your time to pass, you will be reunited with him." However that just raised more questions like, "Why do people have to die?" "Why did he have to die?" "Why was he so young?" etc. Most of the questions I asked were "why" questions. I just couldn't understand and just wanted him to come back.

Cherished Moments

by OULIMATA BA

Bronx Grand Concourse. That's where I would spend my weekends. My dad, stepmom, and stepbrother lived there. Sometimes I felt like it was hard to adjust, to actually call them my "family." But eventually I felt the spark. My stepmom was diagnosed with cancer, breast cancer. This was sometime during 2005 and 2006. Of course, as a child, I wasn't aware of her condition. I only recently found out, and when I did, I was appalled, but then it came to me. All the hospitalizations, the sadness, and the sorrows explained. I truly felt bad for the simple fact that at first I was acting like Cinderella's evil sisters towards her. It was a moment, and to this day, when I hear her name, I have a mental image of this memory. I was coming out of the bathroom and looked to my right. There she was, sitting on her bed in so much pain and with surgical marks on her breasts. That hit me so hard, like how a hammer hits a nail through wood. Ever since then, I cherish all the moments we experienced together. God bless her soul. Bronx Grand Concourse, where my weekends are no longer the same.

Remembering

by JENNA SURIEL

I know I wasn't there, but I was there, you know what I mean? As I walk, I can feel her in the ocean just swimming, playing around, and in just seconds, she isn't anymore. Every time I come to Long Island Beach, it's the same, remembering her steps on the sand, sun hurting in the summer like always. As I walk on this beach, only bad thoughts come to mind like, *why didn't anyone help? Where were the lifeguards?* As my family and I walk, we're so quiet, looking around seeing happy faces, relaxed faces. We see people enjoying themselves while we try to be cautious, worrying whether we're safe or not because no one saved her while she was trying to catch her last breath.

The best part of this trip is when it ends, knowing it is the last time we will be here. We have flashbacks about the last time she was with us alive, her bright personality making everyone around her happy. That's who she was to all of us.

But then I remember that I'm actually standing in front of the beach and my sister is no longer with us...with me.

Adventures In The Dominican Republic

by JAILENE SALAZAR

At a beautiful beach in the Dominican Republic, eating fried fish, watching the calm waves reach the sandy shoreline. My family and I always enjoyed visiting the sparkling, clear, blue body of water. We never failed to come here; the small wooden boats that take nonstop trips to hidden caves were parked, waiting for tourists to go on a wet and wild adventure. One time, we rode a boat that took us to a cave, and we found all types of mysterious sea monsters. We found a pink starfish that poked my hand when I held it. I was afraid to even touch it because I thought it would magically bite me, just like how I'd seen on TV. As we rode back to the beach, I wondered for how long the starfish had been laying on the rock. When we finally got back with this treasure, everyone took pictures of it. We decided to leave the creature on the sand so that the endless waves could wash it back to its starfish family.

Hugs and Kisses

by KAMILA AKABIROVA

It all starts with the drive. Usually the elders sit in the front, making small chit-chat and gossiping like in *Okay!* magazine. The younger ones, including me, sit in the back with an array of pillows and blankets that make us feel like we're on cloud nine. Everyone makes small jokes, looking too happy with smiles reaching their eyes.

The rest stop is one of my favorite parts: the gossip sessions over handfuls of sunflower seeds, making plans about the future beach house, drinking sweet tea, and eating small snacks packed in clear plastic bags.

Once we get to the beach house, we make several trips from the car to the white marble kitchen that is always a hassle to clean. The pounds of groceries and life necessities fill every square inch of the kitchen. The first day doesn't consist of much except for cleaning and watching old soap operas on DVD or any new Turkish show that everyone seems to rave about.

The days are usually spent on the beach, unless you join the more adventurous of the group who walk to the last pier and plummet to their deaths. The afternoons and evenings are when memories are made, playing card games for dares or on the sunflower cushion swing. Many days, if the rain is pouring, everyone is in the kitchen making eggplant salsa or any new recipes someone found on Facebook or Pinterest.

However, when the sun is shining bright and the water is warm, but somehow still refreshing, when laughter fills the air or the sound of water flushing away the sand with each new wave, everything seems worth it. The good and the being together bring smiles to everyone's faces for what the next day might hold.

I Prefer My Room to a Hospital

by EZRI GOROSTIZA

A pillow lays behind my head, comforting me as I'm dragged into the worlds of my books. My room is here to keep reality on the other side of the door. The sounds of arguments and my dog barking outside my room are ignored at first until I realize my parents have returned home from their week-long vacation in Virginia. They've brought back bags filled with food that would probably expire soon, so it is pointless to keep.

It is almost 7:00 PM and my mom isn't feeling well. I watch over my mom as my dad leaves to get himself pizza. It's been about five minutes after my dad has left. My mother is in the bathroom, door closed and locked, and she's violently throwing up. I repeatedly ask her if she wants to go to the emergency room. She refuses multiple times before she finally gives in and agrees to be taken to the emergency room. In a rush I grab my phone and call my dad so he can rush home. My dad gets home quickly, and we rush to get my mother to the hospital.

After that everything becomes a blur to me. I remember the nurses trying so many times to get the I.V. into my mother's arm. I also remember the pain I felt for my mother as I stood there holding her I.V. bag as she threw up. I remember the panic that consumed me; my heart felt like it was in my throat and my hands were shaking like I had been standing outside for hours. I was in the hospital until 2:00 in the morning. My dad deciding to drive me home because I had already gone through enough.

My dad drops me off at home and leaves me there by myself and he goes back to the hospital. I lie down back on my bed, not able to erase the image of my mom grabbing my hand because her hands were freezing cold. I lie there in my bed, letting the comforting feeling of my room relieve me of the stress and panic I've been feeling for the six to seven hours. And I quickly fall asleep.

I wake up in my room with my mother lying next to me. I move closer and hug her. We both lie there and fall back asleep even though it is already morning.

Bulwer Place

by ASHLEY LOPEZ

My mom and my aunt have been trying so hard for three and a half years to get this house. Thankfully on November 30, 2015, my lovely mother closed on it. Calling three phones at a time, my mother yelled, "We got it! We got the house!" I was so excited and relieved that we finally could have our own house. I could finally get my own room, decorate how I wanted, and move furniture without asking my sister if she liked it first.

Right now, our new house is currently under construction. The worker is named Nardo. He really knows what he's doing and does it really fast. He actually finished my kitchen and my aunt's kitchen in two weeks, renewing everything. Our whole kitchen is new. It looks like a whole different house! Oh, how excited I am to sweep our new gray wood floor in our kitchen and to organize our brand-new beige cabinets. Everything just goes together. It all blends in!

When I first saw the brand-new house, I couldn't stop smiling. I couldn't believe that our dream was finally coming true that after nearly four years of trying so hard and almost giving up a couple of times, our house was finally our house. We could finally say it was ours. I rushed to the side door running up to the second floor, which is where our apartment is, zooming through the first floor, where my aunt and her two kids lived, and going to the side entrance of my apartment. The door was already broken down and the staircase led to the brand-new kitchen. My mom, sister, and I were all cheesing, our eyes getting small and our cheeks reaching our ears. I speed-walked to my room to look at my brand-new floor.

I can't wait to paint my new room and not share with my sister. I will eventually miss my old house's neighborhood and location and having stores in walking distance, but Bulwer Place is my home now!

Smoky Halls

by AMAYA CONTRERAS

It was a late August night when my dad dropped me off at home. My dad was leaving to go back to his humble apartment, just over ten blocks away, when my mom began to set up her room so we could watch one of our favorite movies, *My Big Fat Greek Wedding*. Just as we were about to watch the movie, my mom's phone started ringing. My mom answered, slight irritation evident in her face because this always happens. As it turns out, the phone call was from my aunt who lives in the same building as us. She called to tell us to get out of the building because a fire had started on the side of the building.

At first, my mother and I thought my aunt was just joking, but the truth soon became clear. We both dashed to the front door and opened it just to find out that the hallway was clouded to the brim with eye-watering smoke. After slamming the door shut, we made a beeline to my room. Trying to pry open the window to the fire escape was a struggle, but we managed. I rushed to yank on my Ugg boots, as they were the first pair of shoes in my line of vision.

My mom, however, was not as swift with the shoes as I was. She had to settle for a pair of flip flops and was struggling to get out onto the old, rickety fire escape. My mother claims that she saw me bounding down the second floor staircase just as she was getting out of the window. In my defense, I was a terrified nine-year-old, so speed was my only option. Soon enough, I did make it to the ground when I spotted many familiar faces. My aunt and two little cousins stood out because they had a brightly colored blanket wrapped around them. They were sitting in one of our neighbor's cars along with our neighbor's kids.

My mother eventually made it to the ground. I got into the car with my younger cousins while our parents tried to find out what exactly happened. Later that evening, we all learned that apartment 1C was the source of the fire. It was an electrical fire, so there was really no damage to the building with the exception of the charred door, of course. We were never told exactly how the traumatizing incident was caused, but it has stuck with me for years, making me alert every time a vehicle equipped with a blaring siren passes by, and in my neighborhood that's pretty common.

Though the experience was at first a lingering memory with the smoky odor everywhere I went, I've learned to live with it and to learn from it. You can't control everything that life throws at you, and worrying about it won't solve anything. All in all, no amount of stress will affect events of the past, but that doesn't mean that you should forget what happened.

Tears of Excitement and Sadness

by KIMBERLY MARQUEZ

February 17, I walked into the airport with the sound of wheels from luggage being pulled to the check-in. So much excitement is in JFK airport; you're either leaving with joy or leaving with tears on your face. I had been given $100 to do anything I wanted with until I got to Peru. I was nervous to get on that plane because I hadn't seen my family from Peru in years. My thoughts were eating me inside as I worried about what they would think of me. On the plane, my legs were shaking, yet it felt so good to go back home to where I was born.

On March 8, I walked into the airport in Peru with the most important people to me. I checked in with everyone that was going back to New York, Colombia, or Spain. While in that line, sadness started within me. The sadness of it all was that my mom's son, who she had raised, had been missing for days just before I left. My tears were running down my face until I got to the plane.

The Biggest Surprise

by JASIRAH NUR

During the summertime, my mom got really sick. I remember feeling super bad, and I really wanted to be for her surgery. The only issue is that my mom lives in New Orleans. So I was trying to figure out how I could fly out there and surprise her! I told my mom's friend who lives with her that I wanted to surprise her. Let's just say she flew me out there within the next few days. It was so nerve-wracking. I was on the plane all alone, and it was my first time going out there. When I got off the plane, I was so scared. I was in a whole new state that I'd never been to. I called my mom's friend to see where I needed to take the cab to. She told me to me to meet them in a restaurant. When I got out of the cab and into the restaurant, I saw her right away. Her back was turned to me, so she couldn't see me. When I tapped her, her face got so happy. She started crying because she was so excited to see me, and she had no idea about the surprise. It was such a special moment because she was beyond happy.

Four Years Under

by DIAVION BENN

Tall palm trees towered over the pool area, and lawn chairs stretched along the paths. I had just gotten a new bathing suit, and I had completely no idea how to swim. I was about four or five years old and had a floatie and arm floats. I was surprised that they actually made me float, so I went jumping into six-foot-deep pools. My family were all in one huge pool, and I had continued to run and jump in the pool and paddle back to the steps. I did this the whole time.

Then my uncle made me take off the floaties so he could teach me to float on my own. I was extremely scared. When I finally found out that I couldn't learn to float (to this day), I went back to my floatie, continuously jumping into the water. All this time, while I was trying to have fun in the teens pool, I completely missed the children's area.

One too many times I jumped into the pool. Despite the fact that I had really bad asthma, I kept running around and jumping into the pool. The last time I jumped wasn't intended to be my last.

I paddled out of the pool from my previous jump, and I ran around to the side of the pool, my usual routine. As I got ready to jump, the air blew differently. It hit my skin roughly, but I proceeded to jump. While my body was in the air, my floatie slipped off, and my innocent, floatless body shredded through the chlorine water, and for three seconds I died.

I saw everything a four-year-old could go through in three seconds, and I didn't know what to do. Then a girl jumped into the pool after me. She was about fourteen years old and could swim. I grabbed the strange girl's arm and, choking, asked her to bring me to the steps. She brought me and asked me if I was okay. I nodded and ran to cry to my aunt. For the rest of the time, I sat quietly. Even looking at a bucket of water spilling over children became too much.

I've been frightened of water ever since. I hate being surrounded by water. Oh what fun times in Florida, six feet under, four years old under sea level.

Disney World

by EMMANUELLA REINA

It was almost ten years ago, but I remember it like it was yesterday. Going to Disney World is a little kid's dream, but on that night, it was my worst nightmare. I was about six or seven years old, a chubby little girl amazed and in awe in the midst of all the princesses, cartoons, and magic mice that represented and made up my childhood. We had been at the Disney World resort in Orlando, Florida, for a couple of days. I felt as if I was in paradise, riding all the kiddie rides and Ferris wheels, drinking tea with Cinderella, and dancing with Minnie. It was all so exciting and amazing to me, and I felt so joyful and ecstatic to know what each day would bring me.

The resort was fantastic as well. The food court, gift store, and front desk were divided from the hotel rooms by an enormous display of various Disney characters. Buzz Lightyear towered over the palm trees as Mr. and Mrs. Potato Head were shoulder-to-shoulder over the parking lot right by Goofy. They led to a huge gate into the hotel rooms. I was so amazed at all of this, well, for the moment.

That night, we had come home from the park, Epcot. I was so tired but a good tired, and we were in the food court buying milk for my little brother, who was one year old at the time. Being the foolish toddler I was, I started to grow impatient and began wandering around the food court. I casually ended up in the gift store and started fooling around, playing with the stuffed animals and cowboy hats. I tried to walk in the Rapunzel plastic heels and as I swirled around, holding the gold button, and wearing the crystal tiara, I didn't realize it was 11:50 PM. I had wandered off for a good twenty-five minutes. I looked and inspected the huge crowd of happy families, and my parents were nowhere in sight. I retraced my steps and walked around the whole store to see if they were in here looking for me, but nothing. I was trying my best to remain calm but felt my stomach drop and my hands get sweaty. I took a deep breath and walked to the food court. "They have to be here," I thought out loud. I walked through the food court a good three times, inspecting every table, chair, and person in sight. I still couldn't find them. I went to the bathroom and waited to see if my mom was in the stalls, but she was nowhere to be found. I took another deep breath as I felt my face getting warm with fear and anxiety. I stopped in the lobby and thought, "I know where they are! They must have gone to the hotel room."

I jumped up and ran to the hotel room entrance as my Crocs squeaked step by step. I came across the big gate entrance and hesitated. I'd never walked through this long alley by myself before and especially not at twelve in the morning. I gulped as I thoroughly reconsidered this decision. I tensed up a bit as I started squeaking past the gate. Buzz Lightyear no longer looked like a welcoming hero. Goofy didn't look goofy anymore, and Minnie's smile taunted me. These toy statues looked so scary and dark that I shivered. This was the longest and loneliest walk of my life. I finally got to the other side of the alley and went through the other gate with Woody, whose eyes looked into my soul. I ran fast into the gates with relief. No one was in sight, but I was less tense because I made it past the gates of hell. I ran up the four dark and dreary flights of stairs, but I saw no one. I felt so skeptical and as if something was going to pop up and grab me. I felt tears roll down my cheeks as I realized my parents weren't in our hotel room. The lights were off and the door locked, and my heart dropped. I had to go back all by myself. I sniffled as I realized, "You can do this, Emma." So I ran as fast as I possibly could down those stairs and that long alleyway to those gates. I had never run that fast in my life. I gasped for air as I approached the gift store, then I heard my name on the loudspeaker "Again, may Emmanuella Reina please report to the front desk." I sighed with so much relief and I walked to the front desk. There were my parents and brother waiting for me. They looked so relieved, and so did I. I ran to them and gave them a great, big hug. Boy, was I happy.

Aspiring Princess

by HENNESSY JIMENEZ

Growing up as a child living in New York, I was blessed with my little sister, Helen, and older brother, Kenneth, and my mother and father. My mother works as a paraprofessional and my father is a CO in Rikers Island. We all did well in school. We were very social and friendly children. Because of our good behavior, our father took us on vacation very frequently, whether it was two days or two weeks, or even two months. My favorite place to go was Walt Disney World. I remember we went every year for seven years in a row. My dream was to be an actress on Disney Channel. It was my desire to be recognized in at least one of the Disney Princess Plays. Eventually, I was. I was called to volunteer in Cinderella's ball dance. They dressed me up and hundreds of people watched me. The feeling was graceful. I felt like a true princess. I had a purple sparkly dress on, a sparkly tiara, and little heels. My hair was long and curly and my tan made me look foreign. I felt beautiful because I was. Since then I realized I still do want to pursue my career of being an actress. I fell in love with the attention.

The Spotlight

by YAILIN GACHUZ

Growing up, I enjoyed the runway. I enjoyed being the center of attention and dressing up in beautiful gowns. I enjoyed walking in heels, even if it meant enduring the pain later. I liked feeling pretty and being pampered. I participated in two pageants when I was little. The first didn't go so well, but the second was the most memorable experience I've ever had. This pageant was looking for three girls of different ages and ethnicities to represent an Argentinian city. At the time, I was ten, and all I cared about was winning. I only cared about having the perfect dress, the perfect shoes, and the perfect hairstyle. I was nervous and petrified because I didn't want to mess up. In my age category, there were two other contestants. When I was next to them, I felt unsure about myself. One girl was tall and the other girl spoke Spanish fluently and had a million-dollar smile. They had what I lacked. Even though I felt petite and dull, I still tried my best.

The day of the show, I walked the runway with the brightest smile and flaunted my stunning dress. I walked with confidence, with my shoulders straight and head held high. As I got to the center of the runway, the lights and camera were on me. This was where all the magic happened. The stage represented all of our eagerness and excitement we had for the show. As I walked, I realized I didn't have to be nervous. It was just a competition that wasn't going to have a huge impact on my life, so I just walked the best I could, and I was confident.

The other two girls I was competing against were beautiful, but we were all different, and that was my power. My uniqueness was what made me win. I was only worried about myself and understood that winning wasn't everything. I won because of the practice and dedication I had for this pageant. I didn't need to have specific qualities; I just had to be myself, and I was happy with that.

Au Naturale

by JARAI ROSS-MACKEY

Growing up with natural, un-permed, coily hair was hard for me. I remember the first time that I felt self-conscious about my hair. I was about four or five years old in my Pre-K daycare center. I was wearing my hair out in my natural afro, or as five-year-old me called it "Susie Carmichael hair" (from *Rugrats*). I was on the playground when a girl named Jeremy asked, "Why is your hair like that?" in a sort of disgusted tone. Jeremy's hair wasn't even cute; she had these little bunchy knots scrambled all over her head with barrettes clipped to what little hair she actually had. By this age no one was really saying anything about my hair except to call it cute or pretty, so when Jeremy made a comment, it was unfamiliar to me. I responded with a confused, "Huh?" But then the other kids chimed in and started questioning and commenting on my hair. At that moment I just broke out into tears. It felt as if something was wrong with me.

When I entered elementary school, I was also teased for wearing my hair in different styles. I was teased for wearing my hair in an afro, ponytails, mohawks, and even simple braided hairstyles. Someone always had something to say. I went to a charter school on the Lower East Side, so a lot of the kids that attended were mostly white or Hispanic. Each class consisted of about fifty to twenty children, so there were only about four black kids, and out of those four, two of them were girls. Some of the black girls had their natural hair braided, but others had extensions, relaxers, and perms.

When I entered fifth grade, I got a teacher named Mrs. Barfield. Mrs. Barfield was different from other teachers because not only was she black, she was black with natural hair. We used to talk about different things to do to our hair, and she was just one of my favorite teachers.

When I entered middle school, there were still a couple black girls per classroom. There were very few "natural girls," and I was probably the only girl that actually maintained her natural hair all throughout middle school. Around this time, my mother had decided to do the "big chop." The "big chop" was when she cut off her permed hair and started growing out the rest of her hair, and I really admired how my mother did that. Middle school was also when I started getting asked that annoying question that probably every "natural girl" has heard at least once if not more: "Have you ever straightened your hair?" I would always respond with annoyance in my voice, "No, I've never straightened my hair before," and some would say something similar to "You would look so nice with your hair straightened. Why don't you do it one day?" Oh, I don't know, maybe because first, I actually like my hair the way it is, and second, I don't want damaged hair. It was just so frustrating having to hear people ask about me changing my hair, especially when it was the same people asking over and over again.

When I was getting ready to enter high school, I was nervous that there would be some of the same experiences that I had had in middle and elementary school. When I actually got to high school, it wasn't as bad as I thought it would be. There was, for the first time since pre-K, a majority of black students in a more diverse environment, mostly girls, and a good amount were "natural girls." This school was full of black and Hispanic students who wore their hair natural, permed, with extensions, and weaves. I still get asked questions about my hair, but I feel that my hair is more appreciated because there are people who actually want hair like mine.

People should embrace what they have and not care about other people's opinions. Going through the experiences I had growing up, I learned how to embrace my natural beauty and not to get mad or emotional at what other people think of me. It has also made me a stronger person. I wear my hair the way I do, for myself and not for anyone else. While "going natural" may be a trend for others, for me it's my lifestyle because I am natural.

Up at the Catch

by MARYLOU ANDRADES

My body goes numb as my mind spins with my coach's words and the feeling of excitement and nervousness. Waiting at the start of the race course, I feel the anxiety rushing through my veins. Everything goes in slow motion, the water flowing beside me; the coxswain's voice and every movement around me stops. We hear the call "All rowers up at the catch," and I feel the pressure intensify. As I anticipate the call "Attention! Row!" I close my eyes, and I can feel a heavy weight on my shoulders, because if I mess up, it will affect everyone in the boat. The adrenaline overcomes the emotional and physical pain, and every single word my coach has ever told me passes through my mind at once.

"Arms out, body over."

"Accelerate at the drive."

"Stay consistent."

"Don't be complacent."

I stare my coxswain in the eye. She gives a reassuring look that shows she is counting on me, and at that very moment at the catch, we all become one!

It was state championships in Saratoga, New York. It was the biggest and most important race for the novice team because it would be our last until the next spring. That very moment, the start of the race, will stay with me forever. The excitement, anxiety, and chaos taught me to believe not only in myself but also in my team. The big decision on if this sport was for me was at stake. Such a big decision for a fourteen-year-old girl! I knew it would take a lot of hard work and dedication, but I was up for the whole package; I strived for pain and victory. At that instant, up at the catch, I became the athlete I am today.

For Some

by HALEI AVILES

While for some kids coming out as being gay or lesbian to their parents is easy, for me it was much harder. I knew my parents would always accept me as their daughter, but it was the fear of hearing what they had to say. Before telling my parents, I had to actually find myself first. Finding myself took time; it was an actual thought process. I went through the process of thinking, *Is this actually how I feel, or is it just a phase*? I knew I felt this sort of attraction toward girls when I started developing a huge crush on my best friend.

As months went by, I soon developed the courage to tell my parents. Unfortunately, I didn't choose the best way of telling them. I remember it was a Wednesday in mid-April, and I was sitting on the couch debating whether or not to tell my parents. My hands began to shake, and tears streamed down my face as I started a "group chat" via text with my mom and dad. I don't exactly remember what I said, but it was somewhere along the words of "I like girls."

As my phone began to ring, it was my mom. She simply said, "Halei, what's going on?"

All I replied was, "I'm sorry."

She replied, "We'll talk when I get home."

My dad just said, "It's okay; I love you either way."

When my mom came home, she looked at me for a while and said, "You know I love you, right?" then gave me a hug and kiss.

Self-Righteous

by KAYLA NELSON

Self-righteous: convinced of one's own righteousness, especially in contrast with the actions and beliefs of others.

I guess I can say the way I think of myself has changed. I am not scared to be me or to voice my opinions. I am not scared to love myself and where I am from just because others may not approve. I am not scared to feel confident in myself, even if others call me cocky. Truth be told, it took me so long to get to this point of respecting and loving myself that, yes, I can say I'm a little self-righteous.

Growing up in Canarsie wasn't always easy. In my neighborhood was a big mix of all the Caribbean islands. So you have your Jamaicans and your Trinidadians, your Guyanese and your Grenadians, and then a bigger population of Haitians. Not many people liked Haitians when I was younger, so things were harder. I would say where I'm from, and then the teasing would start. People would bring it up, and, I won't lie, it kind of tore me apart.

But then again, I can say that since then the way I think of myself has changed. I am not scared to be Haitian. I am not scared to correct people and say, "Well this is only one part of me because I'm also Cherokee Indian." I am not scared to love where I am from despite what people have to say. It took me years to get here and have so much confidence in my culture, and honestly, I think we're amazing people. So, yes, I can say I'm a little self-righteous.

Not having my father in my life took a toll on me. I mean, he was there for a little while, but he couldn't let the violence go and they took him away from me. As a little girl I didn't really understand—I thought I did something wrong, and it turned into my thinking that I couldn't be loved by any man. Yes, there were other men in my life, like my grandpa and my uncles, but they never matched up to the real thing. I grew up surrounded by family members who have their dads in their lives. Now that I look at it, I'm the only one who didn't have her dad in her life.

But the way I think of myself has changed. I am not scared to say that yes, my dad is in jail but his life doesn't reflect on mine. I am not scared to say that yes, when I walk down the aisle one day, it won't be him by my side. I am not scared to say that now I know it wasn't me, and that my worth is so much more than I know. It took me, I would say, ten years to figure out that my worth, self-respect, self-love, and self-confidence didn't reside in him. And now no one can tell me anything about me because I have overcome the two biggest obstacles in my life and I know now that it's okay to say yes, I am self-righteous.

Serving Hard Time

by JUAN GUZMAN

Words of advice: do not ever steal or else you might find yourself in prison like I did. No television, videogames, friends—confined to a small space twenty-four hours a day. Not to mention a warden whose looks could kill. It all started with a fight at the park.

"Yo Juan, you sissy," shouted Thomas.

"Thomas, just mind your own business, and leave me alone." The words exited my mouth. Boom! Dirt. Thomas had pushed me to the ground. My mind raced. *Should I hit him back? No way! He is much bigger.* So I dusted myself off, stole his basketball, and ran away. As I arrived home, standing at the door was a scary creature, my mother, and she was angry. Argelia, my mom, handed down my sentence, one month solitary confinement.

Stuck in a space the size of shoebox would be enough to make anyone go insane. Luckily I had a roommate, Steph Curry of the Golden State Warriors. Everyday, Steph and I stared at each other, me on my bed, him plastered to my wall. Funny thing is it was a one-way conversation because Steph never answered back.

On my release date, I went to hang out with my friends at the skatepark and grab a bite of pizza. It had never tasted so sweet. Prison taught me that no matter what happens I never want to end up back there ever again.

Nothing to Something

by MADISON HORNBROOK

It was a place I dreamed about. A place I longed to live in. A place where everyone was allowed and accepted. A place with diversity, opportunity, and knowledge—something that, where I'm from, people didn't care about or weren't lucky enough to have. I was stuck. Stuck where nearly nobody cared to put in work to succeed or know what was really out there. From a population of 1,000 to millions. A school of 300 to almost 2,000. Restarted, renewed, and rejuvenated, thriving to go from nothing to something.

I now wake up with a sense of fulfillment and acceptance. I've been given a second chance. A chance to express myself and see what the world has to offer. I am one of the lucky ones.

Moment of Life

by SHANYA WEATHERS

It's not just a regular playpen with trees and children, but it's a place where memories are held. It was called Morningside Park and had a fresh grass smell, birds fighting over crumbs on the ground, and crying babies. This park is where all the action happened.

There was a pretty garden before the gates to the entrance of the park where the birds sang. There were the sounds of the lawn mowers cutting the fresh grass, *vroooooooom, vroom*, which added to the crisp morning air.

I remember everything from the mini quake of people running late for work to the smell of the sweet floral perfume in the crisp air, making the insects jump onto bare skin.

Owww, aaw. Little kids screamed and ran from the buzzing bees. The ants marched one by one to pick up an ice cream cone.

Rrruuuum rrumm.

"Move! Get out the way!" kids shouted as they raced toward each other.

"Mommy, Mommy, Mommy! Come push me!"

Then there was me. I was on the basketball court.

"Pass the ball,"

"Swoosh! Air one!"

The sweat flew from the players' faces to the ground. *Drip! Drip! Drip!* The water bottles' sweat making a puddle of hot water.

"Hey! Move up and fill it up!" The kids behind me complained. "Pass me that one. Tie that one. Move quickly, they're coming, they're coming."

Then *BOOM! S P L A S H.*

All of a sudden I was standing in a puddle, drenched in my own sweat from head to toe. Dripping in water, I had to turn my game face on.

BOOM! Powwow! I splashed a whole bucket of water. Then a cry for help occurred.

A bloody leg.

An argument between the racers.

A crying baby.

A sneezing little kid.

People fighting over seats.

The sun sweating, ball players running, ice cream falling, water dripping.

It's not just a regular playpen with trees and children, but a place where memories are held.

222

by SHANIYA MARTINEZ

February 22, 2014. The morning could not have arrived any faster. My eyes sent piercing daggers at the cheese-cut moon, demanding that it fall out of the ombre purple sky so that the fiery ball of happiness could dance its way to highest peak—taking my anxiety with it. My orbs drooped as I awaited the black solemn box to play the melodies juiced from the brightest warblers that usually brought me unusual waves of anger. I sat up quickly, already dressed from the previous night and made my way step-by-step to the station in which the germ wagon of a train would deliver me to my destination. Three...four...thirty-four minutes of anxiety, thirty-four minutes of excitement, and thirty-four minutes of a baby crying.

Never had I ever been so excited to see the numbers "four" and "two." As I made my way out of the germ chamber, my eyes begged to close; the sun blinded me, but I don't think anything could shield my eyes from observing the massive army of girls straining on tippy toes like giraffes looking for a sign. A dark black car halted at the sidewalk with a screech, demanding our attention. Eyes wide, we all did an about face, and for once Times Square was dead silent.

Hours passed painfully slowly, and everyone was drained of energy and excitement. Migraines pounding and ankles sprained, we still ran from one side of Times Square to the other like a pacer test. Still no sign of the group of five Australian boys. Regret washed over me.

A high-pitched scream, then another and another invaded my already ringing ears. The Janoskians had finally arrived. Drenched in sweat, tired feet, hair wild in fatigue, I needed to make my way to the front. I risked getting hit by a row of cars (which I did later on), but I had made it! I met my idols and held one as all five of them were escorted away from the army of over ten thousand emotionally drained girls and boys.

They yelled; they pushed; they fell but they never gave up.

News spread like wildfire: the Janoskians had shut down Times Square. People had left, but a few stayed, and we all bonded like glue as we stood outside the Westin awaiting the boys. I had loosened up because although these people were complete strangers, they felt like family, and for once I felt like I belonged. We joked and played with each other; ten hours passed easily.

There was this one girl, however, who caught my eye. She had long wavy brown hair with a pair of big, brown eyes to match. Like cat and mouse, our eyes met continuously, then chased away when caught.

Finally, she came up to me and said, "Hey, you're really funny. I'm Bo." As I reflect on that moment, I can't help but feel like it was all meant to happen, the chaos, the excitement, getting hit by cars, etc., because those words were actually the start of an extremely beautiful friendship. Before our departure, we met the boys once more and stayed embraced in a long hug.

Although I haven't seen her or the Janoskians in two years, Bo and I talk every day about everything, and I can genuinely say that Bo and the Janoskians are the best thing that happened to me.

That is why February 22, 2014 is such an iconic day.

My Special Place

by CINDY MOROCHO

It was my first day of Pre-K. I was only four years old. I had woken up promptly at 7:00 AM and quickly put on my crisp new uniform, a short-sleeved shirt as blue as the sky with navy blue pants and a sweater. As I ate my breakfast at the dinner table, my mother explained to me in thorough detail that I would only be staying for a while and that she'd later come to pick me up. My backpack, bubblegum pink with images of Disney princesses on it, clung to my back as we slowly walked to school.

When we got to school, I could see other kids running around. They were the same as me, I thought. It was like a mob full of minions in a *Despicable Me* movie. I saw a girl with her mom crying as she was being dropped off. She was afraid, but I knew that we wouldn't be staying forever. The idea of starting school excited me. My mom had told me about how fun it would be, and I couldn't wait. The building was grand, the color of mint. There were two playgrounds, ours and the one for the big kids, which no one dared to enter. It was uncharted territory that no one wished to explore.

The building was composed of five floors, but we could only go up when told to. My classroom was on the first floor. The room was quaint and miniature like a hobbit's hole; it was safe and warm. We had a sink and fountain for when we needed to wash off paint brushes and palettes. There was a lifesize playhouse in one corner and in the other a big, round carpet that was like a clock. It had many numbers, and every little kid got to sit on one. My teacher's name was Ms. Obrich, but that was too hard to say, so many of us just called her Ms. Orange. Ms. Orange was tall and kind of old with glasses but was really nice. She was like everyone's grandmother at school. We also had a teacher's aid. His name was Mr. Pan, and he was Chinese. His name made us crack up with laughter because it means "bread," but that made it easy to remember. We only had one bathroom with three stalls, and we had to go with a buddy when we asked for permission, but it was cool because it connected to the room next door. It was like a forbidden chamber of secrets.

That day, Ms. Orange explained the class rules and made us write our names on a tag to become better acquainted with each other. Thankfully my name wasn't as long as other unfortunate souls who had theirs written slanted. As we got to know each other I found out that that girl who had been crying earlier was in my class. Her name was Rachel. We became close friends. During play time, I quickly made my way to the playhouse. That is where I met a weird and funny boy. He later became my best friend, Axl.

At the time, school just seemed like a place where I could have fun. I never wanted to miss a single day. Even if I was sick, I knew I had to go. It was painting day after all, and I wasn't going to miss out. As time flew by, school got harder, and although many people regard it as a boring place, to me it was the place where I met my best friend and learned everything I need today. I will always remember it as my special place.

Figment of My Imagination

by TENNILLE CHONG

My favorite place is like a television with numerous channels. I would detail it as popular and exciting, calm, yet untamed. I'd value it because it's my way to get away. I know a couple of people who are fond of this place; maybe you are, too. My place is in my mind. I change the settings all the time, cold to warm, sun to storm. I control how everything will be.

My favorite place is always open. I get comfortable and make my stress go away remotely. I got upset the other day and ended up in Miami, on the beach. I had the best tan. I looked like the sun touched me with magic hands. My swimsuit was cute, nothing anyone's seen before, very much imaginary. The sun was at a set, almost lying over the ocean. I saw everything I wanted in life: peace and comfort. There were even other families of different ethnicities running in the sand, kids playing on the docks, and couples lying in long chairs staring out at the water ahead. It was beautiful.

The only real issue is that you can't stay here. It's like a dream from which you awaken. My favorite place is nothing like reality. It is a figment of my imagination.

WHERE WE'RE FROM
AND WHO WE LOVE

$2.75

by GLADYS BLES

Hundreds of people pass each other by every day, on their own journey, briefly crossing paths, waiting for their train. Standing on the crowded platform, we all shuffle around, inspecting the station for any potential danger and looking towards the tunnel, hoping for a light indicating that our train is here. The mood at each station depends on the borough and time of day. Early morning train rides barely give me enough space to exhale, while afternoon train rides are empty and muted. Evening rides are filled with overworked and irritated commuters, getting off from work or school, mumbling curses under their breath as the conductor announces delays.

Stuck in between two stops with no service, I swipe through my photo gallery of funny screenshots and selfies. I usually take this time to edit a new Instagram picture to post when I get home, taking breaks to choose appropriate songs to fit my mood. Like a true New Yorker, I'm also very aware of my surroundings, avoiding long moments of eye contact and minding my business if I am alone. Occasionally I'm graced with quality entertainment: amateur magicians, guitar players, indie singers, rappers, break-dancers, and salesmen. They sit at stations or travel through subway cars, performing for some change while commuters groan and move back to avoid getting kicked in the face by the break-dancers. Typically I ignore the performers, glancing in their direction once in a while to assess their talent. The New York transit system is home to some gifted entertainers, while others should look into a different source of income.

Riding the train with my friends is a completely different story. We turn into the obnoxious teens on the train who talk too loud and laugh too much. These are the teens that I glare at in annoyance while I raise my music volume to the highest setting in an attempt to drown them out when I'm alone. My friends make the train rides with so-called train traffic, rude women with oversized handbags, and creepy men who stare for too long, enjoyable. The train transforms into a therapy session with my closest friends as we swap stories about our day and mouth the lyrics to the songs we're listening to.

The subway is filled with opportunity and endless possibilities, because every MetroCard swipe is the beginning of a new adventure. I've learned that some situations are not in our control, like service changes that I'm unaware of, and our only choice is to roll with them. Stuck in the Bronx, lost, anxious, and exhausted, I followed my best friend through an endless amount of transfers to make it back to Queens. We navigated through unfamiliar territory with plants we bought from the gift shop at the Botanical Garden, laughing at ourselves for getting stuck in this mess. We embraced the situation like every other ridiculous situation we've been in, whether it be early in the morning on our way to brunch, or late at night after a day filled with good food, good jokes, and good company.

We spend so much of our time focusing on destinations that we often overlook the adventure in the process.

Brownstone

by ASHLEY LAIRD

I always thought of it as our own private building. My friends wonder how someone can live in Brooklyn and not have an apartment number but still not live in an actual house. Our house is over one hundred years old, its stoop breaking down from the cold, harsh New York winters it has had to endure. The interior includes a 1970s paint job, the pink paint chipping away from the walls. I laugh at how some of the building's designs should have changed, such as its old staircase and wooden banister. Yet I still admire its classic features, its hand-sculpted architecture. The man often heard creeping up the old steps is my Uncle Charles. He is a big part of what makes living in this place so special. He shares advice with me, from the importance of knowing street names, to handling being a young adult. In our shared moments, jokes are also translated, including the recurring childhood one about "Gruel Tuesdays," where every Tuesday's dinner is a mystery known as gruel. Over dinner, we move on to discuss moving conversations about politics and history, which might sometimes lead into the same story I have heard a million times about how my uncle could have been kidnapped in the capital of Colombia! Somehow that story also relates to advice on not getting into a car not sent for you at the airport in a foreign country. These special moments do not just occur between my uncle and me, but with my mom, my sister, and my aunt who also live with me.

With four flights of stairs which everyone except me struggles to conquer, I have grown used to climbing this "stairway to heaven," otherwise known as the way to get to my 750-square-foot apartment. Though we have lived upstairs almost ten years, we never made it homey until about two years ago. Before we had a pale, off-white wall, but now the bright peach paint creates a more cheerful setting. The stained red suede coach has now been replaced with a rectangular, more mellow tweed couch. The clunky bookshelf with all my childhood favorites like *Junie B. Jones* and *The Magic Treehouse* is now replaced with a small, six-drawer espresso-colored shelf. Despite my apartment being so small, it is cozy and only makes my mom, sister, and me closer!

My brownstone is special because of all the family events held here, from our annual Christmas Eve party to Mother's Day to my grandfather's birthday. Nothing but laughter and love fill the air. Although we live on a block of brownstones, this one is different … like a blooming daisy surrounded by naked trees in the middle of winter. It is my home. It is my brownstone.

Popcorn Fields

by DAWELYS ALMONTE

I can still feel the wind's soft caress on my smooth, youthful skin, although it must have been a decade ago. The soft, marshmallow clouds were in the blue-raspberry Jolly Rancher sky. The clouds were having a splendid time playing with their wonderful friend, the bright yellow sun. I stood straight on my own two little feet, and the trees in front of me seemed to be tall enough to take a bite from the clouds. Their branches hung low but still higher than my head. They enjoyed mocking me. I would jump to touch them, and they would stand taller in order to stay out of my reach. I couldn't wait to be as tall as them and be able to prove that I, just like a grown up, could touch them. Then, with my newfound height, I would jump on the clouds that looked to be much softer than my bed, but sadly, for now, I would have to endure their soft clowning.

I could hear the little birds speaking their strange language, bickering and gossiping with one another. They could go very high too. They flew in the raspberry skies, over my head, over the trees, and even over the corn fields! The corn fields were never-ending;

they stretched until the end of the world, and I simply couldn't wait to go explore and find my new adventure. I wondered if the sun was happy enough to shine so bright that it would turn the ugly and bad-tasting corn into yummy, buttery popcorn. The old man wouldn't let me play in the future popcorn fields.

He would often say *"Ese maiz es para vender no para jugar."*

I would answer "Sold to whom? There isn't even popcorn yet, so why would anybody buy something that is not yet done?"

His reply would always insult me. *"Tu eres demasiado joven para entender esos negocios."*

I would, of course, feel dignified and answer, "I'm not too young; I can directly see your hairy chest and big belly now."

After that, he would always leave with a mouth full of laughter and resignation. He would leave me gazing longingly at the corn fields and wondering when the popcorn could be finally eaten. For now, though, I could stay under the shade of the mocking *plátano* and mango trees. Although they were from different families, they still got along tremendously well. What I loved the most was my most prized possession that I put up myself. That milky-white hammock was the perfect size for me. It hugged two of the sky-kissing trees, which brought them closer than ever. I would sit on the edge, and my little legs, which could no longer touch the dirty ground, would swing back and forth to create a slow, peaceful motion. I would lie on my white, soft cocoon and see how all things in my little slice of heaven would take life.

For my meddling cousins, this would be too boring and dull; they needed destruction and ruckus to be at ease with themselves. This could never be their favorite thing to do, and this is why this was *my* favorite thing to do. This was nirvana. The bugs did not bother me much; they knew I was the good giant, not one of the angry ones who squashed them just for fun. I was the foreigner, not them; they could, of course, hurt me if they wanted it to, but I would only come to visit their habitat, not damage it, so they steered clear of me and I of them.

My safe haven is dead now. Everything is gone, and nothing is left of it except for my memories. The sun never became brighter; he remained sad for a long time, so the popcorn never came. It always stayed corn until the pests devoured them, just as reality did with my dreams. The trees no longer get along; they now hate each other. The birds no longer chatter nonstop, they are silent and sullen while flying over the blackness that has taken over the once-dreamlike fields. I grew to be the old man's height, but he never saw because he left to live my dream. He grew tall and old enough to be able to jump on the marshmallow clouds. My most prized possession no longer hugs trees and is now being crawled on by the bugs who once avoided me. Nirvana has been destroyed by time's treacherous actions, but now there are new dreams to follow.

Along the Avenue

by LISSETH AGUILAR

It is where I long to be.
It is where I want to be.
It is where I need to be.
This is my Fifth Avenue.

From that moment I sat inside the spewing fountain and dipped my toes to refresh myself from the unforgiving heat, I begged to go back. When the sun was at its highest, I sat with a popsicle in my hand, watching the older kids skate, but when they left and the shadows were past my reach, I splashed into the water when no one was looking just to feel the water trickle down my knees. Soon after, I passed in and out through the arch's threshold every time I wanted to.

This is my Fifth Avenue.

From the moment I emerged from the stuffy subway and circled around the block, a vendor stand stood still before me. I took my first bite of fresh, gluten-free bread from the stand near me, and soon enough, I had indulged in all of the free samples around it. I explored this advanced supermarket: dairy-free cheese, fresh produce, detoxifying teas, flax seed pancakes, ostrich eggs, but my favorite? The apple cider stand. The warm breeze pulled down the people's sleeves. As the sun set, my cider became hotter. This called for a mini adventure through the slim alleyway.

This is my Fifth Avenue.

From that moment, I explored outside school. I passed by a triangular building, and it occurred to me, "Isn't that the *Daily Bugle*?" When I passed by the grandest building in New York (at least according to my textbook) I wondered, "Where were the monkey and the damsel in distress?" When I passed by the lions in their pride, I realized, "Was this where Seinfeld got squeezed by that library cop?" These unnecessary film and television facts were entrenched in my mind, and were what kept me walking along the line as I silently giggled at them.

This is my Fifth Avenue.

From that moment when the tree lit up, I knew that the frost was near. The season caressed the wildness and cheer held from the past year, and translated it to a beautiful language that only the shopkeepers could hear: Cartier, Louis Vuitton, Chanel, Versace, Prada, Bendel's, BCBG, Tiffany's, and department stores galore! After window shopping at Saks and gazing at the huge lights on the avenue strip, the embrace of my friends made the holidays feel like we owned the worth of all the luxury combined.

This is my Fifth Avenue.

From that moment when I met the eyes of a horse stationed at the subway entrance at 60th Street, my ride opened a new world for me. Slowly but surely, I strolled the pathways and crossed the bridges, hopped at every cobblestone, and climbed the sharp rocks at every corner. When the leaves changed, I dove into the neatly combed piles on the grass. When the trees were empty-handed, I sipped my hot chocolate along Museum Mile, marveling at the residential buildings made of gold. When the trees bloomed, the return of the ducks brought back timidity and tranquility, and when it rained, the people sheltered beneath the Terrace. When the lake shone brightly, I lay still on the grass thinking of a bittersweet melody to drift away from the heat.

This is my Fifth Avenue.

From that moment when I discovered the end of Fifth, I had reached the beginning of the river. Along the Drive, I ate the dishes of Spanish and soul food, and walked around with a batido in my hand, taking in the fresh breeze. When the shadows were past my reach, I drove off and left behind a past that seemed like a distant dream.

I sighed.

This is the Fifth Avenue that I longed for and wanted, and where I needed to be.

Brooklyn Trails

by MUSHFIKA CHOWDHURY

I was walking across East Fifth, passing the Windsor Terrace Library, over the bridge, and down the hill. My first journey had come to an end, and my path to tranquility was beginning. I took the same trail as always: slightly up a small hill with large branches scattered over edge of the path and a faded line running through the middle. For some, it was the path they would take to avoid the moms with strollers, guys with dogs, and girls with Nike trainers running blindly through Prospect Park. For me, it was the trail I found as a kid pretending to find Narnia. The trail is where the loners and hopeless romantics roam, hoping to one day come back to the same spot with someone to call their own. The trail that led to the bench near the water, closed off from humanity, was still full of life.

It was where the unexpected made me feel at ease for once. The bench was always covered with something different: white petals from the perfectly placed tree near the water with branches drooped away from the sky, or sometimes scattered with duck feathers. The green leaves lay graciously over the water, moving back and forth with the breeze or frozen from the brutal winter nights. I sat there with clear eyes and a full heart knowing there was no going back. Everyone saw a dirty pond with a scratched-up bench in an isolated corner. The pond was where I fed ducks with my mom as a child, while she held on to my arm for dear life. The bench was where my cousins and I licked ice cream off our innocent play dough-scented fingers. The corner was where I never felt alone. The quiet bench witnessed my rave of thoughts flooding out of the bottle I tried so hard to keep sealed.

I came up to the same trail with a different perspective. The line was almost gone, reminding me of the years that had actually passed. I'm no longer that young girl riding her pink bike through her personal Narnia that most people call Prospect Park. It was a different kind of tranquility. I went there to let my guard fall, making sure that the bench area knew my decisions, and to hold on to the new memories that I have made over the years. The isolation was what they saw with clear eyes and full hearts, which is what I felt and needed.

Jersey City

by ALEXIS CABAN

I remember the way of the block, how loud it usually was from the noise of everyday people going to work and to school and the noises of cop cars, ambulances, and fire trucks.

I remember the park in the middle of the block, across the street from my house. We called it the Barney house because it shared that same deep purple with the friendly dinosaur from TV. The house had a big porch and a very steep stoop. This was the place for porch meetings. A porch meeting was our excuse to go outside. We'd call them when we wanted to be noisy because there was an accident or when we wanted to look at the fire trucks coming down. We'd call them on nice days just to get out of the house, to be outside, and to sneak off to the park. One time when we were on the porch, we had just gotten ice cream, and my aunt's dog, Baby, ran to my little cousin and ate his ice cream right out of his hand. We yelled so loud that we scared her, and she ended up running across the street and got hit by a car. That was a crazy day, but all was good because she turned out to be fine. She also learned to not eat other people's food.

I remember the bakery, Neptune Bakery, on John F. Kennedy Blvd. I always passed it going to school in the morning and coming back in the afternoon. I would bribe whoever picked me up that day to go inside and get me something. It always smelled like freshly baked pastries. As soon as I would come in, the workers in the white aprons would know who I was. Voices that sounded smoother than butter would ask if I wanted to try the cookie of the day or maybe the new cake of the day. Each bite of the sweet treats was heaven, and I can guarantee that anyone who tried them would say the same. I loved trying new treats, but my favorite was their half-white, half-black frosted soft cookie displayed like trophies or awards. For me, they were Neptune's prize possession. I also remember, even ten years later, how those workers in the aprons remembered me, and how those black-and-white cookies were displayed like trophies.

I remember on those hot summer nights, the nights we had the most fun, sitting on the porch and waiting for the lights and power to come back on. My cousins and I would just play out in the front with the other kids on the block, all anxiously waiting for the cool air conditioning to come back on so we didn't have to melt in the sun. The day would go by slowly, and then we would hear that beautiful melody that told us we were going to be put out of our heat misery. The ice cream truck. On those summer blackout nights, the thought of the ice-cold, creamy textures made us wild out and act up, begging our elders to buy some. It was the hardest moment of our lives when they said yes. Choosing the ice cream you wanted on a hot blackout day was tough. There were vanilla, chocolate sprinkles, Spongebob, Dora, and Spiderman. It was so difficult and usually resulted in sharing. After the cold treats were devoured, the sun would most likely be setting, and just as it left, little critters with the brightest lights you've ever seen came out to play: the fireflies. They were so much fun to catch. And if the lights weren't still on, we'd catch some in mason jars and clear plastic and set them up all over the house. We never left them inside for more than five minutes though, or else they'd suffocate. After an hour or so, the lights would go back on, and we'd decide to leave them off.

I remember that the moments when we were unplugged were the best. No games, apps, or devices. Just our imaginations and free spirits, playing with each other. Now, we all live in different states, live different lifestyles, and don't see each other as much. The one thing that we do have, the things that I remember, are those fun-filled days from that Barney house on Bartholdi Avenue in Jersey City.

House of Beloved

by ISIS JANNIERRE BATES

It was bright with love and abundant in care. I would wait here as a toddler for my mother to come home from the academy. The crib that I would occasionally sleep in-and-out of at this point, given that I had grown too big for it, was in what was supposed to be a grand dining room but which had become my room and play area after my birth. I remember the smell of grilled cheese at noon. "Come on, baby," she would say, leading me to the kitchen. Waiting there was a cheese sandwich and a treasure's worth of sweets. "Don't tell your mama, now, or I'll get in trouble." I obliged my grandmother's command. This was a private affair, our secret indulgence unbeknownst to my mother. A paper cut was enough reason to make my mother worry, so heaven forbid she knew about a piece of candy.

I remember the laminated couch covers in the living room and the sound of Elmo on weekday mornings. In the mornings, I would wake in my mother's police uniform shirt (I liked to wear it as a dress before bed). I would go to the bathroom (potty-trained), get cleaned up, and dress myself for the day. My grandmother would approve of my mismatched outfit with a smile and both dutifully and happily return to the kitchen to make breakfast. Following suit, I'd watch quietly as she made my breakfast. My daily meals would alternate between a variety of dishes, ranging from homemade pancakes to sautéed eggs to vegetable omelets with fresh-cut fruit. Waiting anxiously, my mouth would water as I fixed my lips to ask, "Is it done yet?" "Not yet, baby," she would reply. "Almost."

It was like waiting to open your present on Christmas Day. However, every day was Christmas Day in Grandma's house, and love was the cherished, encased gift to take pleasure in.

Night would come, and my mother would return to Grandma's after long nights at the academy. I would run up to my grandmother gleefully, and say, "Mommy, it's my Mommy." The house would light up with laughter and become filled with delight. This was my grandmother's house, and it was the only house where I would learn such love and comfort at this tender age.

Stolen Safety

by CHEVANIE PETER CUNNINGHAM

As we were walking home, we noticed the sun going to rest and the moon slowly taking its place. I was coming home from school, and my mom was coming home from long hours of work at a college. We stopped at the grocery store on our way home, getting the regular groceries. We bought our favorite vanilla soy milk, orange juice, eggs, sugary cereal, and my mom bought the ingredients to make stewed chicken and rice. We took our time carrying the groceries, making sure nothing spilled in the bag.

Mom took out her keys to open the door to the building. The building was full of bright, yellow lights and decorated benches that looked similar to the colorful designs in churches. This was our first apartment, which we had lived in for a year and a half, and we still did not know anyone in that building except for the landlord.

It felt like we were walking up a hill as we went up the small steps to the first floor where we lived. Mom stopped at the silver mailbox to check for mail. After she pulled out the junk mail from the mailbox, we went to the door of our apartment. Slowly, she took her time opening our apartment door since she had so many things in her hand. I decided to grab the keys from her while she was trying to open the door. As I inserted the key into the lock, I noticed that the door was already open. I opened the door cautiously, suspicious of why it was open. I noticed all of the sun-colored lights in the apartment hallway were turned on. First, I looked into the living room and saw papers scattered on the floor. Then I looked even closer and I saw our television was missing. My eyes changed from squinty doll eyes to the eyes of an owl. My mind was telling me to leave the apartment, and my body was telling me to stay. There were soft whispers in my head telling me this was all a dream. I thought maybe my mother or my sisters were pulling a prank on me. I took a long time to process my thoughts. All of a sudden, adrenaline rushed through my body. Next thing you know, I grabbed a huge butcher knife from the kitchen.

I shrieked, "Mom, call the cops."

She was in shock even before I told her. Her face was pale and stiff like the wall. I checked my room and noticed the purple-and-black Eiffel tower jewelry box was broken. The money that I had saved up from Christmas was gone. My favorite gold hoop earrings that had been passed down to each of my sisters were also gone. My mom bought that pair of earrings in her home country, Grenada. They were so sentimental to me because I'd had those earrings since the day I was born. Tears were trying to escape my eyes, but my body was telling my eyes no.

Our palms were sweating, bodies trembling, as we picked up the phone to call the cops in the hopes that they would make us feel secure and get to the bottom of the situation. Waiting for the cops felt like a decade. Impatient and scared for our lives, we called in our super who also lived on the first floor. Mom's throat was so dry that it started cracking as she was telling him the story. I heard nothing but stutters and Mom trying to force herself to yell. He opened his mouth wide in disbelief. He started telling us about how the person who used to live in our apartment was robbed, but the landlord did not believe the guy. My mother and I looked at each other and squinted our eyes because we were trying to figure out why the landlord did not believe him.

Finally, the cops arrived at our house. They took five minutes, which felt like thirty seconds, to search through our entire apartment to look for evidence or any trails that could lead to the suspects. Adrenaline rushed through my body while waiting for the results. However, they found no evidence because the people who had robbed our apartment were wearing gloves. On top of that, the cops came to the conclusion that they came in through our window and left with our stuff through our front door. My heart dropped knowing that we had to act like we weren't robbed and go back to "normal." This was very devastating, especially because no one actually saw the thieves leave with our stuff.

The cops left, leaving my family feeling despondent and perturbed. After they left the apartment we waited no longer; we started cleaning up the useless evidence. Walking into that apartment every day reminded us of the situation as if we were replaying a movie in our heads. From that day on, we hoped that we could move soon because we began to dislike the apartment. We never wanted to go through the same experience again.

My Escape

by KEYANNA SPANN

The general purpose of a fire escape should be for emergency evacuations only; except where I come from, it is everything but. Whether it's a laundry assistant, personal garden, Christmas light display, or, in my case, a hangout spot, the fire escape never goes to waste.

The First Summer

We had tried so many times to have sleepovers at Kayla's (because essentially that's what best friends do), but my anxiety of sleeping in an unknown place kept me from staying past midnight. This time we tried a new approach and moved this two-man party to my bedroom. The next morning we spent what seemed like hours harassing my mother to take us outside to play and be free from the limits of our apartment walls. She repeatedly responded with "In a little while, girls," but our second-grade attention spans couldn't wait any longer. It was the prime of the morning when the sun was at its brightest; Kayla and I weren't going to miss it. Quietly we shuffled to the linen closet and grabbed the largest blanket our little bodies could carry. Together we lugged it down the hallway, past the bedroom, and straight out the window. As the rest of the neighborhood took advantage of the longer mornings, we climbed out onto the fire escape, soaking up every bit of fresh air we could. The day flew by, and we felt not the slightest bit confined. In our minds, this is what life was made of ... forts were overrated.

Last Summer

I've lived in the same apartment since the time I was born as have our household appliances. In 2015, each of them decided to give up on us ... including my air conditioner. Nicole couldn't have picked a worse time to stay over. Our combined body heat and lack of sufficient ventilation made my bedroom the equivalent of a sauna. It didn't take us long to realize that being in this room any longer would lead to our demise. The fire escape was our only option. The cool, summer night breeze kissed our skin as we sat in our pajama shorts, tank tops, and fuzzy socks. We talked endlessly about everything and anything. We found amusement in our unfortunate situation and observed the nightlife surrounding us. There was no Instagram, reality TV, mirrors, or ignorant boys. Just us and the air; we were content in our very own skin.

All through the winter I wonder what new memories my fire escape will bring. New freedoms, new stories, new lessons, new inspirations, new comforts. My home away from home, within my home.

The House Across the Street

by RASHAIL SHAKIL

All my life, I don't remember a single moment in which I was alone. Now, this could be both a blessing or a curse. Living in a two-bedroom apartment with six people definitely felt like a curse. My parents would say, "Stop your whining; it's only temporary." If temporary was five years, I don't know what they thought permanent was. It was my grandmother, grandfather, uncle, brother, mom, and dad. We had to live in and share this extremely small space, which was definitely not meant for such a large crowd.

Summers were even worse. In each room there was only one window that refused to ventilate the area. We were pressed together like peas in a pod. Not to mention the increased body heat which made it difficult to even gasp for some fresh air. "I can't take it anymore!" I screamed as I made my way to the door through my crammed family. It seemed as if I was the only one who expressed how I truly felt about our living condition. I know my brother didn't care; he never minded what went on around him because he was too busy playing video games. I could see that my mother wasn't happy, but she kept silent as she was a traditional housewife, expected to obey her husband and in-laws. However, the one time she did get the courage to speak up, she was quickly shut down by my father and since then had learned to compromise.

My uncle would only come home to sleep and would leave before sunrise to work. When he was home on the weekends, he and my grandmother would always quarrel with each other over the smallest of things. They would scream at the top of their lungs until one of them finally grew tired; most of the time it was Grandma. Afterward, he would slam the door to his room and cause the entire apartment to shake violently as if we were in an earthquake zone. This was a routine that happened every weekend and felt like the end of the world every single time.

I felt trapped, slowly suffocating as my head pounded with their arguments. I wanted to be free, both from the emotional and physical burden I had been feeling for what felt like a lifetime. When I would talk to my friends, they would reassure that I would be able to move out as soon as I turned eighteen. Although that should have comforted me, it only made me more miserable. First, my eighteenth birthday is almost seven years away. Secondly, my parents aren't white. They would not even consider the thought of their daughter living alone all by herself in a country that was fairly new and unknown to them.

Over the next few months, many changes came about. I experienced the death of my grandfather who lost his battle with cancer. A grey cloud of sadness came over us, and every other emotion was suddenly pushed from my being. I no longer cared about the tight space; I no longer minded the sweat rolling down my cheeks as I sat in the house that once felt complete. For the first time, I discovered the feeling of loneliness. The room that once seemed seemed jam-packed now felt vacant and deserted. It was as if there was enough breathing space for the entire city, and, ironically, I despised it.

Soon after that, we ended up moving across the street in a much bigger house. This would have been a dream come true since I was able to have my own room. It almost felt like a luxury. However, I would do anything to go back to the time when I constantly complained about sharing a room with three other people. I did not see the new house as a home; it wasn't homey enough. There were no memories associated with it, and a sense of detachment rose over me. I knew adjusting would take time, and I looked forward in the hope of better days.

Basement Chronicles

by LAURYN VINCENT

It was not a lair nor was it a dungeon; this basement was simply our new home. The cobwebs at the edge of the door told me I must brace myself for the possibility of spiders, and the small window in the basement equaled small views. Small views that all diminished when my childhood ended. I recall midnight playdates with my friends who lived upstairs along and our late-night episodes of sneaking into the kitchen and gathering snacks to munch on as we watched movies. Where we built sheet tents and told menacing stories with a flashlight shining below our faces. We created our own personal cinema in the living room upstairs as we watched *Eight Crazy Nights*, giggling obnoxiously before we drifted off to sleep.

Midday appointments at the school park: the school park where I broke my left arm and had to wear a cast for a month. Trampoline sessions outside in the backyard as we jumped to our heart's content. Running through the house playing lawyer or teacher with glasses on and pen and notebooks ready to take fake notes. All we had in our notebooks were scribbles of our attempts to imitate script. Playdates with school friends were a casual occurrence.

Back to the basement, where my mom would help me get ready for school that morning. Upstairs where she would help cook me breakfast to fill me up so that I wasn't complaining about being hungry all day. Downstairs where daddy long legs creeped and crawled all summer long. Where the pounding noises from the heat radiator tricked my mind into believing a maniac was trying to break in like a monster ready to kill.

Where the footsteps from the family above served as my daily alarm. Where I had my first fish that was killed after my mom placed its tank by the window, which made me very upset that day. It died from too much heat. Where my friends and I pretended to give birth to a baby doll and my mom caught us and was rather disappointed in us for a while that day.

Some of my childhood memories exist in this house. My height markings on the basement walls. The steps where my mother told me, "Don't let anybody take advantage of you, you hear me? Always stand up for yourself." The bedroom where I shared a bed with my mom and watched *Just Like Heaven* or *Ever After* almost every night because those were some of her favorite movies. Where my godbrother and godmother visited us. The friends upstairs in their own world. Where I said the forbidden "F word" when I was four years old. The smell of blueberry pancakes on Saturdays. Someone else lives there now.

The Comfort Inn

by MERCEDEZ TIBURCIO

It wasn't the most ideal situation. "He" left us, and by "he" I mean the man I have wasted words on. And by that I mean my father. My mother, my older brother, little brother, and I were left with mountains on debt, the marshals at the door, and heavy hearts. That summer of 2013 was a wreck. "He" left us in a *wreck*. I was going to start high school mere weeks after he left, and there was not so much as a "sorry." That hurt the most. I had no home, no solace. Do you know what it feels like to be without a place to call "home?" Those two months were the hardest.

We stayed in a hotel, but no one knew. I wouldn't let anyone know. It was an adjustment--actually, an "adjustment" is an understatement. It was like a big boulder blocking the exit of a cave. You are engulfed in darkness with not one drop of light, but you know that behind that boulder there is freedom; there is light and warmth and comfort. Comfort I did not have in the cold, brisk, unhomeliness of the hotel room. It was four solid walls, hollow and unmemorable. Hotel rooms have a way of feeling like that.

Hotel rooms are never places that people remember. They're meant to be vacant until humans take temporary shelter. They're places simply described with colorless vocabulary such as "pretty," "nice," "neat," or "comfortable" or "good." A hotel is not a home; it's not meant to be one, either. Homes are meant to be safe havens. In the hotel I would lay up at night in my own naïvite, wishing my father would honk the horn to his silver Acura downstairs and take me back home.

This hotel was like a never-ending pit stop. There were nights I would wake up and feel as if the four solid walls were closing in on me. The room's ice-cold air seeped into my veins and became the subject of my nightmares. No matter how tightly I wrapped the unwelcoming hotel bed sheets around my body, I would never warm--not without my nana. The one thing I really felt connected to was left forgotten on my mother's mattress after I was abruptly awoken at 8:00 AM to pack all the belongings I could into one little suitcase and backpack. I had never felt so alone, like there was a piece of me that was chopped off and sunken into the depths of the Black Sea's abyss.

Through it all, I put on my sun-bright smile and keep my feelings to myself till the dead of night when no one could hear my cries. "Why, why me?" is all I would ask myself. Wishing I was back in my own perfect little world where I was invincible. That world was not an ideal world, but it worked. It was a place where I could escape to, no judgment, no fear, just peace. The peace I so desperately wanted, a peace that was not in the hotel room.

When I left that hotel room, it felt like a weight had been lifted off my shoulders. I remember sitting on the edge of one of the beds and looking down at a picture on my lap. It was my mother and father in their blissful teenage romance, with raging hormones in a photobooth. It warmed and froze my heart at the same time. Warmed because they looked so incredibly happy, frozen because I never got to see them that happy with my own eyes without expecting a fight to happen that same night. My mom walked in the room as I stared emotionlessly down at the picture and asked, "You ready?" In that moment I was unsure: was I ready? Was I ready to abandon everything? This was no longer about leaving this treacherous hotel room, but about leaving behind something else, something more valuable. Leaving my heart, leaving my dreams of a happy ending, leaving my optimistic mindset and letting realism take over, leaving a part of my life I knew I'd never get back. I looked down at the picture and stuffed it in the suitcase. I felt all emotion leave my heart and all thought leave my mind. I was an empty vessel, nothing but skin and bones. The pain of my decision hurt, and it still does.

"Yeah Ma, I'm ready."

Five-Sided Wall

by YOSELIN SARITA

Those rough, white walls would make you cringe the moment you touched them. The outdoor cement parking lot with flowers on each end made you feel the essence of being at home.

Growing up in the humongous structure gave me the safety I craved as a child. It was hard to believe that every porcelain doll and perfect toy were mine. The one-thousand-plus-piece puzzles that caved into the puzzle in pure perfection. The second story of the house had two rooms and a huge attic that you could walk and play in. The brown windows and green house across the street, looking out onto the pebble road—whenever a car would drive through, you could hear the pebbles scrapping with each other.

I would usually spend my mornings and evenings in that attic, playing with the porcelain dolls my father would bring from America, sometimes even something more than porcelain dolls—things I liked, but never loved. Things I wanted, but never needed. Dolls, Barbies, pop culture toys from the '80s; the man brought everything you could think of. He didn't really mind bringing us anything we wanted since we never spent a whole month with him.

His travels to the United States lasted long cycles, cycles that felt like an infinity curve. But the loneliness didn't cave in until I was actually older. As a child, I was so blinded with the animals, intrigued with school, and more worried about the horses than I ever was about my father. I loved the man, but what is a six-year-old supposed to know about feelings? He loved me, that was all I knew. But I worried more about my toys than I did about anything else.

Those toys were followed by the passion towards my dogs and cats and pigs and horses and cows. My dad ran one of those businesses that sold and produced "resources" that would later turn into what you'll be eating for dinner. Star, my cow as a child, was a pet given to my siblings and me when she became an orphan. Her mother died from drowning in a water hole, but we eventually became her parents. Then it was a horse, whose mother got an infection on her leg and never walked again. And this went on and on as my father's love grew. And so did my dream. The dream of moving and the dream of adventure. The dream of getting away from horror and fear. The new dream away from the old and cycled dream.

But why did that dream die so quickly? That dream died the day I moved. Everything was different, and I saw more than I used to. I saw the deaths, the cancer, the passion, the hate, and the truth. But maybe it is all just a dream I am waiting to wake up from. A new perspective formed that I was not able to see out of. That fifth wall was open and so was I.

Mother Nature, My Friend; Father Technology, My Enemy

by ANITA BRIGGS

I have always had a rather interesting relationship with technology. For as long as I can remember, I have always had issues with it. One time I remember very clearly that I was having internet trouble; I could not get my computer to connect to the internet for the life of me, so I took my computer to my mom. The second I handed the computer over to her, it finally decided to connect to the internet. Then, the second my mom handed the computer back to me, it decided to disconnect itself from the internet. For all those skeptics out there, this wasn't a one-time thing. This happened repeatedly. All of those experiences led me to realize that technology absolutely hates me. If I were a superhero of some sort, my main arch nemesis would be some form of technology.

Because of these extreme issues with technology, I have grown a strong connection with nature. My favorite place in the entire world would have to be deep in the forest surrounded by trees without a computer for miles. It's the one place where you can go to be yourself. There aren't any expectations placed on you when you are out in the middle of nowhere. It's one of the few stress-free environments that I have left. My parents think that this is great. They are happy that I'm not technologically obsessed like most of the rest of my generation. Some of my friends don't quite agree. This past summer, for example, my friends asked me if I wanted to hang out. Because of my obsession with nature, I recommended that we go on a hike on Prospect Park's forest trail. Even the ones that were on board with the idea had to ruin the experience by using their cell phones.

I also have an obsession with camping since it's an activity we can do in nature. I used to go camping every summer. However, a year or two ago, my uncle got a pay cut, and he couldn't afford to take my cousins and me camping anymore. I was so heartbroken when he told me this. Camping, and by extension nature, is my one escape from technology, so I was super upset when I was told that I couldn't go anymore. After all that had happened, my uncle came up to me and said that I looked like he had just killed my dog when he said that he couldn't take me camping. What he said made sense since camping used to be the highlight of my summer vacations. Now if I want to go into a forest, I have to settle for areas like Prospect Park or Central Park.

The most ironic part of my love for nature and my hatred for technology is that whenever someone in my digital photography class has technical difficulties, they come to me for help. Even though all I want to do is escape into a forest somewhere, I can always help someone solve their computer problems. All my years of struggling with technology have left me with the ability to solve everyone's computer problems but my own.

Utopian Getaway

by ELYSE BABOORAM

Not just any island, but Tobago, known as Trinidad's sister island. An exotic place to say the least. I remember it as an island with the most majestic of mountains, where I'd watch the colorful flocks of birds fly overhead with my dad. Oh, how I'd love listening to the chirping in what seemed like harmonious synchronization! I would beam at the beautiful creatures as they would gracefully glide over the towering mountains. I'd always find myself intrigued as to how they'd play hide and seek with the opaque clouds.

Not just any island, but one where the sun rose in brilliance, and I watched as it would set in its crimson tone as dusk slowly approached. Some days I'd procrastinate about whether or not to bathe in its intense radiance or in the calm seas as the scorching rays glistened over the waves in magnificence. On its shy days, I remember how the sun would hide behind the dark, gloomy clouds, while on others it would choose to dazzle us with its fierce resplendence. I remember how its beautiful, simple existence would bring such jubilance to every day of my stay.

Not just any island, but Tobago. I remember the day I learned that it was where the Atlantic and Caribbean Seas would become one. Oh, how intrigued I was by the water maintaining its clear but faint baby-blue tint. I have yet to encounter combative or aggressive waves. On all my visits, the ocean seems to be tranquil and heavenly year-round. How it would allure and fascinate me from any angle our Canon caught. Indeed it captivated my attention with the most charming of shots.

Not just any island, but one with the most peculiar of palm trees. I remember how they would tower over the people and most establishments. My favorite kinds are those that slant in such a way that they provide the best shade and composure when the blistering sun becomes too overbearing. I'd love to watch above as the delicate branches would accommodate the harmless inhabitants and critters that nest there. Oh, how my father loved to rest under the serene and convenient shade! For me, it was the perfect place to find peace.

Not just any island, but one where the food would remain authentic and original. I can't forget how its hint of spices would captivate my taste buds as it managed to integrate other cultures into its cuisines. I especially admired how that unique characteristic contributed to the island's congeniality. I'll always appreciate it for the great hospitality that makes it my ideal location for the perfect getaway.

Located a mere seven miles off Venezuela's northeastern coast in the company of its sister island, Trinidad, lies the unpretentious and subdued island of Tobago. It's the place my family and I love to escape to at any chance we get. Whether we go for two days or a week, its tranquil atmosphere exudes such peace and delight. Tobago isn't just any island, but one that holds a special place in my heart, along with many memories that I cherish.

The Antique Shop

by ALICE SUNGUROV

I have always been exposed to music. From the moment I was born, my parents clogged my ears with Rod Stewart. Throughout my childhood I was infatuated with different sounds, how on one track there could be thirty different instruments playing. In a way, by the time I was eight, I could have confidently said that I had heard it all. My mom would describe me as a sixty-year-old music devotee inside an eight-year-old's body. After my parents first split up, a certain silence swept our home, as if all the music in the world had disappeared and what remained was a sad ballad with a bass note of E-flat minor. The only advent of a singing D presented when I would show my mom a good mark I received from school.

One day my mom decided that she and I needed a change; we needed a vacation. The destination was Paris. It was an amazing trip, but what sealed the perfection was an old antique shop with one single object.

On our walk back to the hotel, the sun was shining on the luminous streets. I took my shoes off and walked barefoot on the chilled cobblestone ground. I couldn't help but smile ear-to-ear: so relaxed. Looking at my mom, it seemed she felt the same way. As we walked along the narrow road something caught my eye, a flicker of light. Turning, I saw an old antique shop with the name "Belles Antiquités" plastered on the door.

Walking inside, I could feel a new energy light up. Looking around, I thought that it seemed too perfect to be real. Everything was strategically placed so that the sun's reflection bounced off the old merchandise. It was, to a degree, like walking into a maze of light beams, so bright and gentle that you could see the dust floating in the air. Naturally my mom and I walked our own paths to observe the antiques some more.

Right as we were about to leave, I heard a sound. Nothing was playing, but I redirected myself to find what had rung in my ear. And as I marched, I saw a small, palm-size object with different pictures of the more prominent French landmarks engraved into it. There, on the side, was a subtle spindle, and as I spun it, small, gorgeous, individually unique notes played. Together they formed the French classic, "La Vie en Rose." I looked up at my mom. She smiled, and at that moment we knew.

The Holy Trinity

by SAMANTHA BERGER

I feel an elbow jam into my side, which is followed by a sudden apologetic look and a sharp pain that will last the whole night. The slightly faded bruise is once more going to revert to a dark shade of purple that will last at least two weeks, and I proceed to question why I am really here and if the pain once more is truly worth it. The voices eventually turn into a chant of the band's name with the crowd's collective agreement that the openers are over and weren't that good. We want the real show. As the crowd gets more anxious for the band, the stage crew coming and going in a hasty rush on stage, merely feet away from me, my mind wanders. I feel the slight air conditioning on my neck which doesn't make much of a difference, and the lingering smell of sweat, beer, and weed, the holy trinity of all pop-punk concerts.

Looking around, I realize I'm just about dead center and start to panic. The center in these types of concerts means trouble. Mosh pits break out typically, and I will likely be hospitalized in the pit with grown men. Reverting to my "strategic" method of getting closer to the barrier, I yell "Vic, oh my god," and say sorry while moving to the first person who turns around to look at me. Knowing I'm safe just about three rows from the barrier, I breathe a single sigh of relief until the crowd begins to chant once more, and the pop-music filler stops.

As the lights dim, the crowd rushes forward, sweaty body against sweaty body in an attempt to get closer to the stage, although it isn't possible. Packed in like sardines, with my thoughts drowned out by the screaming, the lead guitarist plays a G sharp. It has begun, the reason I'm here and where I spend most of my weekends along with the occasional Thursday night. The band breaks into their first song, and I joyfully sing along, or rather scream along, with nothing but pure bliss. When the band's notable song, "Therapy," comes on, the crowd is silenced. Three of the four walk off stage, and the lead singer is left sitting on a wooden stool in the middle of a dark venue with only a single spotlight and an acoustic guitar. I tear up a bit.

Looking around, I see girls crying and phone flashlights swaying with the music, and still to this day, every time I see this, I stand in disbelief. Only concerts have the ability to bring people together to share in this heartfelt moment that is almost godly. This one band has the ability to unite a whole group of people who normally wouldn't have looked twice at each other in passing on the street. At this moment, all the bruises, smells, and heat are worth it, to share in a moment like this, where we are united as one, sweaty body to sweaty body. Concerts like these are a safe haven for many; they allow our voices to be heard, our emotions to be let free, and our faith to be shown in the music. Faith, hope, and comfort is the holy trinity of all concerts, and I wouldn't trade that pure blissful feeling that lasts only two or three hours for anything in the world.

Through the Dark

by GELIA BRADOR

Sometimes, people you've never met can have more of a significant role in your life than those you know.

August 5, 2015. My father, best friend, and I sat in the car, shouting out lyrics as we tightly held on to the pieces of paper that would allow us into the best three hours of our lives. An hour and thirty minutes later, and ahead we saw a structure that became larger and larger. *MetLife Stadium, we meet again.* Off we went. I was wearing a blue romper and a white lace top matched with denim shorts, approaching a place that truly felt like home. I felt comfort in their voices, similar to the sleepless nights where their music was my only friend.

As far as I was concerned, the doors were open and we were on the road again. The feeling was surreal. The excitement I had held in for seven months was finally being liberated. Walking into the stadium where I'd once again see the four people whom I've been supporting for years, I grabbed my best friend's hand and held it tighter. Our blue wristbands were on and our tour books in clear plastic bags covered our heads for a ten-minute drizzle, which came quickly and uninvited.

The night consisted of an Irish accent and three British ones singing songs that I've memorized every single word to. We heard Harry's commonplace jokes, yet still laughed, Niall's speech about "a song [he] wrote with a band called McFly," Liam singing what was Zayn's high note in "You and I," and we saw the joy in Louis when the crowd sang along to "No Control." The bittersweet feeling came along when the guitar on "Best Song Ever" began: "We've been One Direction. Thank you so much!"

The stadium held 89,000 people. Each one of us with different interpretations of lyrics and diverse reasons for holding onto the ones we do. We latch onto these artists and entertainers because they may fill a void created by parents or friends (or lack thereof), or simply because they bring us joy. A band may be just a band to some, but for others it represents much more. It's the light that guides us through the dark.

What Time Is It?

by BONNIE LYNCH

At the time, I didn't feel any guilt; that wouldn't come for another year. All I felt was a confusing combination of excitement and nervousness: excitement for what was to come but nervousness that perhaps things wouldn't work out and we would waste six hours of our lives. My friends didn't seem to share my nervousness as we decided where to sit. We ended up about a hundred feet away from the Barnes & Noble in question, where the book signing would occur at midnight. We set down our chairs and started our six-hour wait until ten in the morning, when the store opened and we could get tickets to the signing.

None of us felt the tiredness from waking up at 4:00 AM or any urge to read or discuss the unfamiliar book we were getting signed; not even the Canadian girl behind us in line, whom we had included in our antics, seemed to feel any exhaustion. We all barely noticed the time passing by, although that might have been because we were talking and keeping each other company the whole time. We barely noticed when the sun rose over the large, nearly empty buildings. We barely noticed when we ate our brief breakfast of pancakes and strawberries, which were especially juicy and ripe because of the warm August weather. We didn't notice when the early risers started walking their dogs, causing quite a bit of hilarity with their cuteness and the fear they brought one of my friends. It was just the three of us girls, plus our newfound Canadian friend, making the best of the most necessary but boring part of our eventful day.

While we did eventually get the tickets for the event, despite the signed books in our hands and the awe of being in the majestic presence of our mission's author, the time we spent waiting on the sidewalk will always be the most memorable part of that day, waiting for a ticket for a signing of a book that even now, years later, I still haven't read.

My Twin

by AALIYAH FAIRWEATHER

If you believe, you can achieve. I'm sure this is what my friends told themselves as they sardine-packed themselves on the twin bed that can barely hold me. The twin "bed," for lack of a better term.

I always envied those that got asked "What's your side?" mostly because the bed is really only one side. Anything from "What's your corner?" to "Where's the inflatable mattress?" more sufficed. Regardless, it was their every intention to make our five hormone-raging, food-craving, overly antsy bodies fit into this small sliver of a bed. On a twin with all of us, there was no such thing as just lying head to toe. It was more like head to toe, elbows to ribs, and knees to shoulders. A little bit of wedging between the hefty mattress and frigid hard brown wooden wall. Even some sucking it up to allow our arms and legs to dangle over the edges, trying not to get consumed with the fear of monsters surging up from beneath us and dragging us down. Screams from any possible attack probably wouldn't have been heard over me yelling to Keria to give me more of the blankets anyway. Jaden shouting, "My neck!" when Keaona plopped herself down on him, not knowing he was lying under the blanket. Mabel crying out, "My knee!" after I knocked her off the bed from playing tug-of-war for the blanket. The twin bed stirred in satisfaction in the breeding chaos, pain, and mania. We were a domino effect of madness, and the bed was unforgiving.

I couldn't blame it though. Some nights, the twin bed laughed at the way my seventeen-year-old, five-foot-six body attempted to fit. "Isn't it time you get a full size?" is what I imagine it saying each time it failed to sustain me as I'd roll off in the middle of the night. It especially had a ball when I figured four others could do the same. But this twin bed that tried to maintain the attitude that I was no longer accepted was my sanctuary when I needed it to be. The double layer of blankets does twice the job of shielding me from darkness, daylight, and responsibility. The pillows hold all of my best to worst to forgotten dreams, nightlong Facetime calls, and tears shed from Netflix binging. The mattress holds my drained body at the end of the day. The white wooden, floral-carved bed that has my extensive collection of Jordans from my mainstream phase in middle school scattered underneath. I couldn't ask for more out of my twin bed. Its limited space provides me with a big world I curl myself within whenever I need to get away and get comforted.

How to Survive a Hurricane

by ARIA FAZIHA KHANDAKER

During my second month of junior year, a hurricane highlighted an incredible moment of my life, a stressless yet absurd moment.

"Andy is what?!" I asked Johanna on the phone, "He's drunk?!"

"I know. I'm going to kill him," she answered. I hung up the phone.

It'd been on the news for the past week that on Friday, October 2, New York City would be hit by one of the worst hurricanes ever. Unfortunately, that did not stop us from taking the B train all the way to Park Slope so we could camp out at Andy's house.

"Why is Andy drunk again?" my best friend, Julian, asked as the rest of our group walked ahead of us on the path to Andy's house.

"I think he's trying to impress the freshman girls that came to his house. I think he lied to them about having a party or something," I replied as I rolled my eyes. "I don't even think he's drunk."

When we reached his house, we saw him coming out with two tawdry girls wearing a jacket fit for a warm summer day in this horrible hurricane weather. Seeing that his eyes were bloodshot red and he was laughing incessantly, he was, alas, not joking about getting drunk. Naturally, I grabbed him by his collar and asked, "What in God's name is the matter with you?! Snap out of it. We need to get inside before the hurricane gets worse!" At this point, the entire group was freezing.

As he looked at his freshman Barbies in embarrassment, he said, "I'm sorry, but my mom's coming home soon," chuckling his way through a single sentence. "But this is Park Slope, guys! Brooooklyn! We can literally go anywhere!" Optimistic and idiotic, he ran down the block and across the street … *"Brooooklyn!"* we heard from a distance.

At this point, we were nearly drenched from the rain. The icy water slapped our faces as we looked for a cafe or any sort of shelter from getting picked up by the wind. My warm and heavy coat was my suit of armor, and the random sound of my friend Declan's camera shuttering every time we stopped at a light made the biting hurricane all worthwhile, as Declan was capturing memories my brain wouldn't recollect. We weren't in the pleasant, "rich" part of Park Slope. We were in the part of broken-but-tasteful delis, chains of fast food restaurants, and several convenience and drugstores part of Park Slope. And I loved it. I loved it because it was broken. I loved it because Johanna and I pushed Andy around angrily for being drunk. I loved it because I felt light … incredibly light.

A solid hour later, after constantly going into random worn-out furniture stores or local Domino's to find some warmth, we found a deli to house eight friends and two annoying girls drooling over Andy's drunken self. We ate paninis and cold-cut sandwiches with no care of what time it was or who was expecting us to be home during the worst hurricane in New York City's history. I didn't care.

I was merely aware of the extent that my life would change in the next couple moments of my life. I had nothing to care about except the fact that my hair was drenched; this chicken panini needed to be eaten ASAP; and that everyone cracked up when I said, "If Andy ever decides to have another 'party' again, we burn him at the stake."

Maybe

by NATALIE GAY

It's hard to be understood when no one knows what's wrong with you. I constantly complained to my mom that my eyes were broken, that I frequently saw flickering dots, like noise in a picture. She made a call , and several months later I was brought to specialists.

I sat in a dull, monotonous room with chairs evenly lined up next to each other. The TV played replays of the same news by the hour, and the wait proved to be endless. The hospital itself gave the aura of health and answers. The previous retina doctor said they couldn't find anything wrong with me, and I should get my cataracts checked out. There, I was surrounded by much older people, people who were most likely older than my mom. The two of us sat there waiting for my name to be called. The static sounds of the TV became irritating, and the sudden call of my name gave me a feeling of relief that I was being rescued from the troublesome noise. After all the tests and questions, I got no answers. They could not find anything wrong with me either.

I longed for answers and intended to get them. Again, I found myself surrounded by older people of retirement age. After the neuro-ophthalmologist examined me, they could not find anything wrong with me, and they recommended I see another specialist. I was overcome by a feeling of despair and a surge of hot blood flowed to my face and down to my shoulders. The thought that it was all in my head entered my mind.

What was wrong with me? Maybe I was imagining these pesky dots, but I've seen them my whole life. Maybe there's nothing wrong with me. Maybe I just think things are there even though they really aren't. Maybe I confused depression and anxiety with clouded vision, that the flickering dots were just constant reminders of my worries and troubles. Maybe all that time spent in the waiting room made me start to believe that things would get better. Maybe deep in my heart I had a sense that hospitals were meant to fix the things that were broken in you, but since they couldn't find anything, then am I forever broken? Maybe, who knows?

The Waiting Game

by ANGELICA LORA

It's like you can't breathe, you know? Your heart starts racing, your stomach feels queasy; you get cotton-mouth, and your throat begins to close up. It slowly contracts until not a drop of air can get by. Then you helplessly gasp for air in an attempt to keep your heart beating, but the efforts are useless. The nerves get to you and engulf you in darkness. All you can do to help is nervously tap on the floor, gnaw on your knuckles, or even pinch them in an effort to distract yourself from the lack of air in your brain.

The waiting room was plain and white, nothing extraordinary about it. A TV screen was playing pointless infomercials and other things that I couldn't hear. My ears weren't in that box with my physical body. Neither was my mind; it was wandering in an unknown plane in the dark, unaware of what would happen next. The white walls blurred in the background as my mind explored the plane. The unknown just made it worse; my heart beat faster, about to pound out of my chest. What did I get myself into? I didn't know getting confirmation of something so small could get to me like this. Maybe it's because it wasn't small anymore since what was once a distant suspicion slowly had become a reality right then and there, in the white box that closed in with every breath taken.

I was snapped out of my daze when the nurse came out and called my name. It curled off her tongue perfectly and sounded like a soothing song. I looked to my left and saw a bright smiling face. A piece of the sun staring right at me, trying to bring light to the near-dark. I sat there frozen; my feet were being weighed down by blocks, and my body was being hugged by the chair. Attempting to get up, I stumbled and dropped everything. It was the nerves and the other stuff. The abyss of darkness and despair launched me into this anxiety attack.

I got myself together and walked behind the ray of sunshine into another dark and dull room. I looked down at my knuckles and saw the blood pounding through them. They seemed as if they were full of energy, red and bright. The doctor walked in and gave me a great stare before changing my reality. "I do believe you fit the criteria for these two disorders." Relief, anger, and frustration rushed through my veins. Speechless, I jumped into the abyss of the plane to escape into a more comforting darkness.

What an Awful Place

by NICOLE QUACH

"Hail Mary, full of grace." That's how all my days started and ended. They made us pray three times a day: in the morning, before we ate lunch, and before we left. It didn't matter if you didn't practice their religion. They made you say it. And when I say "they made you," I mean if you didn't say your prayers, they would scold you. Looking back now, it didn't matter how many times you prayed. The world was still a cruel place.

"What is she wearing?" The conservative Catholic school uniform made me yearn for freedom of expression. No nail polish, jewelry, or makeup was allowed. Whenever I got the chance to wear clothes that weren't my uniform, I took advantage of the opportunity. But you had to be careful with what you wore. It didn't matter if it was one of those days they let you wear your own clothes or if you were outside of school. If your outfit was thought to be too "girly" or showed too much skin (the definition of showing too much skin in a Catholic school environment was defined by a skirt that was just a centimeter above your knees), you would be judged.

But usually it didn't even matter how much you covered up or how cute you looked. Either way you'd be judged by your appearance. Not all Christians are as friendly as you think.

"Pay a $100 fee if you want to eat in the lunchroom." I remember they didn't even provide lunch. In fact, the lunchroom wasn't even that great. It was dirty and smelled like rotten cheese and vomit. The lady watching us was fat and gross. My friend once saw her eat a sandwich out of the trash can. She was also very mean. We had to pay other ridiculous fees too. Our uniforms were over $50 (not including our gym uniforms), and if you were not Catholic, which was my case, you had to pay a higher tuition. Tuition was a few thousand dollars. When I left Catholic school, my parents were thrilled about how much money we would save.

"BFFs forever!" That's what I thought back then. I'll never forget all the people I thought I'd be best friends with forever. One of my "best friends" made fun of me on a daily basis. She'd always say I sucked and that I have no life. Everything I wore she'd insult because it was too "girly," even though it wasn't. The only reason I stayed around was because I wasn't really friends with anyone else. There were a lot of small, unapproachable cliques, and I didn't fit in into any of them. In the end, she was a bad influence and turned me into a horrible human. I became the judgmental bully whom I hated, all because of her.

"Get your things and go." They didn't even give me a chance to explain. It all started when a new girl came to our school. My "best friend" had something against her, so I just followed along. We were talking about her on Facebook and making fun of her. A few days later, we were reported for cyberbullying. I was suspended for three days and was told to get a psychiatric evaluation before going back to school. About a week or two later, my "best friend" and I were drawing and laughing really loudly in class. We attracted attention, and our teacher came over. My friend drew a chainsaw and a dinosaur, which my teacher saw as violent. We were told to take our things and go. My friend got a free pass just because her mother, who had passed away a few years before, had known one of the ladies working in the office. The office worker backed my friend up, while I had no one. I wasn't given a chance to explain anything. The principal just decided to side with my "friend" and blame me even though it wasn't my drawing. My parents and I felt rage like never before. The staff at the school were completely unreasonable and said they had to consult with the Church about their decision. It was then that my parents pulled me out of the school and decided that it was time that I transferred to a public school. The truth was that this school did not care about me, and they would've ended up expelling me anyway. Since it was a Blue Ribbon School of Excellence, meaning it was an honors school, the principal was simply concerned with the school's reputation. He never gave me a chance. To this day, I am sure that the reason I wasn't given a chance was because I am not Catholic. I thought God loves and forgives everyone, but I guess not.

Finding Me

by LIZET CIELO VELAZQUEZ

This is the place where my mind grew up. From 8:00 AM to 5:30 PM, I would enjoy every inspirational lecture, every tedious chapter, and every note that was given. Elementary school passed by, and I saw myself sitting next to a bunch of sixth graders. Little by little, my passion for learning faded away. The change from who I used to be transformed me. I promised to stand my ground and honor my mind, but the world corrupted me and made me lose sight of who I was. Boys would walk by and catch my attention from the corner of my eye, allowing for a new side of me to emerge, the side that I was now exposing as a twelve-year-old. This went on till seventh grade; by the end of eighth grade my mind was in another world. I focused on my appearance and who I was seen with. It was as though my curiosity roamed through the halls of school and triggered me to fall behind. But the habits I developed made me the person I am today. After constant rebellion, wandering, and selfishness, I realized school was no longer my priority. I found myself lost during the summer and needed time. Before I knew it, I was in high school, starting all over again, but this time it was different. I knew my limits and my surroundings. I knew that history couldn't repeat itself, so my mentality changed. Boys would walk by, and I would be in my seat minding my own business. I didn't care what boys had to say about the way I looked or dressed. I knew that things were different and I was different. Although my insecurities were still around, I still continued to enjoy every second I spent in school, because school was where I grew up and was part of who I became.

I Remember School: Middle and High

by KASSANDRA HERNANDEZ

I remember being the shy girl in the corner of the room with no one to talk to. It was a lonely existence: long, unbearable, boring. Misery had its hands around my throat, as if I was nothing but its property. Simply awful.

I remember the cold, prison-like desks that surrounded the herd of brainwashed individuals known as students. I remember the branding of the cattle. The class clowns, the skaters, the anime/manga nerds, the buff boy, the gamblers, the copying machine, the desperate, the hard workers, the queen bee, the unique, the back of class crew, the musicians, the in-love couple, the sports guy, the guy with no cares, the gossipers, the hyperactives, the stressed-out, the singers, the nerds, the truants, the bullies, the people who sleep during class, the Disney-obsessed, the daydreamers, the artists, the vain, the perverts, and the best friends. I never could figure out where I stood. Often I came up with my own labels. Mine was the human answer sheet.

I remember my mother's wise words, "Good grades lead to a good college which leads to a good life." I remember going crazy with the idea. I obsessed over the coveted A. Her words, although simple, took on life of their own within me and molded me into a grade-obsessed student. I remember crying over a C+. It was a computer mix-up, but it hurt me like a knife to the heart.

I remember changing my view on the world and opening my eyes to people and not words. Like a flower in spring, I flourished in my evolution, and I began to focus on things outside of the textbook and instead embedded in the plan of the world.

I remember the staircase in middle school where all the couples used to begin. I remember the library, the place I escaped to and made a second home. I remember the rambunctious lunchroom, my hell filled with the chatter of those who scorned me and isolated me. One of my supposed friends tortured me for a year in that dreaded room. Trivial and jealous, my "friend" tortured me by enticing my only true friend with treasures for a middle schooler. An excess of money corrupted her, and because of it, we became no more than possessions to her.

I remember my bag resembling a turtle's shell. Heavy, round, the container of everything important to me. I remember freaking out when I lost my homework. I cried and pleaded to the teacher, and all she did was say, "Bring it in tomorrow; it's truly fine."

I remember having a group of friends whom I loved and with whom I bonded. We were the smart ones, the unpopular, and the ones the idiots relied on. We were cruel and beyond quirky, but to the outside world, we were dignified and solitary. I remember my class pushing my guy friend and me together because we were so similar. Denial couldn't survive. The shared interests between us were as endless as the Grand Canyon.

I remember my heart growing and skipping a beat for him. He was sweet and smart. My first crush. We grew distant. He was cruel and cold. My first heartbreak and taste of the sadism of the world. I remember my best friend. He was amazingly sweet, and I found myself in his arms every time I saw him. Never did I hug him and not look into his eyes. The only guy who never hurt me and stood by my side. My friend, never more. I remember when the crush grew as fast as a shooting star falls. My first secret. My secret shame. The key to ultimate destruction or ultimate happiness— inner conflict.

I remember when the perfectionist within began to grow and take over the me I had become accustomed to. I remember abandoning all traces of middle school minus my one best girl friend and best guy friend. I remember applying to high school. I was so happy I got into my first choice. I was so happy to rid myself of my ex and my forbidden crush. Graduation day marked a new beginning, a needed beginning.

I remember being a freshman and being Bambi in a field of wolves. I remember being free, having a clean slate, and finally becoming the true me. I remember being a sophomore. Older, wiser, accustomed to the wolves, and of being one myself. I remember being a junior. Older, wiser, a wolf, a nerd, a Disney fanatic, a stressed-out human being.

I remember wanting to tear my hair out. I remember taking SATs. It was hell, but the real agony was waiting to hear my score. I remember finding two new friends who I spent my weekends with. Boys. Crazy. Sweet. Both vanished and both returned. Questions for both that were never answered. I remember having busy weeks and no sleep. I remember wanting to strangle the seniors for not providing a warning.

I remember school: middle and high. I remember it all.

The Gym

by JASMINE BROOKS

Going to the gym everyday was a must. After-school was spent at the gym; weekends were spent at the gym; days and nights were spent at the gym. Gymnastics was my favorite thing to do. Missing a gym day was like dropping the ice cream that you very much wanted on the ground. The gym was my getaway. Getaway from stress, anger, and anything else that bothered me. It was like escaping from jail and being free. Free from everything. Entering the gym made me content. It was like someone paid for me to get more ice cream after it had fallen on the ground. From the leotard that stuck to me like glue to the tight shorts that gave me a wedgie.

Doing flips and tricks on the floor was my favorite. Running fast into my stunt took everything off my mind and made me only think about the skill itself and sticking the landing. It was like I was flying—going so high up into the air and then landing with relief. It was pretty much like that with every event. Thinking about balance was key when on the balance beam, and thinking about holding myself up was key when on the bars or vault. At competitions it felt like all my hard work had paid off. I never thought there would come a day when I wasn't constantly at the gym, like how one does daily routines such as brushing their teeth or taking a shower. It was second nature to me.

But that time came. I wanted to try other things in life, but gymnastics was so overpowering that I couldn't. It was then that I decided to stop doing gymnastics. Saying goodbye to my second home was very hard. Saying goodbye to my team members, coaches, and the different events made me feel so sad. Like the ice cream that had fallen on the ground, but this time it was gone for good. It's a very strange feeling not being at the gym every day, but what I can say is that being out of gymnastics has made me realize that acting is my true passion.

Bigger Than You Think

by SHAROYA BRACEY

Being tall, I automatically feel so close to the ceiling in close spaces, like elevators. At a point in my life I hated them. Why? Well for one, it is an enclosed space. It is so boxed in that the height is never a height where you feel short in it. It is one of those spaces where being in there just makes you feel awkward. It only makes matters worse when rude people remind me how abnormal I am.

My stepmother and I had walked into this elevator on many occasions, but this time was special: a lady walked on to the elevator with us. She was maybe in her mid- to late forties or early fifties. She had on a long, big coat because it was wintertime. You know, one of those older females from your building or street who was always in someone else's business and always loud; you could tell she was coming down the block because she was always talking to someone, and her inside voice is yelling? That was this woman.

She walked into the elevator and awkwardly looked me up and down. I ignored it because people always look, but inside I felt the elevator slowly closing in on me. The walls were getting smaller and shorter. The elevator was going down, and I felt trapped. I could feel her judging me.

Finally, she slightly turned to me and said, "How tall are you?"

How short are you? I thought to myself and looked at her because of her weird and slightly rude question. I replied, "I'm five foot eleven."

The woman smiled and looked forward again, only to turn back with squinting eyes, "Do you play any sports?" *Do you not play sports?*

I gave her the sweetest smile I could, "No, I do not."

She, not realizing her rude question, continued to speak, "Well you should; you shouldn't waste your height."

I looked at her, my eyes piercing through her face with a look so cold that she would've thought she was in an icebox. But that did not faze her. "You should play a sport; you could go to college."

I felt my head now touching the ceiling of the elevator as I went rushing down. My body then seemed too big for this space. My body and point of view were all different. At this point, I knew exactly how Alice felt after drinking the potion. As I was crashing down, I looked at her like she had a flying pig on her forehead, and I silenced myself, only because I knew the words I could say. Saying that my height would be wasted and that would be my only ticket into college is like me saying, "Well, you are short so you don't have any specialty; you aren't anything because you aren't tall."

But I smiled and once again said, "No."

After we left the longest elevator ride ever, she continued to talk about my height to my stepmom as I walked away from them. The saddest part about this story is that that woman didn't know me from a hole in the wall. In that short, small, and awkward elevator ride, she had my entire life planned and figured out, solely based off my height.

I am still in the elevator even when I'm out of it. Every time that woman talked, she brought me to a lower place and made me feel so abnormal and weird in that elevator. However, after that day, that elevator began to take me to a high place, a higher mindset, a higher feeling of myself. It was the point when I realized that I was not abnormal, but different. My being different made her want to pick me out, and I am now okay with that. Elevators used to make me feel so big and awkward, but now I feel empowered, different, above-average, and tall.

Losing Life's Grip

by CHELSEA JAMES

I remember seeing but not feeling. Some may believe it was a peculiar thing, but I didn't know any better. Crying was the only sound that stood out and bounced around the gloomy, solemn walls. Black seemed to be the trending color at the moment, aside from the occasional white pamphlet that lured me and others to the sad location that day. The church was usually a place of praise and refuge for those in turmoil. Today, however, it was a place of sorrow, guilt, and depression. Looking at the body in front of me didn't evoke any happy feelings, nor did it evoke any sad feelings. I was curious, actually. I was questioning why there was the still body of a middle-aged woman in a casket. I had believed that she was sleeping. I was used to believing that the woman would wake up after sleeping, so I was unaware that she would be eternally asleep. Playing with dolls, watching cartoons, and clinging to my mom's leg was the norm for the eight-year-old me, so of course, seeing a still body would make me believe this woman was "asleep." "She is supposed to be waking up, why isn't she?" I thought. I wasn't aware of the consequences that came with the gift of life, the act of passing away in the end. It's a cruel and bittersweet world. I looked back at the casket and stared at the still body of my Aunt Bunny. I didn't remember much about her, but the times I do recall are ones I will eternally cherish. Losing a loved one to cancer is hard, but losing a loved one that you barely had the opportunity to be with is harder. With this memory in mind, I am forever engraved with the idea that you should cherish what you have before it disappears forever. For as long as the world spins and the earth is green with new wood, she will lie in that grave and not in my arms.

Where the Memories Lie

by JESSENIA GUZMAN

It was the other side of the rainbow where golden memories lay, waiting to be remembered. Trees and flowers spread out everywhere. Benches on one side and a playground on the other. A place that held us hostage. A place we hold in our hearts.

Here is where we had fun. Jumping, running, playing here and there. A shiny metal slide where our days passed by. A friend will sit down at the very end of the slide. One by one, we would slide down and pile on top of one another as we impatiently waited for the first person to be pushed off the edge of the slide. Once their body made contact with the concrete floor, laughter filled the air.

Here is where the seasons strolled by, but where winter stayed in our hearts. Droplets of snowflakes dangling from the bright blue sky danced their way onto the ground. Little by little, the snow started to pile up. Each petite snowflake had its own unique design, but each snowflake wanted to be embraced in our loving hands and be thrown off into the air where it once belonged. We had encountered a snowball fight.

Here is where he confessed to the extra beat in his heart when he thinks of me. My face was the canvas, and the pigmentation created by his words that adorned my cheeks was the art. I remember how his tender lips felt against mine. I also remember that right after that my friends dropped water on us to "make it rain," because who doesn't want a kiss under the rain, right?

But … we grew too old for the slide. That snowball fight isn't as much fun when you get hit across the face with a snowball. And his beautiful words vanished into thin air as we parted ways. Those little children running around the park grew into young adults. "We should meet up," we would say, but we never did.

Memories

by ASHLEY JAVIER

I remember the third football game of the season, filled with friends, family, random people just passing by. It was impossible to find a familiar face in such a tight crowd. The September air had a pleasant breeze to it, and leaves were scattered all over the sidewalk, a clear indicator that fall was right around the corner.

I remember the blazing sun hitting us directly over the bleachers. I remember watching you, focused, a look of determination plastered on your face. It was as if nothing else mattered, just you and the ball. I remember when my heart swelled with pride, watching you on that field. I remember the roaring and cheering of the crowd on my side of the bleachers. I remember the feeling of concern washing over me when I saw you get tackled. I also remember the feeling of relief when I saw you jump back up.

I remember the all-too-familiar smell of french fries and hot grease in the air as I waited for you, sitting at a McDonald's booth. My best friends and I shared fries and caramel frappés, nervously looking towards the door, waiting for you and your friends.

I remember walking behind the field late at night, holding your hand, feeling safer than I ever have before. The air had a chill to it, the streets quiet. Our friends' loud voices trying to overpower one another broke the silence of the night.

I remember sitting side by side on the bleachers, watching another team play. Your friends passed around an Arizona bottle filled with liquor, trying to flirt with my friends. I leaned against you, and you rested your hand on my knee. I felt at home, there, with you.

I remember when you walked me to my best friend's house later that night. You kissed me goodbye, and I felt the butterflies inside my stomach as they collided against one another, drunk with emotion.

I remember that November morning when you told me you needed space; things were too complicated. I felt the butterflies disappear all at once.

I remember when I saw you with her two weeks later. She was your "friend."

I remember when I loved you more than anything. I don't anymore.

Love and Growing Up

by TREYSHA ROBINSON

December 2014

I was sitting on a bench in the middle of one of my favorite parks in Manhattan. I've always felt a warm security there. Good things always happened there. But it was one crisp winter morning that truly illustrated this sentiment.

He seemed to be in a rush. I didn't know at the moment why I felt so compelled to hang on to his every movement. He was fascinating in every way imaginable, and all I wanted to do was walk right up to him. However, being my typical teenage self, I did no such thing. As if in response to my thoughts, however, he turned and met my gaze. He smiled. I think I smiled back, but it may have been an awkward smirk. He, surprisingly, walked up to me. There was a semi-awkward introduction, flirtation, an exchange of information, and the start of a very startling relationship.

January 2015

This guy.

Every daydream is consumed by the image of him. It was not just in school. It was every free moment mymind had. I lost sleep sometimes and missed my train stop once.

He engulfed every part of my mind; it was like he owned it. He had me wrapped around his finger, as every free thought was focused on him. He had me, and I didn't think I wanted to let go ...

March 2015

This was no longer a teenage crush ... this was passion and lust on the fullest scale. No one could make me feel what he made me feel. These feelings seemed to be nothing but dangerous. Whenever he held me, I felt like a tidal wave of complete ecstasy rolled over every micrometer of me.

Now it may seem like this was anticipated or fated, but it was just luck. The park. The look. That park was us in a way-- often changing with the times, never remaining in one state for a prolonged period of time. But when we could, we would take in the beauty of it all and hold on to it as long as possible.

Every time I saw him, every time he spoke to me ... I can't even describe what came over me in those moments. His voice as smooth as caramel; it hooked me on every word. Every time he looked at me with his hazel eyes ... it was like I was put in a trance.

He may have become a minor obsession ... I tried to distance myself because this could not have been healthy. But he reeled me in every time with his smile as cunning as the Cheshire cat's.

April 2015

The park. It was our place. We shared some of our darkest secrets and desires on the benches of this park. We had some sort of connection to it that I couldn't explain. But somehow, we always found ourselves sauntering into the park hand in hand.

Inner Thoughts

When I first met him, he became the only object of my affection for the first few years I knew him. He was this magnificent creature I could only look at and not touch. Every time we spoke, I couldn't get a full sentence out. My whole body shook in his presence. Really. Head to toe. These feelings made me nervous. I was still a child in the eyes of most. But I needed to grow. My sapling self needed to grow straight into a tree.

    I don't admit feelings like that. Why? I don't know. I might be afraid of rejection or maybe what would happen if he shared those feelings. I do admit that I have a big issue committing romantically because it's hard for me to own up to my feelings. I've never been in a relationship where I was fully committed to the guy I was with. Relationships are the only things I consistently fail at.

    But I wanted that now … and I wanted it with him.

June 2015

I had just gotten home from school one day. I remember it vividly, as it was the day the nature of our relationship changed. If someone were to ask me what I had learned that day, I would have no answer. He was the only thing on my mind. So I picked up my phone.

Ring, ring …

The anxiety. The anticipation.

"Hello."

My heart skipped a beat.

"Hey," I said. "I know this may sound crazy but I can't stop thinking about you."

Long pause …

Why did I go and open my stupid mouth?

"Then I must be crazy too," he finally said.

I laughed. "You had me scared there for a minute."

He laughed this time. "I'm sorry, babe. I'm just mad I didn't get to say it first."

"Heh heh. I'm lucky this is over the phone because I'm pretty sure I have the goofiest look on my face," I said.

We stayed on the phone a few hours talking about our days, school, politics … You know, normal topics of conversation. That's why I was surprised when he asked me …

"Do you wanna go out Saturday?"

"I-in public?" I asked.

"Yeah. I mean, it's not crazy, just … different," he replied.

"Umm," I said, searching for an answer.

"It's okay to say n-," he started.

I cut him off. "Of course, sounds great."

I sensed a smile in his voice. "Okay, cool. I'll text you the details," he said. "See you Saturday, baby."

"See you Saturday," I replied.

I hung up the phone and started nervously playing with it. I was anxious again and anticipation crept up my spine. I noticed the clock. 10:32. I started smiling.

Inner Thoughts Part Deux

This was the day that my eyes finally opened. The day that my heart opened. I actually opened up myself to someone who was a complete stranger only a few months before. The park was always my safe haven. But now I had found my serenity in his arms, his eyes, his smile, his every look, his every word. It was on this day that all of my connections to my childhood seemed to be completely severed and the sapling finally became a tree.

The Boy in the Trails

by TYLER ROARTY

I remember agreeing to meet him in the trails just like every other day. This time would be different because it was our last time together before I would lose the sight of his smile because of hundreds of miles of separation. We got lost for hours in the middle of the woods because we had hoped that that would make time stop. I remember that it was pouring rain, and I had hoped that the deafening sound of the thunder and rainfall would drown out the screaming reminder that I was falling in love with my best friend. I remember the exact spot where we were in the trails when he stopped me and gave me a box that contained the necklace I would wear every day since then. It used to be his grandmother's, with whom he was very close. He had received it after she passed away and wanted me to have it before I left. I remember how badly I wanted to melt into his arms and be frozen to his lips, but I believed that this would never happen because he was my best friend and nothing more. I remember when we got into a fight a couple weeks after I left, and we stopped talking for a little over a year. I remember thinking about him each time I put on the necklace for all 438 days that we did not speak. I remember when I slowly began to force myself to forget him. I remember that once I decided this, he messaged me again, as if he knew that I was forgetting about him and did not want to be left behind. I remember we started talking again. I remember when he asked me out a few months after that. I remember every moment we have spent in the two years (and counting) since that moment.

Cocoon

by NATALIE ULLOA

Four walls conceal my natural habitat from the world. My desert-colored walls give me comfort and absorb all my emotions. They hold secrets and laughs, slumbers and sleepless nights. There is always something to do in my limited square footage. My walls expand with my aspirations and imagination. Although I am confined, I am not constricted. My space may seem dull to others because of its size and content, but it still manages to inspire me, to influence me, to support me. Anything is possible in my world because my walls don't judge. These four walls have seen every emotion has leaked from my body and seeped into the hardwood floors, sometimes splattering onto my rectangular brown rug placed in the center of it all. My tears, after getting too emotionally attached to a compelling song; my smiles, after witnessing the adorable actions of my favorite boy band; my anger, after being misunderstood by my family with no one to turn to; and my laughter, after watching the constant *Friends* reruns that are always flashing colors onto my TV. These are the things that have built up my walls, brick by brick.

I am able to shut the world out and be completely as I am, how I was meant to be. The anthems that fill the air create a soundtrack to my existence. My dance parties to Justin Bieber and Arctic Monkeys don't require a plus one. The only observer of my talents is myself and her reflection in the mirror, strung with lights around its perimeter, attached to my bureau, which is topped with fragrances and hair products. This place is so diverse and accepting. I feel most confident being alone and admiring my own features at my desk which is supposed to be used to admire homework. The wavy brown hair that brushes my shoulder blades, my sculpted eyebrows, the hollows of my cheeks that shape my face. My vanity cannot be exposed to the world. I can also feel like the world, including myself, are my worst enemies. My insecurities cannot be exposed to the world.

My beige and dark brown accents, along with the massive canvas of a ballerina and the many photos that give insight to the journey of my coming of age, are decorations to my chronicles in solitude. My space is lit up with all my memories, tangled up with my worst nightmares, made in my sleep but also made from feelings of tight-chested panic attacks and hopeless moments of anxiety. There's so much more to my simple little cocoon, more like a metropolis to me, but all you need to know is that these four walls, they hold me up.

WHERE WE GO AND WHAT WE CARRY WITH US

Myself Again

by IYANNA WEBSTER

Something important to me keeps me warm at night, shows me comfort. I would rather be here than anywhere else. In the morning it's the hardest thing to leave, and at night it's the best thing to come home to. The feeling I get when I come to this place is like no other. I can be myself here whenever I feel like it. This special place I have in my heart is my bedroom. The dreams I have here are sensational. In one dream, I was in a place by myself underwater breathing, relaxing, being my own person. If I screamed, no one could hear it. It was like I was myself.

The Sunset Painting

by NICOLE APARICIO

We walked inside the art museum, the cool, air-conditioned air hitting our faces as we made our way inside. The cement-gray tiles gave a contrast to the black boots that my cousins and I were wearing. The see-through glass walls clashed with the sun as it created a beautiful rainbow on the floor. I took a map and skimmed through. To my surprise, there were eight floors. Starting with the last, the eighth floor, we went and worked our way down. Natural sunlight filled the rooms as we stepped out of the elevators. My boots made a padding sound. The area was vast as I walked into a room with little screens built into the wall. I was on my tippy toes as I tried to look through the rectangular slots. Clips of wars were shown. *How is it that clips of war can be considered art*? I thought to myself. That was just one question out of many that were lingering in my head. The fifth floor might have been one of my favorites. There was an interactive art piece. Hesitant at first, we lay down at the center and looked up at the ceiling. Clouds and a pale blue sky took over the screen. Slowly a dark blue sky with tiny little stars appeared. I felt as if I had left the atmosphere, although I took note that my body got tense and my hands clammy. This must be its purpose, how our emotions build a certain way of feeling toward experiences.

After we got up and entered the next room, to our surprise, we saw a monitor of the interactive art installation that we had participated in, but in this art piece you were able to see the thermal energy of each individual. I felt exposed the slightest bit and confused knowing that people had been watching me. But at the same time I felt great knowing that I was a part of the art that someone saw. Coming back from my train of thought, I speed-walked and linked arms with my cousin, and before I knew it we were in the outdoor gallery. There were little groups of people who were taking selfies or pointing off into the distance. I smiled knowing that I would be doing that too but also knowing that these people love art as much as I do.

"Let's go to the roof," my cousin suggested excitedly.

We followed his lead onto the staircase, nausea rising in me, not knowing how high up we were and the cars and all this open air around us. My eyes concentrated on his Canon camera hung around his pale neck as we made our way up the stairs. The breeze and chill of the afternoon hit me once we were on the roof. The beautiful lilac and orange sky was set on the horizon as the bright sun seemed to be in the center of the calm waters and the sky. I took in the full beauty of the view and snapped pictures of it for memory. Although I can't capture the serenity of that exact moment, it will always be with me.

Up

by DANIEL CRUZ

In this crowded city, filled with hate, violence, corruption, and death, I can only look for a place to escape. But where shall I escape to in this endless maze? If I take a right, I will be lost. If I take a left, I will be lost. Each corner and turn is split in half. I feel warm and seamless in one side, then cold and lost in another, and as soon as I take myself into another space, there I am out in the open, my every step watched, judged for my looks and actions, but not for who I am.

In Up, I don't have to be funny for the cocky kids. I don't need to be too cool for the cool kids, and I don't have to be super manly for the jocks. I can just be myself. So why not just open up, close my eyes, and go to Up? Up is where freedom is actually freedom, where rules don't exist, where I find peace, where I feel serenity and enlightenment. Up is my utopia where colors of all sorts exist, where darkness is not indeed my fear nor my danger. Up is space, and to have space is to have everything. Up is my nirvana, my heaven; Up is paradise. When I go to Up, it doesn't last long, but I'm free, and nothing is better than that feeling. Up is my chance of spiritual and mental exploration. Up could be cold or could be warm. When I go to Up, it's never the same.

Up is a handful of emotions and thoughts that could empower you or enslave you. Up tests me and pushes me to my limits. Up makes me want to give up on everything but still manages to make me keep going. These emotions are some that I have never felt and never want to feel. Up brings these distant memories—some warm, some cold, but these places inspire me and show me who I am, who I'm bound to be, and, lastly, who I will become if I were to throw it all away, the cold truth, the truth you do not want to hear about yourself.

But the thing is, once you go Up, you never come down because even the bad things in this place, the thoughts that make you doubt yourself, the fears that hold you down, the mistakes that you make, are not thrown and shamed upon you, because you're free when you're in Up. In Up I see the past, the present, and think about my future, and use it all to better myself. This place is my weakness, but it's also my power. Hopefully, you can go to Up as I do and feel your divinity.

Night Marmalade

by PARIS JEROME

Light shines from the clear window wall into the deep baby-blue colored room, sometimes a pure white or beige. Despite this room not being fully claimed by years of mementos, colorful pillows, and cute figurines, it always felt like my own place. On occasion, the trees outside would graze against the window as rain slammed on the pavement, but it just fueled me to drown deep into the huge warm duvet. I visit this place frequently, on the train listening to music, doing my hair, walking home, or when zoning out in class. I always looked forward to going back to that place. The room changes from rural scenery to urban to suburban, depending on how I feel, but I still feel at peace. I can imagine a lilac and marmalade sky pouring over the home as the room gives a gradient to the orange and purple hues. In the abyss of black, the moon rises enough to see the neighboring apartments shine in a sea of sparkling stars and house lights. This room will always remain until I'm too old to dream of it or until it all comes true, my ideal dream bedroom.

The High Line

by NATASHA SANTIAGO

As we went back and forth, yelling and saying things we didn't mean, all I could think was, "Why is this happening? I don't understand." Once the final word was said, my anger overcame me. My face said my anger overcame me. My face was red, my body was numb; even though I was angry, my eyes were watery. There was only one place that brought me peace and serenity.

It starts on 13th Street and ends on 30th street. It is by the river that separates New York City and New Jersey. It is full of beautiful art and crowded with plants. My favorite part is a little city where a man has anyone draw, paint, whatever they want, and he takes their art and puts it around the city. It brings merry smiles. As I walk, I see more art. As I look at the art, I start to feel calm. I lie on the wooden bench and watch the sunset. The sky is pink and orange. My body and mind are completely relaxed, and I call them and everything is fixed.

Enjoy and Appreciate

by STEPHANIE PUJOLS

I've always enjoyed the outdoors, cool breeze blowing my hair across my face softly and accidentally slipping strands between my lips and into my mouth. "Ew," I always mumbled to myself. The sun was beaming down so warm and bright. My legs walked on their own, ready to be free and lead the way into the Central Park entrance on 100th street. Central Park stretched its warm arms from 59th street to 110th street and was filled with many things to do like the zoo, parks, open fields, a pool, ice skating, dog walking, running, biking, etc. Something for everyone.

Shoulders side-by-side, my sisters and I walked, shortest, medium, tallest. We seemed to always walk in size order which surprised me but also made me laugh because my oldest sister is, ironically, the shortest. The bright, blue sky was above us, and the birds were flying so freely, chirping their way through the sky.

"Where should we explore today?" asked my younger sister excitedly. "I want to get lost and try to find our way back home on our own," she added with laughter after. We all agreed, and soon enough our legs were guiding us through the long park ahead of us. I always liked doing things outside of the box. I don't like doing small things; new things always excite me. Looking around smelling the cool, warm air, I thought about how beautiful life really is if you take the time or one simple moment to appreciate it.

The Island of Excitement

by BIANCA JACKSON

Imagine that as soon as you get off the plane and walk out of the airport, your heart melts at the beautiful sights and excitements of nature. Then all the old memories build up and bring smiles and giggles. You drive down the busy roads filled with people off to their duties, some ignorant, some friendly, but the majority good-hearted people. You see entrepreneurs on the road selling anything they could get their hands on, things like cut up pineapple, mango, coconut trash and/or coco water, or sweets like peanut chew bags, juice, etc. They launch your taste buds and just make you feel so good. These entrepreneurs are just one little part of why you enjoy the islands. The island isn't all fun and games, though. So many hardworking people make sure that they make the best out of the little they have, especially with a good smile on their faces and so much positivity that it makes you look at your life and appreciate what you have. The roads even tell stories, stories of how your great-grandparents survived and made the best out of what they had. You tend to not realize how much greatness you have inside and that nationalism brings out the inner you and the pride you have for what you believe in. In America, stuff is often taken for granted because they're imperialist and have industrialized, so everything they needed was already taken, so they already have help and don't need the extra bargain to succeed, but back in the islands everything is earned. You'd think they'd have a BJs or Sam's Club, but they basically had a bank-like store that gave them a minimal supply of basic needs, and if you worked your way to the finer things, so be it. Life is what you make of it, but in Jamaica the loving people have a big rubbing on that.

Tropical Paradise of Nassau

by ALEXANDRIA HAUGHTON

After all of the security checks and metal detectors, we finally got inside. The wait felt like an eternity until the gates opened. We showed our tickets and strolled through the carpeted hallway to step foot onto our soaring bird. We took our seats and ordered drinks and food for the remainder of the trip.

After a long period of sleeping and music, we'd finally reached our destination. The smell of the tropics in the air made it feel like paradise. The murmurs of conversations filled my ears. I came to realize that my family members had arrived before us. I got bone-crushing hugs from my aunt, uncles, and cousins that I barely know. Eventually, I was led up to our room and fell straight into bed.

My favorite thing to do was go to the beach and swim in the water. I changed into my bathing suit right away after reaching my room and putting down my luggage. I ran with urgency down the hotel steps to get there. This place reminded me of peace in a sunset. The smell of salt water filled my nostrils. That may not be a pleasurable smell to everybody, but it actually smelled great and kept me calm. I don't know what's better: the soft sand beneath my feet or the serene sound of crashing waves. Hearing the seagulls cry added more peace to the atmosphere. *Whoosh*! Sounds of the waves beating against the rocks in the water. After walking along the shoreline, collecting washed-up shells and clams, I found a perfect spot to sit and lie back under the breeze to let the sun kiss my tanning skin. As I played with soft, squishy sand beneath my feet, I thought about my life, family, and future. However, my thoughts were interrupted by screams of my lovely aunts whom I actually knew and I stood up to give them and their children hugs. I could tell this was going to be a good four days with them.

The days spent up until the reunion banquet were fun-filled. My cousins and I went to the beach, played in the hotel room, and went to buffets. It was like a movie whenever all of the cousins reunited. Whether we played in the hotel rooms, got hectic from Nerf gun wars to hide and seek, to just wilding out and dancing. With just a few more hours until the banquet, I took a shower, washed my hair, curled it, and then got dressed for the event. The banquet was the actual reunion party where the whole family came together and celebrated with one another. We also performed dances and songs and recited our own poetry. Everyone was dressed in casual yet dressy clothing to impress the other family members. Tonight was the night where we all rejoiced, then departed the next morning with the reunion of the family in our memories and hearts until the following year. This beautiful, relaxing reunion of my family in the Bahamas was like a cool breeze with rays beating on sun-kissed skin where happiness turned into serenity.

First Time on the Road

by MARIA PAZ GUERRON

It was 5:00 AM, and I was super tired. Getting only four hours of sleep wasn't a good start to the trip, but I had to get myself ready for the long day ahead. I quickly changed from my PJs to my light-colored jeans, my Minnie mouse t-shirt, and my white Converse. I washed my face, brushed my teeth, and pulled my hair into a ponytail. I had forgotten to pack some of my things, and I was behind schedule. I was supposed to leave at 5, but I overslept. My dad went downstairs to pull up the car, so I dragged the luggage downstairs. As I walked out of my building, I noticed the floor was wet. It seemed like last night it rained. I carried my luggage to the trunk of the minivan and quickly ran back upstairs. There were two more suitcases sitting in the living room, but I had to get my dog ready, so I put his leash on. I grabbed my bag and quickly went through a mental checklist to see if I had everything I was going to need for Florida. It was 5:20 AM, and my sister and mother were still packing a few things, so I knew we were going to be way off schedule. I yelled at them to hurry up, and finally we were all set to go. I closed all the curtains in my house, locked all the windows, turned off all the plugs and outlets, and walked out the door. In the lobby we could see that it was raining again. *Shoot!* I thought to myself. I knew for sure we were going to get soaked, so I had to make a run for it. I picked up my dog and dashed to the car. Once inside the car, we were safe from the cold rain, but thanks to my sister being so slow she got the car wet. Once everyone was inside the car, I pulled out my dog's bed, laid it on the floor, took his leash off, and put him on his bed. I made sure in the back of the seats I had my essentials like a brush, toilet paper, Clorox wipes, and my blanket.

It was 5:30 AM, and finally we were on our way to the first state, New Jersey. An hour flew by, and we were still driving in New Jersey. I was so sleepy, so I pulled out my pillow and blanket and went to sleep. Then something bright was shining on my eyes, so I woke up and looked outside the window, and saw a bunch of cars and a big, blue bridge. I went on my phone and looked up my current location. It said we were on the Delaware Bridge. I was so fascinated by how beautiful the bridge was and the view of the bridge that I no longer was tired, but I was really hungry, and so was the rest of my family. Once we crossed the bridge and got to Delaware, we found the first gas station. By that time, it was 7:20 AM. My dad got out of the car and went to fill the tank with gas, and I took my dog for a walk around the gas station. Then I went inside the gas station to use the bathroom and then went to order food. I ordered four bagels with cream cheese. My parents got coffee, and my sister and I got orange juice. We ate in the car and continued our trip.

The next stop was Maryland, which wasn't so far. The view was simple; trees and lakes and houses were everywhere. Around 9:15 AM we got to Maryland, and I was so surprised by the beautiful houses and old vintage buildings. I had never seen anything like it, and it was all new. We kept driving and made it to Washington, D.C., and I was totally in shock. When I saw the big skyscrapers and the big Capitol Building, I was so amazed. Then we drove quickly by the White House and Lincoln Memorial. I will never forget the beautiful structures in the nation's capital. The traffic in Washington, D.C. was really bad, so it took a long time to get to Virginia. When we arrived in Virginia, it was 11:33 AM, and I was super hungry. So I made my dad stop, and I went into Burger King and only bought french fries to snack on since we planned to have lunch around 1:00 PM. Virginia was so beautiful; it had an old vintage type of vibe, and it was filled with nature. I loved looking at the rivers and lakes as we went by, and it was so interesting because all you see in New York are huge buildings but no farms and wild animals. Virginia was so big that it took so long just to cross it, and at 2:00 PM, we made it to North Carolina. We stopped at the gas station, and again my dad filled the tank while I walked my dog. As we kept driving south, the temperature was rising, and soon I was sweating. I begged my dad to turn the A/C and I turned on the radio. The music was super annoying; all they played in that state was country music. I was scrolling through different stations to find pop music but nothing, and it was so weird to hear that type of music. In South Carolina, there were so many fields, and it looked beautiful with all the horses and animals. It was such a different environment than New York.

At 5:09 PM we arrived in South Carolina, and I was so tired and hungry. I felt bad for my dad because he was the only one driving, and my mother was talking to him. I really concentrated on the environment, and it sort of made me miss home, because everything was different and the life over there was different.

In the gas station, everyone seemed to know that I wasn't from around there, and it made me feel awkward. I just really wanted to get to Florida and take a big nap. Around 6:00 PM we stopped at McDonald's to eat and once again followed our routine. We were still two states away from Florida, and we were miles away from the next state, Georgia.

At 8:00 PM we left South Carolina and entered Georgia, and it was getting dark. The sun was setting, and it was so pretty to watch, especially how it disappeared behind the trees as we drove on the empty highway filled with a couple of big trucks. Around 9:00 PM we stopped at McDonald's again, filled the car with gas, used the bathroom, and walked the dog. The funny thing about Georgia is that everyone there has a country accent. It was so funny to hear, but they thought my accent was funny, so it was a weird but humorous situation. We stopped at a supermarket outside the gas station and bought Georgia peaches, and they were delicious. They were so sweet and yummy that we ended up buying a basket of them. The thing I hated about Georgia was the huge bugs; they terrified me. The biggest bug I had ever seen in New York was a cockroach.

Georgia was a big state, too, and by 10:00 PM we made it out and finally arrived in Florida. The bad news was that my uncle lives in the middle of Florida, so we had to continue to drive for a couple of more hours. It was so dark in Florida that you couldn't even see the sidewalk, but we made it to downtown Florida, and, OMG, it was so incredible. The buildings were so nice, and they had so many lights. It almost looked like Las Vegas, and I couldn't keep my eyes off them. Around midnight we made one last stop to once again fill the car up with gas, walk the dog, use the bathroom, and buy food. By the time we were close to my uncle's house, my dad was so tired that he had skipped a toll and didn't even realize. There were train tracks on the street, and we passed by so many motels and Wal Marts. By 1:00 AM we had finally reached our destination, and everyone was so tired, which was weird because my dog and sister slept the whole way and only got up to use the bathroom and eat. Either way, I was so relieved that we made it, and that night I dreamt about all the wonderful new places and the new experiences I had encountered that day. This was my very first road trip, and it was something I was never going to forget.

The Best Memory

by AALIYAH CASTILLO

Many memories come when I go to the bright, open backyard. I remember the time we, my grandparents, aunts, uncle, parents, and the kids, celebrated my fourteenth birthday. It was a bright, happy day.

I see the backyard as a remedy for sadness. It was a fun day because we were in the big, deep pool that smelled majorly of chlorine. Then, after a while we could smell food! As we continued to play in the pool, grandma asked, "Who wants to eat?" All the kids at the same time yelled, "Me!" Then all the adults begin to laugh.

After we ate, we sat with our full bellies, big as balloons, but hard as rocks. Later on in the day, we went back into the pool and played tag and Marco Polo and competed in swimming races. We ended the nice, mellow night singing "Happy Birthday" to me. Everyone yelled and I was standing there looking like a happy, but lost, puppy. You can relate to that when people are singing to you and you just don't know what to do with yourself. The night sky was pinkish purple and beautiful, just like the family portrait we took.

My Little Blue Beach

by KELFRI BUENO

My beach, my little, blue beach. The Dominican Republic is rich and rare to me, but my favorite place is my blue beach: Boca Chica. Memories of family fun and the breeze hitting my brown, smooth skin. My mother sitting, looking at the sky while I sit next to her, telling her she's beautiful; her little smile and fat little cheeks with dimples so deep. My mother, my best friend. She laughs at my thoughts and then tells me she loves me. My mother and I sit, watching the sky turn dark. Night-so-bright and beautiful stars shine like little light bulbs. I gaze up and think about life and the people around me. I look at the moon, and it's my favorite thing to look at in the night sky. It looks as if there's a face on the moon as I gaze into the night sky. It reminds me of my uncle, who has passed away. The view of the moon, especially while sitting on the beach, is so much more beautiful. My mom always taps me and says, "Look, there's a face on the moon." The only thing I keep to myself is that the face on the moon is my uncle's. I decide to keep it a secret because I like being the only one who sees him. When the time of night comes, when I am too tired, I decide to walk around the beach. The moonlight hitting the clear water makes it shimmer as I spot the fish swimming happily. The little sounds of my little, blue beach, my most favorite beach. When the end comes and my mom screams, "*Vámonos, mi amor!*" I say, "Until next time" to my little blue beach. On the way home, riding through the hills with the beautiful sights of the water, the breeze hits my face and I start getting sleepy. It feels amazing. My bed at home waits for me to dream about my beautiful day at my little, blue beach.

My Fire Escape

by FIONA BRISEÑO MEYER

Right above everyone, but not too above everyone, I'm right in between the coziness of my own home and the street where everybody else is living. A very well-known neighborhood called Soho. Broadway and Lafayette, where you see the street style kids, the tourists, the Sunday brunchers, the shoppers, even people dressed in suits. I see people dressed for all occasions, looking like they're heading to different destinations. I like to listen to the cars, the people. I like to observe the city. The cold metal touching my skin. A little adrenaline rush from the thought of an extremely old fire escape dropping at any moment. I like the rush. You wouldn't think it's peaceful, hearing ambulances and people screaming, "Taxi, taxi;" and "The next stop is Delancey" coming from the automated train voices that make their way up through the grates. But I love sitting on this fire escape. I love thinking, sitting, writing, even taking pictures to capture the beauty of New York City, the still, and the not-so-still. Building after building, they are all different, and some are sky-high, with one million windows and billions of different faces. There is always something new here. This fire escape is my not-so-quiet quiet place.

Boardwalk

by ELIZABETH CANELA

It takes a long trip to get to my godmother's house. I speed-walk from my house down the street to catch the "C" train to 34th Street. Finally it's my stop at Penn Station, always crowded like the HSF elevators. I read a black and white sign that reads, "NJ TRANSIT." I stroll towards the sign and buy a ticket to Perth Amboy. I ask the nice lady what time my train comes in. She tells me 3:30.

"Thanks," I say with a smile.

I take a look at my watch, which reads 2:40. *Ugh*! About an hour until my train boards. My ticket says my train is boarding on Track 8, so I keep that in mind. I take a seat at the waiting area and look around to see everyone else on their pocket-sized computers. I think that these people are robots. My phone reads 3:20. I get up just like everyone else running to Track 8. They look like a flock of birds trying not to miss our train or have any delay. I dodge everyone on my way into the train to take a seat and rest my feet. The train ride is about an hour long. During that ride, I look out my window and observe the wonderful view. The trees in such a delicate green; the rivers and lakes shimmering in blue; and the sky is such a wonderful baby blue.

"Ticket, please." I, startled, look to my left to see a man dressed in all black. I hand over my ticket. Click, click, click. He hole-punches my ticket. I sleep away the minutes I have left for my ride. "Next stop, Perth Amboy" wakes me up like music to my ears. Grabbing my things, I hop off the train. The cold winter breeze hits my cheeks. Brrr! I shiver my way to my grandmother's house a few blocks away from the station.

Ding-dong. Peeping through the window, I see a shadow come open the door. I enter the home, and the smell of rice and beans eases me. I give hugs and kisses to everyone my eye lands on. I zoom up the stairs to my temporary room to drop my bag. I fly back down to party with my cousins. Red, blue, green, the bright lights light up the Xbox controllers. Shooting over here, there! I play *Call of Duty* with them. The graphics of the game are great. After a while, I wander around the kitchen for some food. The rice and beans are served on a plate. I chomp on every grain and bean, savoring every part.

At 9:30 PM, the day has gone by. Then I remember my favorite reason for going to visit my godmother: when my godfather comes home from work, he takes my two younger cousins and me to the boardwalk. I enjoy it because it's quiet and I can think to myself. I wait anxiously for his arrival. Around 2:30 AM, I know he is on his way, and it is time for our daily boardwalk. He comes to make himself something to drink. We exit the house and stroll down the maze of dead streets to the boardwalk. About ten blocks downwards, upwards, left and right to the boardwalk. Once we see the white boards--short, tall, big and small--we are close to the boardwalk. We come across a nice, oak, wooden platform with railings. That's when we know we are at the boardwalk, and from that boardwalk you can see the ocean's dark blue water swaying left and right to the speed of the wind. We walk off the boardwalk onto the sand that is cold and moist, grainy and tannish. From the boardwalk you can see all the city lights: yellow, white, red, green, and many more. It reminds me of Times Square but far away. Sitting on the boardwalk benches you can feel the breeze blowing your hair in every direction. Now my favorite part is the silence of the night. It allows you to hear the creaks coming from walking on the boardwalk. We will all be exhausted from our wonderful adventure, just to do it again the following day. We end up arriving back home from the maze of streets at 5:00 AM. I really enjoy the walks.

The Lost Sister

by SAMANTHA ALVARADO

The room with the big brown couch, white walls, and memories that reach at each corner. The room where I gained a bond with my sister and the place where I later lost her. She was thirteen, while I was six. We would play our favorite video games whenever she came over. I remember the smiles upon our faces; her blue eyes lit up the room. I had looked up to her. She was my big sister. All I ever wanted was to be like her. Whenever I'm in the living room, I remember all the little memories we shared and the way that she fell asleep with her eyes open; it was pretty creepy, but I thought she was the coolest. As the years passed, her visits shortened and shortened, and at the age of sixteen she and our father got into an argument and that was the end of it. It's been seven years now, and the living room remains with only memories of her. I loved my sister. I looked up to her. We spent many days in my living room, and that's all I'll ever have. I try to reach out to her, but there's never a response, never any happy birthdays, simple hellos, and most certainly no I love yous. One of the worst feelings in the world is caring about someone so much and for them to just leave your life for good.

And it all took place in my living room.

The 17ᵗʰ of January

by CLAUDIBEL BATISTA

As I slowly awoke from my sleep, rubbing my eyes, I suddenly turned onto my side and started to check my phone. As I went through my social media, I realized the day and time. As today was a special day, everything was prepared. I quickly jumped off my bed upon the cold floor. Opening my bedroom door fast but quietly, I walked down the small hallway to my parents' room. I opened the door, peeking in like a lion watching over its prey. As I expected, my mother was still snoring at 12:00 PM on this special day, her birthday! For about five minutes, I stood there frozen, just trying to decide my next move. Perhaps I should wake her up. Maybe she won't yell like usual, I thought to myself. Finally I decided to jump on the bed and wake my mother with a big hug and a "Mami stop getting old, you're twenty-four now, right?" My mother's response was a big, warm smile. My mom is my everything; words wouldn't explain my love for her. Her smile brightens any stormy, grey day. Knowing my mom as well as I did, I knew her sleeping session wasn't over. The clock ticked 5:00 PM, and at that time, I was in bed cuddled up with my blanket and on my phone. I heard footsteps!

"The birthday girl is finally up!" I said into the phone. As I stared at my mom getting all dressed up, all her movements suddenly were in slow motion. I asked myself if she would like the letter I had prepared for her. This letter was very special to me since I described how important she was to me and thanked her for many things as well as apologized for others. This letter was a big accomplishment. Because of my inability to express my feelings other than crying, this letter took me two days:

As I get older, I realize more and more how much you have done for me and continue to do every day. There's no bond quite like ours. You know me in ways no one else ever will. You also see in me all the things I don't and can still become. You are my biggest fan, my mentor, my confidant, my hero, my turn-to person when my world comes crashing down...

Trying to figure out the right moment and right way to give my mother the letter was the most difficult part. With this letter she would be introduced to my mind, which scared me. Then I had the idea to put it in the mailbox like a regular letter and wait for her response. Once everyone was dressed and ready, we were out to eat! At the dinner table, everything just felt right. At that very moment, problems and disagreements disappeared. I wanted this feeling to stay forever!

A Place I Used to Call Home

by SHANIA JAMES

I was out of breath, reaching for the golden knob on the old, chipped-paint wooden door. When I walked into the apartment, I began to feel a chill race down my spine. It was quiet, which wasn't normal. There was no smell of home-cooked soul food, but the smell of incense lingered in the air. Joy no longer filled this house, but sorrow was here to stay. It wasn't always like this. In 2014, my Aunt Marilyn passed away and ever since then, everything has changed.

This house holds history. My great-great-grandmother got the place many years ago when she had my great-grandmother, who has never lived anywhere but this house her whole life to this day. She then had my aunt and my grandmother, who had my mother, and they all grew up and were raised in this house.

My mom always told me stories of the old times when she was growing up in the house. She always described how, in the mornings, they would have farina for breakfast, kind of like the porridge from "Goldilocks and The Three Bears". They all gathered in the living room after supper to watch their favorite cartoons on the old black-and-white TV with the antennas at the top. She also told me about the times when they still used pagers to get in contact with one another, and funnier stories from when grandma still had her teeth.

I always loved coming here. It still has an old spirit to it—no WiFi, box TVs, and cool antique phones where you have to spin the dialer in order to put a number in, which is much harder to use than an iPhone. The main reason I liked coming here, though, was Aunt Marilyn, whom I called "Aunt Boog."

I loved spending the night in my great-grandmother's house just to be with her. She always cheered me up and kept me laughing. She consistently had a joyful spirit, and she was good at keeping everyone happy. Everyone knew and loved her. She saved me from getting in trouble all the time and was always there for me wherever and whenever I needed her. She saved me at five years old from choking on a chip. She rushed me to the hospital when I had my first allergic reaction to kiwi, and she reassured me everything was going to be all right.

My best memories with her are when we would stay up together till 3:00 AM, watching Lifetime movies and eating cucumbers with vinegar at the kitchen table. Every time I was around her, she would be cooking soul food and listening to her favorite artist, R-Kelly. She was the one who threw all of our traditional family get-togethers every year, which were the only times when all of my family who grew up in the house would come together. Little did I know, her funeral was going to be the last time all of the family got together.

One night at 1:30 AM, the phone rang, and I could hear the doctor's voice on the phone with my mom saying, "There isn't anything else we can do. I'm sorry." My aunt had been in the hospital for kidney and lung failure. She was doing alright at first, but it seemed like every day she got worse. I always begged to go to visit her in the hospital, but they always told me no because I was too young. When they would go to visit her, I sat at grandma's house anxiously waiting to hear how she was doing.

The day she died, my happiness died. I never got to say goodbye, but I always sent a message that I loved her every time my mom went to visit. On her last day, my mom finally sent a message back: "I love you, too." I cried and cried for months. I dreamt about her every night. She was really the only aunt I had. My other aunts were in rehab or no longer in contact with our family. I never wanted to go back to that house after her death. My great-grandmother always asked me to visit, but I refused to.

Months went by, and tears were shed, and I found myself walking up the stairs to that door again, 3B. Out of breath, I reached for the golden knob on the old, chipped-paint wooden door. Walking in the apartment, I felt a chill race down my spine. I was quiet and you could hear the subway rolling by. I looked outside of the window where I used to watch the fireworks with Aunt Boog, and I stared at the Coney Island Ferris wheel. I was scared to be here; I actually didn't want to be here, not if she wasn't here. I didn't want to go into her room, so I sat at the kitchen table while everyone else did. Sitting there brought back so many memories and thoughts. I was tired of sitting there alone, so I worked up enough nerve to go into her room. Walking in, my eyes examined all of the pictures on the wall. I inhaled the smell of her perfume still wafting in the air. I hit one of the rusty buttons on the old, broken-down radio, and her R-Kelly album began to play. I looked around the room and everything remained the same. It was like she was just here yesterday. Everyone may have just seen an old room walking in there, but I could still see her sitting there singing and laughing like the old days, when things were much happier.

R.I.P. Aunt Boog

Long-Lost Grandfather

by FANTA KANTE

The streets were covered in dirt roads with sparse grass. The sidewalks were made with fruit and vegetable stands and cattle with groups of lambs.

"What do you guys think?" my uncle asked in a thick, West African accent.

"It's different," I said. The window of the Range Rover rolled down, and the moist Malian air whisked my hair. We stopped at a compound that looked like a village. A path of pebbles fought my pumps as I tried to get through. I tapped my brother in shock as a big-breasted woman came running towards my mother.

"Thom? Thom! En Allah!" she called out to the heavens as she bombarded my mother with hugs. *Uh oh, it's my turn*, I thought. My aunt smothered me with kisses as her breasts suffocated me. She dragged my family and me to the main house in the compound. A group of unknown cousins and other relatives ran towards me like hungry birds flying to bread. The smell of lamb stew filled my nose as I walked into the living room. *Wrong day to wear white heels*, I thought with exasperation. I looked down at my shoes, now dirty with red mud. An old limping man with an aged beard and useless arm sat on the couch glaring at an old TV box. I heard my mother's heels approach behind me.

"Papa?!" she started to tear up.

"Thom! Allah I can walk again Walai," the old man spoke to God. The old man dropped his cane and leaped towards my mom. They rejoiced and a dam holding twenty years of absent love broke down.

"Fanta, meet your grandpa," my mom said with glee.

It hit me like a pound of bricks. My grandfather ... for sixteen years ... my last living grandparent, finally.

My mind was blank.

Bonds

by SHAZIAH LA VAN-SMALL

Around when was I six years old, a brother-sister bond was created. That year, my grandma was having a Thanksgiving dinner party. It would be one of the first Thanksgivings that we would have with my brother since he went off to college. My grandma's house was always *the* home to go to if anyone needed anything. Everyone knew where her house was, regardless of if it was years since they last visited. It always smelled of burning incense or the smell of something delicious cooking in the kitchen. No matter where you lived, this was considered your second home. Generation after generation were raised here until old enough to leave. I remember being so excited for this year's Thanksgiving just because I would get to see my big brother, Jamaal. Tomorrow was the big day, and it couldn't come any slower. When tomorrow became today, I was too hyped, the sort of hyped a kid is on Christmas morning. Though it was early in the morning, my mom and grandma were already preparing for the big meal. They always had this bond. Cooking was a big deal in my family, and the both of them loved to do it. It seemed like forever until my family would arrive. I tried keeping myself occupied by doing little things for my grandma like setting the plates and silverware, but this only took me about five minutes. I then tried convincing my mom that I could help cook in the kitchen. She quickly refused, so instead I asked for my favorite snack, Goldfish crackers. My mom had brought a big box as a little snack for me to eat while we were at my grandma's house. She reached for the big box on top of the fridge and poured some in a small bowl.

"No more Goldfish or you're not going to be hungry," she warned. I walked away with the small bowl, brushing off what she had said. "Don't ask for any more either!"

"I'm not!" I hissed. At this point I just wanted people to arrive already because I was getting anxious. Suddenly, I heard the door open then slam shut. I ran out of my grandma's bedroom to see who it was. My eyes dropped to see that it was only my sister. Not that I didn't want to see her, I was just hoping that it would be someone that I didn't see every day. Not too long after, I heard another door open.

"Hey, family!" I already recognized this voice. I ran into the living room once more to see that it was my brother.

"You're here!" I squealed. I ran into his arms excitedly. After letting go, he told me that he missed me so much then walked in the kitchen to hug my family. While in the kitchen he tried sticking a finger in his favorite sweet potato pie.

"Not yet," my mom caught him just in time. "These pies are for you to take back with you, and I'm not making any more."

Soon we were ready to eat. I didn't want food yet, though. I craved more Goldfish crackers. The sound of laughter and stories filled the house and for a while it felt like all the problems that we may have had vanished because all that we felt was love. This was how our family bonded, just through good old conversation and laughter. The sound of metal forks scraping glass plates must've been music to my grandma's ears. She loved the feeling that someone enjoyed her cooking. This was when I decided to make my big move. I walked right into the kitchen and reached for the box filled with my kryptonite. Not far behind me was my mom. I had been busted.

"Don't even try it. What did I say? Put it back right now." I was furious. I stomped out of the kitchen and back into my grandma's room. As I passed through the living room there was nothing but silence. Why couldn't she just let me have my way? I only wanted a few more Goldfish. My face was hot and my eyes felt like a hundred pounds. Suddenly, I heard a creak from my grandma's door. I quickly tried wiping my eyes before the door fully opened. I was relieved that it was only my brother. He said that soon he would have to drive back down to Delaware. Then that's when he got closer to me and saw my face.

"What's wrong?" he asked. Without much hesitation I explained everything to him while sobbing loudly. I wasn't sure if he could make out what I was saying over my short breaths. "Hey, you have to stop crying before Ma makes you go to bed early." This made the tears come harder. I didn't want everyone to be having fun without me while I was asleep all by myself. He left to go back into the living room to start saying goodbye to everyone else. I lay down on the gigantic bed feeling sad that my brother would soon be leaving. When he came back into the room to tell me goodbye, he reached into his basketball-patched leather jacket and took out a paper towel and reached out and gave it to me.

"I'm sorry it's not much, but it's all that I could sneak." There was only about a handful of goldfish in it, but I didn't care because I was just happy that he thought about me. I was so overwhelmed with joy. "Just don't tell Ma," he said. This day helped me to realize that my siblings and I always have each other's backs. That was our bond.

San Francisco

by TAMMY LEONG

San Francisco to everyone else might be like any other city in the world, but to me it is a whole different place. I fly six hours every year to spend two months of my summer there and return to New York City before school starts. I call it my summer home. In my book I have two homes: one where I spend most of my time each year back in New York City and one where I get away, relax, and spend time with my grandma and uncle after not seeing them for a whole year. There is something about San Francisco that is different from New York. Maybe it's just the people or the environment or maybe it's me. There is always a memory when returning to my uncle's house every year in San Francisco.

I remember waking up to a beautiful sunny day. My uncle had just left the house for work, and it was just my grandma and me. I begged her to go into the city with me so that I could take some pictures, but she refused. She continued to clean the house. As I was ready to walk away, I saw her get light-headed. I ran to catch her before she hit the ground. I put her to bed and immediately read the instructions my uncle left for me in case of an emergency. I remember it saying really clearly in my uncle's messy handwriting, "If she feels light headed or has a headache, give her two white pills in the drawer and call me!!" I grabbed my phone and the pills and called my uncle. My uncle rushed home and got my grandma into the car and drove about thirty minutes into the city where my grandma was treated before. The car ride didn't feel like thirty minutes. It felt like ten. Everything was happening so fast that I couldn't wrap my head around it. I was sitting next to my grandpa in the backseat as my uncle drove to the hospital. I could hear my uncle trying to catch his breath as he drove. I looked outside the window of the car, and I saw cable cars going up and down hills as my uncle drove by. I had to remind myself everything was going to be alright. I could feel tears trying to escape my eyes. I quickly wiped away my tears so I wouldn't scare my grandma more than she already was. As soon as we got to the hospital, my grandma was rushed to the emergency room. By this time she was unconscious and was rolled away in a stretcher. I waved goodbye to her. We waited a while. I remember my uncle telling me my grandma was going to be in surgery for a while and not to worry, but I could tell he was holding back and not telling me about something. He drove me home, and I got to visit her in the ICU once before I had to leave early to go back to New York City. I had overheard my uncle on the phone with my parents, telling them that it was too much stress for him with my grandma in the hospital and taking care of me. He bought me a ticket, and I flew back the next day. After a few months of my grandma in a hospital bed, my uncle finally gave my parents some good news that my grandma had a long way to go, but she was going to make a full recovery.

Going Bananas for Bananas

by AMENCIS BERQUIN

Grandma's house is where I always go to get away. It's in between my parents' houses. Not too far from the train but not too close. So when I don't want to be home, I pack my bag and go to my grandma's. I never have to tell her in advance; it's practically my own home.

All the magic happens here. Every phase and milestone I've ever gone through has taken place in that very house. Sometimes when I'm lonely, I pop up to Grandma's and stay for as long as I like. Many things go on at Grandma's house, but there's one specific thing I remember that makes it so special and close to my heart.

See, my grandma makes the best banana pudding, but she would never give the recipe to any of my cousins or me. Brini, Jojo, and I ask her almost every day about how to make that creamy goodness. The reason we ask so much is because she only makes it once in a blue moon, so I want to be able to make it myself without having to wait twice a year. My cousins and I didn't think it would be hard, so we decided to make it ourselves with our own recipe.

I got the blender, and my cousins proceeded to cut up bananas and toss them in. I heard a noise, and we knew we had messed up. The blender top wasn't placed on correctly. When it was activated, it splattered all over the place: on the walls, on our clothing, on the floor, everywhere but our mouths! We tried to clean it up, but my grandma was down the stairs.

This was when I realized the significance of this place. We got our phones taken away, and we were yelled at. I felt like I belonged. It's my own home. Did I ever get the recipe? Well, I did, but I lost it the same day and never got another opportunity, so I wait for those two days out of the year to enjoy Grandma's banana pudding.

The Day My World Stopped

by EMILY MARTINEZ

March 4, 2016 was the day you came home from jail. You were in there for so long; we've missed you. Now that you're back, everyone has been happy. The whole block welcomed you home with arms wide open. We celebrated with parties that reminded me of our summertime days. You would always bug me about my outfits if they were too "inappropriate" as you used to say. I swear you were like the older brother I never had …

Now you're gone.

March 20 was the worst day of my life. We had just gotten you back and now my brother, my heart, was taken from me. I would rather you be in jail than my having to say R.I.P. to my angel. Whenever you were around us, it was nothing but smiles and laughter. You were so little, my little munchkin. For months on end we were screaming, "Free my brother!" Man, life is short—too short. As I walk through Webster, everything becomes dull. Even on Park Avenue things will never be the same. Your candle lighting is there on Webster next to the park every day. I walk past it and it brings tears to my eyes. Not even two weeks you were here. I never really understood the fact that others judged you without even getting to know you.

For some reason, on March 31, I couldn't bring myself to go to your funeral. I regret it. I will always regret it. You were a big brother to everyone, and I found it hilarious that you were so little acting so tough. Some people will never know pain until they lose one of their family members. Now that you're gone, it seems like everyone is leaving. A bunch of our guys are gone but they'll be back in a few years.

March 4, 2016, my world was going 'round and 'round. March 20, my world stopped. Before you had gotten locked up, someone had stabbed you. Wrong place, wrong time. He stabbed you right in the kidney. I remember while you were bleeding out on the floor, you emptied out a clip and a half on him and his friends. *Bam! Bam! Bam! Bam! Bam! Bam!* We were all outside when the shots were fired. I froze. I didn't know what happened. Our friend threw himself on top of me and we both fell. He was protecting me.

They carried me home, and the next day they told me what had happened. Oh my God! I told my mother and she was heartbroken too. I stood in the hospital every day with you, and I didn't want to leave you. When you got better, they took you away from me for having an unlicensed firearm and a few dimes and nicks on you. You didn't get time for emptying a clip and half on the guys. The judge took it as self-defense. Thank God!

After you came home, you were smoking too much and everyone told you to stop. You said, "Oh, no, I'm fine," and, "I'll be good." You were always the big brother and the protector, but every time someone tried to care for you, you denied it, so you didn't take our advice. You smoked an eighth on March 19, 2006 and around 12:00 AM on March 20, you fell asleep and never woke up. Heartbroken tears flowed down my face. I didn't want to be spoken to; I didn't want to be touched; I didn't want to eat or drink. I feel like I could have prevented it.

Sleep in peace. Gone, but never forgotten.

Heroes and Happy Endings

by JULLY PATEL

Hospitals are so weird. One day, they bring smiles, happiness, and life, while other days they bring sadness, tears, and death.

I was really young at the time, maybe about five years old, when I came home from school to find him gone and my mom home early. I asked where he was, and she said he went to the doctor's for a visit.

"When will he be back?" I asked.

"Soon, very soon," she replied.

Minutes turned into hours, hours turned into days, and days turned into weeks. He wasn't back. I couldn't really remember how long he had been gone, though I remember visiting once or twice after school.

He was there, in a big room with white walls, on the big bed connected to many machines, sleeping, pale and bony. But alive. My mom would talk to him, but he couldn't hear us or respond. Then my aunt, uncle, and cousin came to visit. I never asked why they had planned to visit when they lived hours away.

"Honey, wake up. We have to go to the hospital." That's how I woke up that morning. Tired and sleepy. Before leaving, we lit candles and said our prayers. I remember burning my thumb while lighting the candle. It was cold here in Chicago, a little too cold.

The memories of the drive to the hospital and the walk to the room are vague and blurry. Opening the door I initially saw my mom on the floor, crying, wailing, while my aunt rushed to comfort her. I stood there confused, not knowing what was going on. I saw him asleep, with no wires attaching him to machines. I sat down next to my mother, and I noticed the two drops of blood under the bed, staining the white, clean floor. I could hear my uncle talking to the doctor. The doctor said something about him coughing up blood and his heart collapsing.

I guess that was when it set in that he wasn't going to wake up again. He wasn't going to braid my hair for me. He wasn't going to cook me food. He wasn't going to draw or paint with me anymore. I wouldn't be able to hear him encourage me to climb up higher on the trees at the park. I wouldn't see him take pictures and videos of me doing stupid things. He wouldn't be in our lives anymore, and I wouldn't have the chance to grow up with him around.

That was the moment the tears started falling. Seeing your hero, so weakened and fragile, is hard, but not knowing if you'll see him the next day, awake and smiling, or if you'll have a chance to tell him how much you loved him is even harder.

I guess not every hero has his happy ending.

Do You Know What I Mean?

by NATHALIE ROSARIO

In 2005 when technology wasn't really out there, summer afternoons were spent with the whole family in 189 Park. Video cameras are where the real memories were kept, but nothing can beat this at all. Food, beach chairs, radio, and dominoes kept us close. Happy expressions everywhere I go. Why is life right now not like that anymore? Everywhere I go, no expressions, only everyone on their phone. Back in time, that's where I want to be.

Happiness is nowhere near, and now smiling has disappeared. Time...time has changed. If only we could arrange how life would be. Can you see what I mean? Life is nothing without good memories. Now...do you know what I mean? During that time, I was five years old, running around the park with my cousins, going down the slide, screaming and laughing from the rush of excitement from playing tag. Also, the game cops and robbers felt real, like I was a real police officer protecting the citizens. Hearing my mom's voice calling me overfilled me with joy. I chased after her voice to see her holding a camera and saying, "Hi, Nathalie! How old are you?" I held out my hand to show that I was five and started to walk away slowly. My dad grabbed me from behind and began tickling me until I screamed way louder and couldn't breathe.

The sun was setting, and my dad called everyone in, saying, "Come in, everyone! Let's take a family picture!" More than twenty people were in the photo. My father counted down, holding the vintage Polaroid camera. I looked around. "Three!" Smiles. "Two!" Happiness. "One! Cheese!" That's what I see in 2005. All good memories. This is how life was for me without technology.

A Day in Times Square

by TIARA MORENE

I remember last summer when a group of my friends and I had a full day of exploring and just doing fun things. The day started out as normal as ever. I was bored, so I texted the group chat with all my friends. We decided to meet up around 10:00 AM. We all met up at our old middle school park. Then from there we took the train to 42nd Street, laughing and joking the whole way. When we stepped out of the train station, the skyscrapers rose high above us like looming giants, and the businessmen and women were quickly moving to their destinations while the crowds of tourists stood idly gazing up at the giant LED screens throughout Times Square. My friends and I proceeded to go to *Toys "R" Us*.

We weaved through the never-ending swarms of people dressed as characters from our childhood to get there. We raided the *Candyland* part of the store. We bought three bags of candy and walked around Times Square, stopping in stores, giggling from time to time, and having a good time. That was when we all started to get pretty bored. There was still so much time in the day that we couldn't just go home now, so we went to the movies. We bought popcorn and other snacks along with the candy we had. We watched one movie, then another (we snuck into the second movie). The second movie was pretty crowded, and we were beginning to get worried that someone was going to walk up to us and tell us to get out of their seats. Luckily that didn't happen, and by the time we got out of the theatre, the sun was setting, and the flashing bright lights of Times Square became the only light illuminating the streets. Our final destination was a comic book store tucked away on a corner from the main street. We needed to climb a small staircase to get there, but when we stepped into the store, it was amazing. We browsed the endless rows of comics and collectables, stopping to look at the things that stood out to us. We bought a few things, and we all went our separate ways. I went home happy and smiling about the crazy day I had with my friends.

The Hood Called School

by CELINE PICHARDO

School. Where you met your first best friends and first jumped out of your parents' arms. Your individuality and persona started to form and your curiosity sparked. *What does the boys' bathroom look like? Where do babies come from?* All questions in the mind of a child in the second grade.

School. You'd lost all your baby teeth and now have braces. Your peers treated you like some sort of celebrity because of this. You'd always been a dedicated student that earned above average grades, but you'd never guess that it would blow up like it did. It was fifth grade, and your teacher casually told you you'd been selected as valedictorian of your graduating class. No way! You'd never thought you had the potential to reach such heights. At graduation, everyone cried as you gave your speech. Elementary school was over and done with. You didn't realize it then, but you'll definitely miss the innocence and childhood you left behind.

School. Junior high was not what you had expected. You made a lot of new friends, but the unnecessary drama that came with that? Arguments out of pettiness and jealousy every month along with the common melodrama: "OMG, you like her better than me?!" or, "One of us is mad at her so let's all ignore her." You could have gladly done without all this. Let's not forget about your first crush. When that ended, you thought the world was crashing down on you. Silly, twelve-year-old you. However, you never lost focus on the important stuff and made it into the National Honor Society. But, of course, there was still fun and games. Throughout the many trips you attended, you made unforgettable memories. Like the times you laughed so hard you peed on yourself and when you played ManHunt in the Park. But nothing could compare to Junior Prom: Best Day Ever! Your date was a boy whom you'd had your eye on for a while. You guys were color-coordinated, and he even got you a corsage. Guess who turned out to be your first boyfriend? But anyway, on to the next one.

School. You got accepted into your dream school: the High School of Fashion Industries. Dreamy. Not so much. Unlike before, you were more aware of your surroundings. Who to become friends with: the supportive, real group of individuals or the backstabbing, negative-influences crew? By now, you definitely knew where babies come from and were surely staying safe from that. You've learned everything from Trig and Earth Science to how to write an essay, but you didn't only learn the basics. School threw obstacles at you and played a major role in your successes and building your street smarts, everything that forms who you are today. But school, most of all, indirectly taught you how to survive in this game titled "Life."

A Tragic Night on the "B" Train

by JADA LEBELL

I ride the train every day. I always sit in the middle seats so I can see out of the window because it reminds me of when I was a little girl. I see the same people every day, and I listen to the same music on my playlist: rap, 90's, soca, and R&B. I know I have a very boring life, but when I went on the train that day, it was a day like I had never seen.

The train moved slower than ever that day, and I realized that the people I saw every day on the train were not there, which was weird. There was a Jewish man reading his Torah, a group of kids gossiping about school, an old lady sleeping, and three women talking to each other. As I sat down on one of the middle seats, I decided not to listen to my music. So I closed my eyes, and the loud taps of the rock music that the man next to me was listening to annoyed me. As my annoyance with the man grew, the sweat slowly trickled down the back of my ear. The train stopped, *chhh*, and the wheels on the train made a sudden, loud screech.

I quickly opened my eyes, looked out the window, and noticed that we hadn't even reached the end of the stop. The Jewish man looked up from his Torah, and everyone, silent and confused, looked at each other. I was nervous and confused. My legs were shaking like a baby holding a rattle, and I noticed that the faces of the people outside the window looked weird. They looked shocked and almost out of words. After a few minutes, the group of kids looked out the window in confusion. "What happened out there?" "Did someone get shot?" After panickedly sitting on the train with no idea of what was going on, I heard the conductor say, "Ladies and gentlemen, sorry for the delay, but there has been a suicide death that occurred in front of the train…"

I was shocked. The old lady who was sleeping woke up like she had been listening the whole time and started to raise her hands up like they do in church. "Sweet Jesus, come watch over me…" She sang as she rocked back and forth and sang hymns I remember singing when I was a little girl. It was dark on the train and my phone was almost dead. The train moved up after about an hour, and I quickly got off and ran up the stairs. I passed the old sleeping lady and the three women all still talking. It was dark outside and a little gray. With only a few streetlights and moving cars, I could see the ambulance lifting the body cart into the back. There were people everywhere, flashing red and blue lights from the police car, and the sounds of cars honking at the other cars, because everybody wanted to see. It was a very confusing and tragic day.

When I got home, I quickly turned on the television to News12. It said on breaking news, "A Harlem principal jumps in front of a train."

The "B."

The Angel

by ANNIE DONG

As I walk with my friends along the way, breathing in the fresh, minty air, they chat away about the usual things and teachers. I smile and think about the person I can't wait to see. The streets are crowded and noisy, but I don't mind as long as I get to see that smiling face that greets me every morning when I walk in. I remember the first time we met: her skin was pale and smooth like porcelain. She was definitely pretty, but when I looked at her face, it was emotionless. Her face was cold and icy without a single hint of warmth compared to the other teachers who were greeting their new classes with smiles and overflowing warmth, yet on my side, she was as still and solemn as a statue. Fear began to build inside me. I wished I was around that blonde and bright smiling woman who taught English and was already getting along great with her students, but I couldn't do anything. This year was going to be long with this teacher who always wore a stony face. How would I survive? She seemed mean and unwelcoming.

Days went by, and things started to turn more than I expected. She gradually started changing. She helped me overcome my fear and released her true self. She was supportive, encouraging, and the first one who I found to have infinite patience. Being a person who doesn't trust easily, I wouldn't open up and I tried to avoid her, but she told me that she was always here for me and that I could always talk to her about things. I thought it was weird for her to say that to me only because I clearly had no intention of talking to her or confiding in her, but something in her voice gave me a sense of security; I could see sincerity in her eyes. I wanted to quit so many times, but when I looked at her and thought about all the patience and effort she put in just to help me and to ensure that I understood, I didn't have the heart to give up.

I loved those moments when it was just the two of us alone in the early morning, our special moments when we joked, laughed, talked, and smiled. I loved her soothing words whenever I cried or became discouraged and frustrated. Whenever I saw her smile or her smiling at my work, it brightened my day. When she was absent or gone, I got worried and nervous, expecting to see her when I walked in. I didn't want anyone else to come and take over the class. They couldn't compare to her. I just wanted to be around her, that special person who brightened my day, our laughs and smiles. We talked through my many tears, and my work was only between us. It was only between us. How pretty her smile was and her eyes were-- the eyes were soft, flowing with warmth, and the smile as pure and pretty as a diamond that shone bright like thousands of twinkling stars in the night sky. Every compliment and smile lit up my day. Her motherly warmth, care, and love were huge.

The angel brought me out of my shadows and took me under her wings. Her wings of love, security, trust, and patience drew me to her. Her gift of knowledge, how important and precious it was. She took me under her arms when I needed guidance and brightened my horizon; she saw the potential in me that I couldn't see. She was the shining star who guided me through difficult times. The day she left, it hurt. I could feel the tears threatening to fall, but I wouldn't allow it. I had grown attached to her, and I loved her. She had become a part of my life. She told me that she wanted to see my smiling face, but at that moment I couldn't smile. I held it in until I was alone and let it out, tears flowing uncontrollably until there were no tears left. My eyes hurt like a bee had stung me hard, and I felt so tired that I could just lie down on my bed and sleep. I felt as if I was being slapped in the face. Something was gone and could never be found. Something was broken but couldn't be mended.

When we arranged to meet up again, I was shocked and stunned; she agreed! It was just like a dream come true. When I got the email, I began jumping up and down, all smiles and skipping without caring about anything else. Now the only thing I cared about was the visit. To have the chance to go and visit was such a honor. I could not mess up. I was so excited and nervous to meet her. *What will she be like? Will we still get along? Will she still remember me the way I still remember her*? She must have gotten prettier; she was always lovely from the first sight of her. *Will our bond and connection be like how it used to be*? I was so nervous that I went to ask my two teachers, who were also caring, patient, and funny and always had good advice. With their advice, I went on my way to see her.

Standing in the lobby, I could not contain my excitement and anxiousness; I kept pacing back and forth. The school day ended and the other teachers let their students out. I watched with a smile, well my smile was not for them of course, my smile was for my angel. I looked down at my watch counting the time. *How punctual will she be? Will she be late or on time? Is this a trap or a joke?* The thought of it being a trap or a joke increased my anxiety so I decided to stop and stare at the floor as if it was so interesting. When I looked up, she was there looking at her watch. I smiled to myself thinking how I was just doing that a few minutes ago. She looked different, but that skin and hair color must be her. When I called her name, she looked up with that amazing, charming smile, the warm, soft eyes, and the lovely voice just as I had remembered. The smile that first melted my heart and that lovely voice that had given me the sense of security. The warm, soft eyes with sincerity which got me to open up to her. The rest is history. She was just as pretty as I remembered. She looked younger and her soft, silky skin seemed to glow so beautifully that I almost couldn't recognize her. Thinking back to the day when she took me for pizza, it felt unreal. It was too good to be true, but when I pinched myself, I was wide awake. So it was real. Her looking at me while I ate made me nervous. Was there something on my face? Did I eat too slowly or too fast? But she just gave me her bright smile, and her nurturing gesture when she handed me a tissue to wipe my mouth, since the tissue I had was clearly stained with sauce, made me feel warm all over.

Her hugs were so warm that I almost didn't want to let go; it was a protective shield. The bond and connection were definitely strong--we still connect as always. If it was in the beginning I would have never imagined this, but now I embrace it. Where would I be without her? I can't imagine. Looking through what she wrote, I smiled reading it. I will not quit. I will continue on because of her. My angel, my shining star who gave me strength and courage. The one who had faith and confidence in me, because of her I know I can conquer obstacles that come my way, and I'm capable of doing anything as long as I set my heart to it. The one who influenced me greatly and also the reason why, whenever I fall, I will get back up on my feet and persevere because there's nothing that can stop me. The person who can make me smile my brightest and who accepts me for who I am despite my flaws. I love her and look up to her. I will never forget her. I will always remember her even as years go by. Without her, I would be lost and so confused. She's the one who has enabled me to come this far. I have changed and grown, but I am still the same person who loves, admires, and respects her. Time changes, but the one thing that doesn't change, and can't change, is my respect, love, and admiration for her. My angel, my shining star, and my mentor. My role model and partner in crime, I will love her forever and ever.

Getaway

by ZUAIRAH ISLAM

Getaway. Everyone has one. A place that they would rather be than anywhere else. Where people most likely go to refresh their minds, let loose, have some quiet time, or just sit and think. Wherever it maybe, whether it is an attic, a café, a closet, or even a roof, this is their happy place. My getaway? The crusty old fire escape outside my kitchen window.

At first, I would rarely ever go to my fire escape. There was always snow, rain, leaves, or bird poop. Sometimes the stairs were too cold, and sometimes they were too hot. There would always be something restricting me from even setting foot on that thing. But see, when you have a connection with something, whether a person or a thing, you'll always end up finding your way back to it. Although I don't go on my fire escape much, when I do, I'm in my happy place.

I would go out countless times a day. Each time was a new experience. Sometimes it would be early morning, right at dawn. Watching the huge bushy trees while hearing the birds chirp and fly was really breathtaking. Other times I would go really late at night. That would be an adventure, mainly a dangerous one. Since my neighborhood isn't technically "safe," my parents would never let me go that late, meaning, I would have to sneak. Every night after they fell asleep, creeping to the kitchen past my mom and dad, and getting out the window was an absolute thriller. Then going out with a blanket and reading a good book, just staring at the view, thinking, or talking on the phone until 2:00 AM was in a way very peaceful.

Surprisingly, I've only ever been caught twice. Guess I am as sneaky as I portray myself. After those times, my parents would start locking the fire escape at night. After a while though, they stopped, and I was back to sneaking.

Everyone has an escape. It could be a place, a person, or even their own mind, where they find inner peace and relaxation. The late night phone calls, early morning summer breeze, mid-day book reading is mine. We all have a getaway. You just need to find yours.

My fire escape.

My getaway.

Old San Juan

by DANIELLE JEAN-LOUIS

It was hot, hotter than any other place I'd ever been, at least. I'd just come from the pool when I felt a wave of extreme hunger come over me. They'd told us that we weren't allowed to leave the hotel after 9:00 PM without an adult, but everyone was busy in the game room, the workout room, playing knock-knock-ditch, or they'd gone out to dinner without us. Rebecca and I were the only ones left. We were told that San Juan wasn't the greatest place for a female to be alone at night. They'd warned us that there was slight gang activity and a large number of homeless people who hung around the neighborhood. Being with Bec I might as well have been alone. We strolled through the streets looking for some place that had workers who looked like they spoke English. It was really hot, and I'd grown impatient. I couldn't wait to finally get back into an air-conditioned room. We finally agreed to go to the Burger Shack we'd seen a few blocks away from the hotel. It was pretty late, so we decided that we would just take the food to go. I'd noticed a scary-looking man with big, bulging eyes staring from across the street. I'd chosen to ignore it though. We'd almost reached the hotel when I noticed the man was right behind us.

"*Disculpe!*" he yelled. They'd given us a few Spanish words that we should know in case we ever got lost or something. But *disculpe* wasn't one of them. I didn't know what to say, and neither did Bec. She looked just as confused and afraid as I felt. So we just kept it pushing. The man seemed to realize that we didn't speak Spanish, so he'd started to call out, "Excuse me miss, do you have fifty cents?" It was then that I realized that Rebecca, being Rebecca, was holding the rest of the change we'd gotten from the food in her hand. Smart. He was about a foot away from us when I'd grown tired of being followed. I'd decided to just give him the money so he'd go away. But by the time I'd gotten a chance to turn to Bec and tell her to give the man some change all I saw was the money on the floor and Rebecca halfway down the block screaming, "Run, Danni! Run!"

I'd never run so fast in my entire life.

School

by IYNN LEE

For the last ten years, I've been getting up in the morning from Monday to Friday to learn something new. In this place, we learned how to read and write; we learned algebra and geometry, drugs and sex, and the history of our world. We learned that a2+b2 = c2 and how the United States bombed Hiroshima and Nagasaki in August of 1945 to end WWII.

In this place, on the end of West 24th Street, a daily routine of Fashion Industries has begun. Here, we learn how to use the Pythagorean theorem and the quadratic formula more than we learn how to paint or sew. On the walls of HSFI, there are "soaring" facts on every floor to encourage us to be better students. Teachers put up posters in their rooms to help us learn better and accept ourselves for who we are, but students judge us based on our skin color, and teachers judge us based on our grades.

This daily routine must go on for another two years, until we wear our caps and gowns, hold our diplomas and flowers, and start a new life of routines when college has begun.

Removing My Appendix

by CARMEN SALAS

I gripped onto my bear, Humphrey, tighter, his soft fur comforting me. There was no traffic at all. I looked outside the window and noticed that everything was closed and that the sky was still dark. I was going to experience the scariest day of my life, and the rest of the world was still sleeping. There was a long wait after arriving at the hospital. I sat for a few hours, but it felt like many hours. Every minute felt like five, and my heart was beating harder and harder. Nurses talked to me about the procedure and how it would go, but I was still worried. A therapist came to talk to me. He assured me that everything was going to be okay and that it was normal to be anxious. He said I would be asleep and that I wouldn't feel anything. I tried to stay calm, but my heart kept beating harder. My parents told me to take a nap and that they would wake me up when it was time, but I couldn't fall asleep. Although I was tired, I was also jittery. I thought of all the things that could possibly go wrong.

The moment finally came. I'd been dreading this moment for weeks, counting the days that led up to it. The nurses came to pick me up, and it was time to leave my parents. I hugged them, and I was left on my own, just Humphrey and me. My heart was beating quicker and louder. The doctor opened the door to the operation room, and there was a bed for me to lie down. It was like a scene from the movies. They allowed Humphrey to stay with me. They placed him next to me so I wouldn't be alone; it was more comforting to have him there. The doctor said it was time to go to sleep. This was when I would go under the anesthesia. She placed the mask over my nose and told me to take deep breaths in and out. To distract me, she said to count backwards starting from ten, and that before we reached one I would be asleep. She started to count, "Ten...nine...eight..." I felt my heart beating slower and slower. My eyelids became heavy, and my thoughts stopped. All my worries were gone. I felt calm and all the scary thoughts I had went away. I didn't focus on the sound of my heart anymore. I could only hear her voice, "Seven...six...fi-" That was the last thing I heard as I fell into a deep sleep.

August 5th

by CHARLIZE TORRES

The heavy feeling of desperate anticipation filled up my entire being from crown to toe, and though I wish I could have done something about it, I couldn't. I was stuck, trembling in bliss. That is, until complete darkness fell upon us and matched the color of the starry night. My whole being screamed along with my voice and thousands of others in and out of sync of perfect euphoria. The introductory video slowly came on the massive screens, and the screams were what we considered mild and controllable until suddenly the video ended, leaving us with a split second to gasp in one large breath of air for what happened next. The gasps released, and the music and the beat of my favorite song began to play over the sounds of fifty-six thousand screams and majestic fireworks popping. Once my eyes looked past the lens of my eyeglasses and landed on the four faces that make my world go 'round, my heart felt as if it wanted to burst out of my chest and my body could die, screeching and shaking off immense amounts of ecstasy. All of it, the buzzing sounds of screams, the happy positive and lovely atmosphere, were all enough to make my heart pound uncontrollably each time, harder and harder and faster than the last. The deep thumping of drums and the static of guitars radiated throughout the entire stadium, doubling the screams. Whenever it grew silent enough to hear the angelic voices of our precious entertainers speaking to us in British accents ringing from their microphones through our ears, fifty-six thousand hearts swelled in harmony. Before the end of it all, the darkness emerged, we each cried in bliss and sadness and then the music stopped. They were gone, but the memory of it all, of that special place, will stick with us, with me, forever.

Overdramatic

by KIARA HUSBANDS

That day I could feel the negative vibes in the atmosphere, but everyone else seemed oblivious to it, as if it was affecting only me. I sat on the couch and looked out the living room window, watching my father and uncles go back and forth to the moving truck. And again I felt that negative vibe surround my body. I didn't understand why everyone was walking around so nonchalantly as if nothing was wrong. I was going to get murdered! My dad and I living on our own was not going to be a good idea, which I realized once I learned about all the dangers that could occur. I was only nine years old during this time and I was very gullible. My older cousin told me that people who live on their own get killed, robbed, or kidnapped from their homes. The thing that scared me most was that there were only two of us on our own. When we got murdered, who was going to come and help us?

When we moved in, I couldn't sleep at night because I needed to be prepared for my murder. But my murderer never came. After a couple of months, I forgot about all the things my cousin told me, and I began to realize how much better things were. I no longer had to fight and argue with my cousins about whose turn it was to have the TV remote. I watched what I wanted when I wanted. I no longer had to share or fight over my toys. I could use them any time I wanted. Everything got better for me. It was the start of a new chapter for me.

A Drastic Change

by ONJALIK RASUUL

The bells rings, and my teacher, Ms. Sargent, calls for the class to line up. Everyone grabs their cubby and gets in line with their partner. Walking down the steps, exiting the school building, I see my mom across the street. I tap my teacher and run across the street to my mom. Rushing into a big hug, she gives me a bag full of goodies and a few dollars. I take out an ice cream sandwich and begin to eat it. My mom walks me to my favorite park. I like it because of the size and the number of activities. My mom always takes me there after school. It is my happy place. Well, my mom is talking to her friends while I play hopscotch with the imaginary boxes drawn on the ground, and the sound of glass shattering interrupts. *Pow!*

"Oh my God!" a lady screams.

In a daze, I notice a bald man wearing a white tank top who is waving a gun. Suddenly it goes off again, but this time it hits my friend on the see-saw. He falls off and hits the ground, his body shaking. Then it stops. Someone pulls me by the back of my shirt. It's my mom, and she slides herself and me under a bench nearby.

I don't know how to react to seeing one of my closest friends bleeding out pints of blood. The shooter takes off at the sound of the ambulance and police sirens. Police escort my mother and me into our building. Yellow tape starts being put up all around our projects and especially at the scene of the crime. The police put his body in the back of the ambulance, even though they know it is too late; he bled out before they got there. I glance over at his mother, who has broken into an extreme meltdown.

"No!!!! Not my baby!! Why me, Lord?" Everyone surrounds her, and that's when I start to put two and two together. One of the coolest boys I've ever met is gone. Dead… forever! I start feeling overheated, and my eyes start to water. Tears creep down my face.

I have thoughts of the park and how Jose and I used to play on the swing, our scooter races in the handball court, and me trying to keep up with his tricks. Before I know it, I'm bawling. Jose was like a brother to me and without him, things won't be the same. There isn't a day that I don't think about how things would be if he was still around, and how different big moments in my life would have been, like sweet sixteens and even my future wedding.

SEEING OURSELVES
ABOVE THE CLOUDS

Behind the Big Walls

by KEILYN MERCADO

I woke up and everything changed. Everything around me felt different, but I couldn't quite put my finger on why. Even though my mind was underdeveloped, I could still recognize that hole that existed in my life. The thing that glued my whole family together and made the Mercados who we are. That person was gone, and I had no idea when I'd be able to see him again.

It was a bright, sunny day in the Big Apple. The chilly air whisked against my skin, allowing the hairs on my body to reach as high as the sky. The coat that protected my body was useless; the rawness of the air found a way to infringe. My mom held me protectively while my sister stood by her side. Suddenly, a dirty white van with big wheels approached us. A tanned old guy came out and opened the back door for us. My sister climbed in the back, my mom following right behind her. People of different races, ethnicities, and colors surrounded me. Men, women, and children were all in that van. I was in a truck full of strangers. Where was I going?

The whole setting changed. Suddenly, I was in a big dull place. The walls were rutted, murky, and lifeless. The air was as copiously hot as a sauna after the heater was turned off. Different types of men lurked through the room. They ranged from slim to chunky, bald to hairy, dark to light, hairless face to wolf face, big belly to none, tall to short. The only thing that made these men look different from us was their clothes. They wore these huge gray and beige suits. They didn't wear any other type of clothing but these gray and beige suits. Was my dad one of these weird uniformed men?

Suddenly, there he was, in those long grey pants with the bulging shirt to match the suit. He wore a tired look when he walked down to us, yet once his eyes locked with mine, his whole persona changed. That amazing smile I grew to love appeared on his face, smiling from ear to ear. Once he saw me, he picked me up and gave me the tightest hug ever. He gave me a bunch of kisses and told me how much he loved me. He did the same with my sister. Once it was my mom's turn, however, he had a gloomy look in his eyes. His eyes held a melancholy glare, yet his smile was plastered on his face to obscure his true emotions. My mom sent my sister and me to a little room that had a mid-sized TV and a big table with a bunch of coloring books. I sat and began to color. Little did I know that would be the last time I would see my dad for years.

Reconnection

by KADEEM AARON LAMORELL

The Plane

The first time I went to Trinidad was when I was two years old. My mother sent me to live there with my grandmother for a couple of months. She sent me not because I was too much to handle (I was a bit of a crybaby) but because she wanted me to spend some time with my family down there. When I went down there recently as a teenager, I heard endless stories about how I used to be as a kid. But we're getting a little bit ahead of ourselves. So, here's some background around this recent trip and why it was so important. Leading up to the trip, my mother was a bit rocky on her status. Initially my mother came to the US as an "illegal" immigrant. She came here on a tourist visa to visit family and ended up staying for twenty-six years. She couldn't leave the country for that duration of time. However, one year before she began planning the trip, she got her green card after years of running around with lawyers, filing paperwork, and just plain ol' patience. When she showed it to me, it was met with sort of a quiet excitement. On one hand I was happy she didn't have to traipse around under the radar; on the other, I didn't realize the effects it would have on me.

We started planning the trip in the beginning of 2015. My mother sprung it on me out of nowhere. I was a little apprehensive at first because I hadn't been out of the country in a long time, and I barely remembered my family down there. Everyone was so grown up now and on their own paths, so I didn't know how I could get to know them. We booked the tickets a month before summer and then had to reschedule because I needed to get my passport. I had some anxiety about flying as it got closer and closer to the date: I kept researching plane crash headlines, and death, and the mysterious MH370 crash. I was trying to calm myself by looking at the positives of the trip and the fact that traveling by plane is way safer. Eventually the fear dissipated once we got there. We had to a do a whole run-around with the bags, paying extra because we over-packed and throwing clothes into other suitcases to balance out the weight. We went through TSA and finally got to the terminal. We were surprised no one was there, but we just sat and waited to see if anyone else was coming. Eventually, I went to check the board and it turned out our terminal was changed and was across the airport. We had to rush all the way to the other side of the airport to get there. We got there just in time as they were beginning to board the plane. As I boarded, my fear began to leave completely and, as the plane took off, it was actually relaxing to me. I fell asleep listening to music on my phone and woke up three hours in. It was pitch dark outside.

The Experience

We got there early in the morning. When I got outside the terminal I felt the humidity almost instantly. The first thing I thought was "My hair is going to get frizzy." We waited for my uncle to pick us up, and he drove what seemed like forever to my grandparents house. My grandparents didn't even know we were coming, so it was a surprise. In the morning, my mother went up and surprised my grandparents by saying, "Hello, Hello, Africa." I was still fast asleep during this time. I went up to the kitchen at about 10:00 AM, and everyone was so surprised to see me. I was met with a barrage of "Wow, You're so tall," and "Do you play basketball?"--the common questions I get when I see my family again. The days went by slowly as it got closer to my grandparents' fiftieth anniversary. I got to talk with my cousins after years of not seeing them. They were pretty cool in my book. They were in high school or secondary school just like me. They dealt with the same things: school, work, relationships, all that jazz. It was nice to be able to reconnect with them as a teenager. I walked around the town a little, went to the movies, went to the beach. It was a fun experience. By far the most fun and terrifying experience for me was going into the Pitch Lake. They were spreading tales about how if you stepped in the wrong place, you could get your foot stuck and die. So, obviously, I didn't want to go anywhere near that death trap. But guess what, I decided *why not*? and went in with my sister-in-law. Bear in mind that the only reason I even went in was because she was going (she's the only one that was as tall as me). My cousin decided she'd just wait in the car. As we were walking in it, I couldn't help but be extremely cautious, almost to the point of pulling her in a couple of times.

We eventually made it to the bathing spot where my other cousins were playing. The water was warm and clean. It felt like I was in a natural jacuzzi. However, the most memorable thing was my grandparents' fiftieth anniversary. I was running around helping prepare for it. Decorating, taking out the food, setting up candles, putting out chairs, greeting guests, the whole nine. People started to arrive and fill up seats, and the ones that remembered me all came up to me with, "This is Kadeem? I remember you when you was only this size." The event started, and the host began to make jokes to entertain guests. People started coming up to talk about funny moments with them. Everyone was laughing, drinking, eating, and just having a good time. It was so beautiful when my grandparents exchanged rings and kissed. I saw that, and it was just so inspiring to me. I just thought, "Man, I hope to have something like that one day." Having grandparents that are still together in a stable relationship is such a blessing and a model for how I want my love life to be. It was definitely one of the most memorable things that came out of this trip.

The Other Side

There's always two sides to one family tree, the mother's and the father's. I've always known my mother's side of the family. I frequently spent Christmas with my uncle who lived in Maryland. I also went to see my aunts a lot. However, I never spent too much time with my father's side of the family. I always talked about the more superficial aspects about his side (he's mixed) but never actually got to know them too much. This was my chance, I thought. My grandmother had invited me to stay over for a day or two just to get to reconnect with my cousins on that side, who were pretty much my age. I was apprehensive about going because I was attached at my mother's hip the whole time. But I decided to go because I thought family was important. I got to know my cousin Kirdisha a bit more, and, in a lot of ways, she was just like me. She wanted to study music in England and leave Trinidad, feeling isolated there. Her mother, my aunt, didn't want her to study that, believing it was insignificant. Although, I was always supported by my mother in my endeavours in being a fashion designer, so I connected a little bit with that. My father specifically had wanted me to be just like my brother—a man's man, into playing sports, girls, all that masculinity jazz. I told her she should break away and follow her dreams; she'd regret it if she didn't. I don't know if she went or not, but I hope she did what was right for her and not for her mother.

Departure

It was hard to leave, knowing I wouldn't see them again for a while. There were goodbyes, hugs, and a lot of pictures. I said goodbye to my cousins and my grandparents. I said goodbye to the dog outside that was too busy barking into the night. I said goodbye to the big house, to the island breeze and the palm trees, to the place I grew to love in such a short time. We left late at night. We packed our stuff in my uncle's car and said our last good-byes. I sat in the front seat looking at the lights of the towns far and near. My headphones were in, and my mind was just blank for a moment. It felt satisfying not to think for a minute, to not really feel anything and just exist in space with no worries. We got to the airport, moved our bags into check, and passed through the checkpoints to wait for our plane at the terminal. I fell asleep and woke up to an unending shivering from the cold air in the airport. I boarded the plane and sat back, headphones in again, only this time, I was reflecting on my time there. It was truly a memorable experience. I drifted off into sweet sleep again and awoke to an almost blinding light. It was heavenly, looking out of the plane window and seeing myself above the clouds. Amazing and surreal.

What Is No Longer Ours

by KIANNI BRADSHAW

The secrets of the bed uncovered
The bed now outgrown
All that lies under now are the dust bunnies that inhabited under
the bed
It no longer belongs to us...

What my brother and I thought was a normal bed wasn't—it became something more. "Kianni, come in my room," my brother would say. I went into his room and searched all around, but I couldn't find him even though I knew he was in there. The mattress lifted up, and my brother appeared. "Come under the bed," he said. This was the moment the bed became something more. The wood was smooth to the touch, and the pink carpet was rough and became uncomfortable after some time. We stared up at the wooden planks that held up the mattress. There was always a constant need for a flashlight or another source of light because of the paucity of light underneath the bed. Why go to the theater for movie night when underneath the bed was all you needed? The times my brother hid from my mother and she couldn't find him, my lips were zipped, but this became an old trick. Nothing lasts forever. The wood became vandalized from boredom, the carpet stayed more or less the same, and the planks grew wobbly, some even out of place.

The secrets of the bed uncovered
The bed now outgrown
All that lies under now are the dust bunnies that inhabited under
the bed
It no longer belongs to us...

A Little Bench in the Big Apple

by MAYA DELLA

The calm surroundings and the faint sounds could just be heard throughout the park. The beautiful ponds were filled with ducks, turtles, and fish along with the nice, watered green grass with the sun's light bouncing off it. Central Park: most New Yorkers would find this park dirty and not interesting at all, but it holds so much value to me. This was the spot that my father and I would always turn to whenever it was a nice day, and we were outside, bored. When my father was alive, we would spend our time at that very place. It wasn't as lavish as other places that New York has to offer, but it didn't matter where it was, as long as I was with him.

Every time I think about that place, it reminds me of a time when I was younger and my dad suggested that we go on one of our weekly walks through the park. I recall that day being beautiful and sunny which made it the perfect day to go out. I had asked my dad if I could bring my toy shovel to the park, thinking I was going to dig up some treasure, but my father just looked at me weirdly, wondering what on earth was going on in my head.

That day we had an adventure through the park, coming across unusual-yet-usual things that are normal for New Yorkers. When our long walk ended we headed to our usual spot, which was a bench in front of a huge pond. We ended up here after every walk. On that very small and wooden bench we would always talk about everything together, and we would even gossip about my sister as well as our entire family. Even when I got older in my early teen years, we would still take some time off from our schedule to chill out and take in our surroundings. I rarely go back to that park now, but if I did, I would head straight to that special bench and reminisce about every trip that we took there. Whether it was with the whole family or just between me and my father, whether it was a short trip to that bench or a long one, I will always cherish every moment that I spent with my father.

The Hallway

by ALEJANDRA DELEON

Thanksgiving is the one time of year when you're forced to hang out with every family member, people you don't necessary like and people you haven't seen since you were younger. All the new members, like babies, new boyfriends or girlfriends, etc. Every year your family goes to your great-grandmother's house—it was a tradition that started when you were younger. Once the front door swings wide open and you step in, you hear many kinds of voices, from people yelling at the TV to yelling at each other about something very dumb. As you walk down the hallway that once seemed enormous when you were younger, you can smell all sorts of things, like the food that's getting its final touches in the kitchen or all the dessert my mother, aunt, and cousin like to bring. As you head into the living room you smell the wine and beer that all the adults are drinking while they blast Spanish music.

As the adults do their own thing in the living room, the kids make their way into the long, narrow white hallway. For as long as you could remember, that's what all the kids did. There isn't anything special about the hallway. There are no windows, just a mirror and two paintings that are all the way near the living room. In the middle, where the bathroom door is, is usually the darkest part because the light is never on. The walls are painted white, with a heater that is also white and a light switch at the end by the front door. The hallway was the kids' territory; it was the place where you could talk and play without the adults bothering you. When you and your cousins were younger you would take off your shoes and climb the walls. Leaving black and gray marks as you climbed to the top, you would see who could touch the ceiling first and who could stay up the longest until you got in trouble.

Your little cousins would run up and down the hallway, screaming like they were in a horror film as someone flickers the lights. You never understood why they would do it, but seeing them laughing so much as they ran would make you smile. The adults would come and scream at you for being loud. Once the adults had enough they would take some kids into the living room, but no matter how many times they would pull the kids apart, you would always come back together in the hallway.

As time went by and the kids got older, the hallway didn't seem as fun. The older kids started hanging out with the adults, while the younger kids still hang out in the hall. But they don't do the same things the older kids used to do. Now they just sit on the floor with their phones, silent like mice. The adults get mad at them for always being on their phones. They tell them stories about how the older kids used to climb the walls and socialize with each other. They would all laugh at the end of the story and talk about all the good times they had. You secretly wish you were still playing in the hallways, but things just stop being fun when you get older.

A hallway once so magical, once filled with so much imagination, is just filled with memories of what you used to do on Thanksgiving.

Memories Can Happen Anywhere

by SHANIQUA BLACKWELL

Can you remember the last time you saw a seesaw park? The old-fashioned teeter-totter—the long, flat, floating board with handles on each side? No? Neither can I. But I remember the bitter cold and being bundled up head to toe with heavy winter gear by my mother. Raheem (my older, unintelligent brother) used to say I looked like Ralphie's kid brother, Randy, from *A Christmas Story*. On December 16, 2005, my two sisters, Asia and Shauna, took me out of my after-school cooking class early to drag me to this unfamiliar place with their friends Diamond Crohns and Patricia Lewis. I was yanked by my arm through an old, dirty grassland, heading to an abandoned building complex. My arm started to feel like it would disconnect at any moment. I was complaining, really complaining, kicking, screaming, biting her fingers to get out of her death grip. I was pulling back with the force that made me think my arm was going to be pulled out of its socket. I won our game of pull and pull; she let go of my arm, and I crashed to the ground like a plane crashing from the sky. I fell hard. My shoulder hurt, and I began to cry. I couldn't help it—I was only five dealing with controlling, aggressive teens.

My sister's friends complained about my being there, and I wanted nothing more than to tell them off. Asia grabbed my arm again, in a gentle manner this time, and whispered in my ear, "Be good, listen. You're embarrassing me. Calm down; we're almost there." She said we were "almost there" as if I knew where we were going. I had no clue. I was stuck following behind my older sister just like every other younger sibling. It was dark outside, and the cold wind was smacking against my face, and I was tripping on dirty rocks and grass to keep up with the group. I looked up to actually get a view of where we were heading. The scene was narrowed by a barbed gate. Ahead was an old rusty park with the usual jungle gym, slide, and something else I hadn't seen before. I looked at Patricia Lewis and asked her what the big metal object was. She laughed and replied, " A seesaw, two people or more go on and you can see who gets off the fastest." I nodded my head, and everyone dumped their book bags on the ground. The surroundings changed, and it felt a little bit warmer.

I ran to the see-saw, hopping on and almost falling over. My sister and Patricia climbed onto the other side, resulting in my being lifted high in the air. I screamed with excitement, swinging my legs. My sister hopped off and the seesaw dropped, along with my stomach. It felt like being on a roller coaster dropping you into a "free-fall" state of plummeting down a hill. We continued our fun for about an hour, then it was time to go home.

I never experienced such a rush before. I thought maybe following my sister into this abandoned park wasn't so bad because I had a great time. As the years went by in the first, second, third, fifth grade and all through junior high, I would visit my seesaw park with a friend, and together we would experience the thrill, of being in this off-limits, forbidden place.

Around the seventh grade my mother got sick; she was told she had diabetes. Many don't realize the seriousness of the disease. I cried a lot after researching all the health problems associated with having diabetes ... cancer ... heart disease ... heart attacks. One day, after another rough day in school, I wanted to clear my mind and think off some of the problems occurring in my life. I walked to the see-saw park only to find a newly made parking lot sitting in its place.

Sol

by NATALIE CANDELARIO HERRERA

I remember the feeling. The cold, unforgiving New York winds that ruthlessly hit me with no mercy and left without remorse. I don't remember the plane rides, but I do remember the air pressure of my beautiful Hispaniola and how it suffocated me with the excitement of my arrival. I remember the air. The warm embrace that welcomed me with open arms as I approached with newly opened nostrils. I remember sitting across from my grandmother and how I'd listen to her faint, silvery, yet always compelling voice tell me: "*Los novios se encuentran, se botan, y se encuentran de nuevo.*" I remember picking mangos. I remember picking limes. I remember the dalmatian that'd always bark whenever I did. I very much remember the mosquito bites and the inevitable slab of *vivaporú y sal* that they'd always slather across my puffy limbs with the occasional but always much expected joke of: "*Es que tienes la sangre dulce, a mi nunca me pican.*" I remember waking up to the cries of roosters. I remember waking up to the *campesinas* who carried fruit above their heads in baskets and in their wombs, yelling out in voices only at home in our land. I remember waking up to the bittersweet sun and Mami's bittersweet reminders of what a blessing it was to see it. I remember playing card games en *la galería* with Mama. I remember domino nights. I remember our lunches and how there was never a day that the food wasn't ready at 12:00 PM precisely. I remember how Papa always loved to sit at the head of the table. I remember Mama and Papa's naps right after lunch; I would always dread the everlasting hour of boredom that I'd have to endure while they slept. I remember that one summer Mami and Papi sent Adrian and I alone. I remember how Papa had switched the door lock to be inside out to keep us from going out onto the balcony, but Gaby, Adrian, and I switched it back just to watch the orange sunrise every morning. I remember pressing my face against the glass window while we drove by the *cancha* in hopes of seeing my cousins. I remember the trips to the beach. I remember the blue skies. I remember the cerulean hues, the glimmering blues of the water. I remember the water, a water so clear, so captivating. I remember the water, a water so reflective of its country's beauty. I remember.

My Personal Little Bubble

by MILEIDYS MOSQUERA

After school I just want to get home and ignore everything and everyone. I get home from a whole day of school to end up in my bedroom, dropping everything from my coat to my school bag on the bedroom floor. I greet my mother with soft kiss on her cheek and move towards my bedroom with my bag in hand. I get my tablet out of my bag so I can read the rest of the fan fictions that I have found.

My room consists of a bunk bed that is next to the door and a single twin size bed by the two windows, with a view of the street of Pennsylvania Avenue and the sound of the train. The twin bed is for my older sister Mindrys and the bunk bed is for me and my other sister Maria. The bottom bunk is for my sister and the top bunk is mine. Most of the time, my sisters are never there, so the room is kept for myself. The top bunk is like my small safe heaven. It has the space that I need to be alone even when my sisters are in the room with me. Around my bed there is a curtain hanging from the ceiling to cover my bed from the light that is in the center of the ceiling and the looks that I get from my family when I get home. The wall next to my bed is full of paintings and drawings that I have done over the course of my high school years, things that my family would never allow to be posted on the living room wall. That small space on my side of the room is like a safe bubble that keeps me from the judgment that my parents have toward me because of every opinion I have toward society. I close myself off as I stay up on my bed to ignore. On my bed there is a body pillow, a small fan, and the extension cord I use to charge my phone at night. My bed space is like my little box of creativity that makes me get inspired to create beautiful designs that come from my personality, almost like the painting that I have of a girl blowing bubbles underwater. My bed is where a place where I escape reality that goes on around my life every single day.

Just Get Up and Go

by PAULA FERREIRA

"Beep… beep… beep" is the sound of your obnoxious alarm clock going off at 6:15 AM. You can only snooze a few times before you are late for school. By 7:30 AM you are done and ready to start your daily commute. You get on the train and put your headphones in to block out the loud talking, crying babies, and the annoying guys yelling "showtime" in the subway for forty-five minutes. You stop on 23rd Street and walk. On the corner of 24th Street and 7th Avenue lies a big school called the High School of Fashion Industries. As you enter the building, swiping your ID, you hear a jolly voice from a tall, slim man saying, "Good morning!"

It is 8:45 AM, and you hear a swarm of loud ratchet girls yelling, sounding like a flock of birds gathered around the student elevators. You roll your eyes, because it is too early in the morning for all the ruckus, but over time you manage to get over it. Throughout the day you follow your daily schedule as a junior: first college applications, then chemistry, lunch, visual merchandising, US history, English, and trigonometry. Although it may become exhausting, you have to get through it. Momma wants a successful, prosperous young woman, and that is what you have to be. The jokes, the laughter, the good, chill vibes, the gossip, and the bond between you and your friends will keep you going through the day, I promise. Don't forget, education is the key to the door of success. So on that note, don't think twice about getting up at 6:15 AM.

Lunchroom Best Friend to Everyday Sister

by TENIA POOLE

I remember the day my best friend became my best friend. It was freshman year in the cafeteria. It wasn't as loud as usual, and the weather outside was nice, so I was already in a good mood. We sat together every day. I would tell her everything and she would do the same. We got into line to get lunch on this day. As we were waiting, I said to her, "I have to tell you something important."

She immediately asked, "What happened!?" with wide eyes, as if she was ready for me to spill all the tea.

I then said, "You're my best friend!"

She had the biggest smile on her face after I said it, and from then on we've been best friends. Yeah, we go through times where we don't talk, but only for about a day or so. We always bounce back like rubber does when you do something to it.

Who could've known that I would find my best friend in a lunch room? Except now I see her more as an older sister rather than just a best friend.

A Colombian-American Education

by ANYELA CORONADO

First Grade

This was the year my mom finally wasn't busy and had been successful in her dream of having and directing her own school. Of course I was the first one enrolled in it, so no more "You have to stay here because school is Monday to Friday, and on the weekend you can come home if I'm there." I was finally an official student at my mom's school.

It was hard enough starting at a school where all the kids knew each other except for you. Yet it was even worse having your mom as your teacher, because the times when you accidentally call your teacher "Mom," it wasn't a mistake.

Second Grade

It's awful to think that I only lasted a year in that school. The explanation was, "You're going to have to transfer in fifth grade either way, but at least this way you get to start learning English earlier than planned." Yeah, it wasn't great being the new kid all over again, but at least this time my mom wasn't my teacher.

I made good friends, learned a lot, and had a good time in that school. It was a private Catholic school; so it was super strict. "Prayers must be said every day; skirts have to reach below the knee, black shoes always clean with knee-high white socks; ties must be worn at all times and hair pulled back in a ponytail! Oh, and no Spanish shall be spoken during English classes." That was all I remember the nuns saying.

This was the year I almost peed my pants in English class because I hadn't memorized the line, "May I go to the bathroom, please?"

Third Grade

We said prayers, prepared for our First Communions, started the swimming and horseback riding classes, where I almost drowned and fell multiple times. They took two weeks out of our two-month vacation to do all of this. This was also the year some crazy kid pushed me off a park slide, which led to me cutting open my chin and bleeding for two hours and holding ice to my chin because I refused to go to the hospital and get stitches.

But the two most memorable things that happened in school that year was an eleventh grade couple getting kicked out of the school because they were caught making out in the hallway (and this was a big deal in Catholic school) and also a girl almost setting her hair on fire during our First Communion while trying to light the candle. Maria Jose was and still is one of my best friends since then.

Fourth Grade

Fourth grade was kind of intense. It was the year I felt I belonged. We had our own clique; the girls were Julia, Maria Jose, Laura, Erica, and me, and the boys were Nicholas, Ruben, Juan David, and Chihou. As more students started to arrive that year, we all kept our circle very close, giving almost no one the combination to enter in the locked gated community we had created. This was the year I felt more comfortable. I was so comfortable that when I saw my science teacher was failing everyone in the class and giving 10/10 to her favorite student (who just happened to be her boyfriend's nephew), I rebelled and got the whole class to riot and yell "Justice! Justice!" in the middle of her class.

My mom was not happy to have to leave work in the middle of the day to come sit at the principal's office with me. The teacher eventually got fired, though.

But then this year was the year that broke my heart, my soul, and my spirit. My grandfather—the most important man in my whole life, the man that basically raised me when my father wasn't there, even though I knew he was here in NYC working to bring my mom and me there. My grandpa was a very big paternal figure in my life. When he died, my world fell apart, and I cried for what felt like years. I missed him so much, but there was an upside to this, the most horrific situation in my life: it made me realize how important my friends were, how much they loved me, and how much I'd underestimated the power of our friendship.

But of course, just my luck, this was also the year my parents decided to move me to the United States. My goodbye was the worst. Everything happened so fast. All I remember was telling my friends and, later on, being at the airport crying my eyes out because I did not want to leave. In New York I had to repeat fourth grade again because "Eight years old was too young to be in fifth grade." It was truly the most confusing and intense year of my life. I didn't know whether I was miserable, bitter, or if I just loathed, despised, or disliked the whole idea of this place.

Fifth Grade

Everyone was so annoying. No one would speak to me in English because I came from a Spanish-speaking country. Some dude kept making immigrant jokes, and some girl even asked me if my dad was a drug trafficker just because we were Colombian. But, I thought, ignorance is everywhere and I was bound to find it someplace sooner or later.

Sixth Grade

All I hoped was for was the same annoying and ignorant people to not follow me to middle school; they didn't.

I made new English-speaking friends who were cool. Not much happened that year.

Seventh Grade

This was the year of boys! Girls were getting their period, and guys were getting mustaches. This was the year I said goodbye to tween Anyela and hello to teen Anyela. I was as comfortable as I could ever feel in this country and everything seemed to be turning out great.

Eighth Grade

This was the year of lost friendships. Those friends that I had acquired in sixth grade were gone; we grew up so fast and we all took different paths. It didn't even make sense for us to still try to be friends when the truth was we'd grown apart and could not be put back together, not even with superglue! It was the year of being brave, like when I punched a boy in the face for throwing food at me because I needed to show people how even though I always walked around with a smile on, that didn't mean they could do anything and I wouldn't get upset or react to it.

This was also the year of graduation, prom, senior trips, and the year I got to go back to Colombia! I was so excited I just wanted to go straight from graduation to JFK.

When I went back I was scared, not because it was dangerous, but because I started to realize that some people went from seeing me as a native, a Colombian, a neighbor... to seeing me as a tourist, "La Gringa" like they would say jokingly, but I knew deep down they meant it. Even though I would laugh along, those words would sting my soul like a bee would my arm. I also carried with me the terror of my friends treating me like the other people did. We had spent a long time apart, and I wondered if my friends from New York and I grew apart while we were in the same state, how would it be here? Would they shut me out? Would they not remember our long, late-night Facebook conversations? Our long Skype sessions? Will they treat me like a tourist just like everyone else? But of course, like always, I underestimated the power of our five-year-old friendships because to them I wasn't a tourist or La Gringa; I was simply Anyela, their Colombian friend who lives in New York.

Ninth Grade

Remembering freshman year is hard. I didn't do much but get to know the city with some of my new friends. That's all I remember other than making friends with this really annoying girl who used to sing really high pitch noises for everything! Any time and at any place. I would constantly tell her to shut up!

She transferred and we never spoke again. That was a friendship I was okay with losing.

Tenth Grade

I loved my fashion class. I got a sewing machine for Christmas, and all I did was sew and design. Maybe I'll be a fashion designer; it's something I'll love to do. I already love sewing.

I went to BookCon and it was the most wonderful experience of my life. "Let's make this a tradition," my friend said. I thought it sounded amazing.

I couldn't wait to be a junior!

Eleventh Grade

I decided I did not want to pursue fashion as a career.

"No, I don't hate the world. No I'm not angry. If I look tired, maybe it's because I am!!"

I really can't wait to graduate.

Remember

by RUTH CABRERA

You're not sure if you're more tired of being forced to attend a place you're dying to get released from or of having to bump into your waking nightmare in the hallways, staircases, cafeteria, and bathrooms. You wonder how is it that in the ten floors and over a thousand inmates, you could possibly be running into that mutt over and over. When you walk past her, a sense of rage and the urge to extend your arm and use all your force to mark five fingers right across her mouth rises, but I suggest you don't do it. Think. Remember where you are. Don't let them take away your privileges.

For a second, remember it's not your fault. You have good taste. How can you blame her? But it's still not okay for her to have done that with him. They're both disgusting. You were too nice. You trusted them. They were sneaky, but still, try to remain calm. Although you may never forget what she did, just be glad he had the courage to confess and allow you to finally open your eyes. She was grimy and evil. As much as it hurts, do not show that you're affected by this. Remember where you are. You will be held accountable for anything you do. They don't play that game in here.

Remember, you won't find real friends in here because it's filled with ninety-five percent fake, evil females who do not care about you. Don't trust those who follow that mutt around either, especially if they only try to approach you when she's in her cage. On your release date, if you still feel like you need to remind her of what she did, get that palm of yours ready and swing your arm like never before into her face and whisper to her, "Now you'll learn to never try and take what's mine again." You'll walk away with the best sense of release, and she'll always remember your name.

The Struggles of Being Me: Overcoming Stage Fright

by CHASTITY GLASBY

I remember the deafening silence and the heated stares of the people around me. Calculating, waiting for error, and ready to cheer for you or go against you at any given moment. I remember my rapid heartbeat, sweaty palms, and the voice in my head going over every step and move, so I knew that when I started I wouldn't be the one to mess up. I remember closing my eyes and taking a deep breath, mentally preparing myself, and then drifting into calming thoughts so that my fear diminished and I was ready to cheer. I remember that as a cheerleader, you have to get used to being the center of attention while avoiding stares, as well as keep your composure by smiling like no one's watching (even though they really are). When it's time to compete, I take one last deep breath then focus on the wall, where I can pretend to look at the crowd when I'm really not, and start. After a while, I lose focus on the wall and actually look at the crowd because, despite the deafening silence, the anticipation, and the gaping mouths and wide eyes of the crowd, on the cheer mats is where I feel at home.

When Mean Girls Attack

by TAMMY FONG

Many girls are tomboys when they are young, primarily in elementary school or middle school. I, too, was one of those girls. Back in elementary school, I loved sports and was really competitive—I still am. I used to play soccer every day with my friends during recess, in the small area that separates the playground and the basketball court. My time spent in that area playing soccer was one of the highlights of my childhood, but there was this one time that I did not enjoy it as much. There was a girl in my grade whose name was Althea, and calling her a mean girl would be an understatement. She was one of the worst girls in my grade at the time because she was stuck up and had a terrible personality. One time she felt it was necessary to make fun of my friend who had a disability and refused to stop even when I asked her to (she proceeded to make fun of me as well).

One day, there weren't any soccer balls or any balls that we could kick left in the equipment pile. My friends and I were pretty bummed, but my friend Jeffrey noticed that Althea had a ball, but she wasn't playing with it or anything. She just stood there holding it while talking to her friends. Jeffrey suggested that we go up to her and ask if we could use her ball. My friends and I stared at him in horror.

"Dude, that's like a death wish," Brian said.

Jeffrey shrugged. "What? We want to play, don't we?"

I frowned. "Yeah, but would it be worth it?"

"Only one way to find out."

He walked over to Althea and her friends, and we could only watch as they spoke. After a few moments they walked over, and we all took a deep breath.

"So, I heard you guys wanted my ball." Althea sneered.

I nodded.

"Well, you're gonna have to play me for it."

"What?"

"You heard me, us four against you guys, but you will have to lose a few people, or it won't be fair."

My friends and I exchanged glances, and I smirked. This was going to be easy. We decided that Brian, Jeffery, Alan, and I would play Althea and her friends. We headed to our usual spot and got into position. I played offense.

"Alright, first team to get ten goals wins," Patricia, who was the referee, announced. I extended my hand out to Althea to shake.

"Good luck to you and let's have a fair game." She glanced down at my hand and with a "hmph" turned her back on me and walked back to her friends. Wow, what great sportsmanship! We started the game and, let me just say, it would be an understatement to say that we completely throttled them! My team scored seven goals in a row while Althea's team only scored one goal when Alan tripped. I could sense their desperation as I was about to kick the ball because Althea charged at me to block the kick, as she's seen me do many times in the match. You would have to be some sort of idiot if you expect to block a kick from me without getting excruciating pain in your shins. Nonetheless, Althea continued to charge at me when I kicked the ball.

"Owww!" She screeched as the ball hit her. See, what did I tell you? She immediately bent down to clutch her shins and cry while her friends surrounded her.

"Uhh… are you okay?" I asked out of obligation. She looked up at me, anger clear on her face. Her friends were glaring at me, and I could feel the tension from my friends as they prepared to defend me. She got up and stormed towards me.

She yelled, "Ugly!" and pushed me. I barely stumbled as she turned and hobbled away like an old woman while her friends threw dirty looks at me before following her. Awww, looks like someone needs to put ice on her little boo boo, and I'm not just talking about her bruised shin. My friends and I stood in silence as we watched them run away.

"Sooo … looks like the ball is free for us to play," Brian said hesitantly.

"Yeah, let's just play since she left anyways," Kelly said with a nod. We all murmured our agreement and started a new game. Althea and her friends never came back.

Later on in the day, at dismissal, I groaned when I realized that I had math tutoring and that Althea and her friends were going to be there. Great. My friends gave me sympathetic looks as they left and Jeffrey patted my shoulder.

"Tell me if she does anything to you, I'll break her frickin' fingers for you."

"Haha thanks, but I don't think violence is the answer."

"Still, tell me anyways, 'kay?"

"Gotcha."

I waved goodbye to my friends and waited for the moment of truth.

Invincible

by BRITTNEY IDEHEN

In middle school I went to a school where the majority the kids were Jewish or Russian, and there were about four African-American kids. There were actually more people of color at the school, but even though some of them had skin as dark as mine, they didn't get bullied because they weren't African-American like me. Sometimes I don't get too mad thinking about why the other kids with brown skin didn't leave me alone. If they didn't make jokes about me, then they would have probably been bothered like me. Somewhere along my middle school journey, I met these three girls. Sometimes they got joked on for being Muslim. During lunch, instead of staying in the lunchroom by myself (where I would usually sit in a corner and read) we would just sit and talk. Well, they would talk in a language I didn't understand, so I was I was back to sitting and reading. I would sit and wait for someone to bring up a topic or ask my opinion on something.

After leaving my friends, I began going to the library for lunch, but it never changed what happened in class, mostly art. We had art four days a week, but two out of four of these days I had an extra math class that I loved. I was bad at math, but I really liked the teacher. Her name was Ms. Lemani. She was friendly and amusing, and we had almost the exact same personality and she always pointed it out. Now back to art. In art I sat with a group of boys that were my friends; one of them was my best friend, and another one became my best friend when we got to high school. Even though everyone at our table was my friend, my "friends" would make jokes that hit home and I would just brush it off. Since they were kind of my friends, I don't like to use the word "bullying." Talking is talking, and I was really grateful that I wasn't stuck in the back table with Leonardo and Ronald. Those were two kids that didn't speak English, but I often sat with them before I made friends because I didn't have anywhere else to go. When I got to eighth grade, the jokes started to get more annoying.

The most annoying one was the one that the kid who sat next to me used to you say, he would hit me with the drawstring to his sweatshirt and say, "Pick the cotton." Because of the jokes that were made toward me in middle school, I now under no circumstances find it okay for anyone who isn't African-American to say the "n" word or make the slightest joke about black people. There was another kid in my class who whispered a random joke to me about the Klu Klux Klan, and out of nowhere my guardian angel of a teacher, Ms. Friedler—who, like most of the school, was Jewish—stopped the lesson, turned completely around, and went off on this kid for what he said. For the first time in all three years of middle school, I was being defended. My teacher often told us that she heard everything we said but almost every teacher said that. It was like saying, "I have eyes in the back of my head," but after she somehow miraculously heard what he said to me. She even included how he would have been considered a slave too.

As weird as it may seem, that kid and I became good friends after that. One of the things we realized after becoming friends was that we both loved an artist named MGK. My favorite song was "Invincible," and because of that song, I always felt a little better. I actually made two best friends, and even though they both spoke Spanish, they never spoke it around me because they knew I would feel left out. After middle school, the three of us stopped speaking as much as we used to, but I'll always appreciate their friendships and the time we were friends.

Ms. Friedler stopping the lesson that day made me want to be a teacher. I want to be a teacher so that I can defend all of the kids with a voice as loud as an empty room to make sure that they never go through middle school the way I did. Maybe I'll even inspire someone.

Memories from Granite Street

by JUSTINE COOPER

My earliest memory on the block was falling off of my grandma's back porch. It was completely cement, about six feet high. There were black metal bars, like a railing surrounding the top. Instead of running down the stairs to play out in the front, everyone used to jump off the edge of the porch. But I always ran down the steps. But one day I decided to jump like my friends. Michael was in front of me, and he jumped. So I was still on the porch, but he was at ground level. The last thing I remember was looking down at Michael and him looking up at me. I jumped and fell. I rolled all the way to the garage. I had big cuts all over my face. I came into the house, and I saw my grandma and my mom talking in the living room. My mother turned and glanced at me, but then she did a double-take. They both started to scream. They frantically asked me what happened. I told them I fell. The next thing I remember, we were in the car on the way to the hospital. I was three or four then. I still have a scar underneath my left eye and a scar right above my left eyebrow.

Ninety-five Granite Street was my father's childhood home. My Grandma Nell lived there until 2003 when she got remarried and moved to Pennsylvania. When I was in pre-K, my dad moved out of my house and went to live there. My grandmother often visited after she moved, so when I was younger, I spent a lot of time there as well. The street was a dead end, so the kids on the block played together all the time. There was a whole group of us. There was Michelle and Michael Richards; Jayson, Jasmine, and Justine Esquilin; and Jasmine, Amy's little cousin. Occasionally Michelangelo used to play with us as well. I didn't realize it then, but I was the baby of the group. Jasmine Esquilin was the oldest; then there was Michelle; Justine and Jayson were twins; then it was Michael, the other Jasmine, and myself. Maybe that's why they picked on me from time to time. But that was mostly Jayson and Justine. I remember feeling like an outsider sometimes, considering that I never actually lived on the block. Michael and Michelle lived right next door to my grandmother. The other Jasmine lived on the other side of my grandma's house. Two doors down from Michael and Michelle was the Esquilins' grandmother. But even though the Esquilins didn't actually live on the block, same as me, they lived up the block and around the corner, on Furman Avenue.

A memory I am not so proud of was the time everyone went to swim in Tushar's pool. I didn't even know who Tushar was, but I asked my grandmother if I could go anyway. Like anyone can imagine, she said no. I was upset, but I quickly got over it with the help of Michelangelo. Just because I couldn't go didn't stop all my friends from going. So it was just me and Michelangelo outside. He couldn't go to the pool either. I don't remember whose idea it was, but I remember us throwing their bikes and scooters on the ground. Some kind of food was poured over them, and we just made a huge mess in front of the Esquilins' grandmother's house. We ran back to my grandmother's backyard and waited for them to come out. I was only six or seven at the time, and I remember Michelangelo asking me if I would be his girlfriend. I said no, and we waited in silence. They finally came back and asked us what happened and who did it. Before we could answer they asked if it was the boys from up the block. Michelangelo and I looked at each other and we looked back at them, hesitated for a second, and then agreed to their version of events.

But perhaps my favorite memory from that block was the day Michael Richards and I kissed for the first time. It was freshman year of high school, and he and I had been "talking" for about a month. I wasn't completely sure how he felt about me then, and I convinced myself he didn't like me so if that turned out to be the truth, my feelings wouldn't be too hurt. It was a rainy day in April, and instead of going home after wrestling practice, I came to the block. The plan was for my dad to drive me home from there. When I got on the block, I texted Michael and told him to come outside. I waited in the doorway of my grandmother's house for him to come. I saw him out of the corner of my eye. I walked down the steps and over to him. He had a huge black umbrella and was wearing a red sweater. I remember him teasing me because my umbrella had a hole in it. Eventually I moved under his umbrella. So it was just us under his big umbrella on this rainy, rainy day in April. I got up on my tippy-toes and leaned up to him, but he wouldn't lean down to me. I leaned back down. I remember doing this two or three more times before he actually looked down at me and kissed me. But once we started to kiss we couldn't stop. I felt almost like we were a scene in a corny, cheesy romance movie. Just two teenagers kissing in the pouring rain.

Memories at the Park

by DEREK RONDA

There's this park. The park is located in the west side of the city, on the banks of the Hudson River, overlooking New Jersey. I haven't been to that park since the last time I was with her. This park brings back memories, memories that I wish would come back again. I had the best times at that park with a special girl. We would go to the park and sit on the bench at the spot where we sat the day I first brought her here. We would talk about everything and open up to each other. She would make me happy, and I would have this great feeling that I can't even explain, but all you need to know is that it just felt amazing. Once time went by, things started to change. Feelings started to fade away, and our hope for each other disappeared. But whenever I think of her, I always remember our great moments at the park and how everything was just perfect. I would take those days back anytime, but at the same time I can't force her.

The Sunset

by YING LIU

Remember what I asked you that day? I do.

I remember the day you promised to hold my hand everywhere we settled. No one can replace the value of each word you delivered. I remember your shiny eyes holding my heart, dazzling it with brightness. Until that day. I remember your warmth turning into a black hole in my world. I remember that soft hand of yours turning into a diamond with no sense of life, only the hardness of hatred that I now contain for you.

I remember every step of your timeline, but now it doesn't matter anymore. My caring has turned into your reasons, the reasons you used to crumble me. And now I will burn all your reasons.

The lonely path I took as I wandered downhill, parallel to the sun. Our love became so dim, just like the sunset. Day by day I waited. Day by day the sun went through the same irony. As the sun set, your shadow became more visible. But as the sun rose, you slowly camouflaged into a world where I could only be blinded with all your beautiful lies.

Your promises, your lies, all vanished with that sunset.

Personal Narrative

by JARLYN ALVAREZ

I remember the hot summer, when skin gets darker, days get longer, and drinks get colder. Music gets louder, and so do the sounds of voices greeting, singing, and gossiping. Oh, how wonderful New York is in the summer. I remember the happy vibes at every corner and the blocks one walks by. I remember waking up early to go to the beach, sleeping outside as the morning's soft air touched my skin with soft care. Feeling the breeze flow through my long, silky black hair as I made my way through the highways and tunnels of the Big Apple. I remember all the barbeques and picnics filling my heart with ease and happiness.

As I sit in the cold, freezing, waiting for the bus, and hesitating to walk the two blocks home, I remember walking everywhere and not even thinking about a bus ride in the happy, joyful summer. After this rough, skin-drying, pale winter, all I need and desire is a hot, shining sun. Now all I can remember is that there are only two more months until another summer in New York City!

My Island Experience

by SAGINE TEERATH

Trinidad brings back joyful memories for me. Every time I go there, I have a blast and can count on having an adventure. The taste of my grandmother's fresh coconut water always puts a smile on my face. I remember the relaxing feeling I had when I lied in a hammock. As I swung back and forth, I felt sleepy. Trinidad has beautiful oceans that can compare to no other place. The light blue water glistened in the sun. I felt the cool, crisp air brushing against my face. I sunk my toes into the light beige, smooth sand. My skin tingled from the touch of the salty waves. Whenever I am in a sullen mood, I can always reflect on these moments in Trinidad to regain composure.

My Epiphany

by AKACIA THOMAS

Sometimes we take family for granted, and I was at the tender age of seven when this revelation came to me. I grew up living with my cousins. Imagine having a slumber party every night—it sounds super fun, right? It most certainly was. I remember being such a tight-knit, close family. My cousins and I woke up and got dressed together every day, ate breakfast together, and many times, at a young age, we'd even shower together. Our favorite place in our apartment was definitely the living room. For starters, it was the biggest room in the house, which meant plenty of space for playing, which clearly was our forte. We would build forts and bridges and many other extravagant, adventurous, little kid things. Also, our living room had the biggest TV, which for us was like watching our favorite cartoons in a movie theatre.

I was having the time of my life. So imagine my heartbreak when I found out we were moving. I don't really remember it happening; it was kind of like a dream. One day I was living with my cousins, and the next day I wasn't. The move was extremely drastic and painful. I mean, that apartment was all I knew for the first years of my life. The move was kind of like losing your phone and getting a new one, with no photos, no contacts, and no memories. It feels so foreign. So no matter what I did while living in that new apartment, no matter how fun or cool it was, all I could ever think was, "I wish my cousins were here…"

Trading the City for a Moment of Bliss

by ANA SANCHEZ

I can sit here and write about how much I hate high school or the little sleep from how many cups of coffee I drink, but I would rather tell you about something other than NYC.

I remember getting to North Carolina after a nine-hour road trip. I remember looking at that big resort covered in shiny glass. I remember walking in and seeing a fancy curved staircase, a warm fireplace, and a whole lot of people at the lobby with their suitcases—including us.

I remember exploring the first few days, and on the third day we went up that mountain. I remember being the last to wake up; I was really dreading the climb. I remember freaking out. I didn't want to go up. I really thought I was going to get lost or injured possibly even eaten by a black bear. I remember it took my friends a long time to convince me to go up that thing. I remember it looked huge! The floor was wet, and there were branches everywhere. I remember slipping and falling every couple steps. I was barely able to keep both feet on flat surface, so walking on top of a slippery ground was definitely almost impossible for me. Ugh! Thank God my friends kept me up and alive.

I remember stopping halfway to to a small shop for water and snacks. Silly me thought I wouldn't need any of those, so I bought nothing but a small key chain. I remember every sound of crunching and popping the branches would make when we stepped on them. I remember that bloody knee some girl got from trying to run up. It was her fault; no one told her to go up running with all those twigs and branches on the ground.

I remember that after all that struggle of getting up there, we finally saw this mouth-opening view. I remember seeing everything really tiny from way up high. I remember the white fog slowly fading away and revealing all the other mountains. I remember every mountain covered with snow at the tip and a white sky. I remember the smell of fresh air up there. I remember that moment of bliss I had when I sat down on a rock and just stared at that view. I remember not wanting to come back to the city. I remember wanting to stay there all of November. I remember everyone taking out their phones to take pictures. I remember sitting there for a long time without moving, wishing everyone I knew in NYC could see what I was seeing.

How to Hold Your Depression Just a Bit Too Close

by SPENCER AYVAS

Wake up to the sound of an alarm beeping in your ear and fingers running down your spine. You'll want to stand, you'll want to turn it off, but Depression will put his cold hands on your shoulder, dig his talons into your skin, and whisper. He'll say not to get up. He'll say that five more minutes in his arms is just fine. You'll listen to him; you'll listen to what he says because you have no self-discipline, and he'll wrap his arms around your body in an intimate embrace that lacks everything intimacy should have.

Five minutes pass quickly.

Suddenly, you're ten minutes late to leave the house. In your panic, you rip away from his arms and rush. Reprimand yourself for listening to him, swear that you never will again, even though you both know that you'll listen to everything he says, always. You have no self-discipline, after all.

When you get to the bathroom, he'll be there. Slithering on the counter and over your shoulders. He will card his hand through your hair and whisper smoke that goes in one ear and swirls behind your eyes; he'll say that you're losing a lot of weight. He'll remind you how bad it is. He'll remind you of the very real possibility of death. He'll say that you look better and better with every bone that protrudes from your skin when you breathe. He may drag a hand over your ribs. He may put a hand on your hip bone. He may feel your collarbones. You may be dying.

Your head is more smoke than thought.

You take the train to school; a short ride, usually, but you have taken to riding the train back in the opposite direction to the very first stop on the line in order to guarantee yourself a seat. Your commute should be around forty minutes long. Using this method you've managed to extend it to a whopping hour and a half. You don't care. You need a seat.

Depression follows you; he's recently taken to sitting on your shoulders, the perfect spot to whisper your insecurities and put his hands around your neck and laugh as you try to act like you aren't being strangled by an incorporeal demon whose hands are made out of tar and who bleeds acid. He sits on your shoulders, and he is heavy. He weighs you down; your spine feels like it's collapsing under its own weight. You feel like your bones are breaking, but you have to act normal, don't let anyone see him, and he laughs. You've started sitting on the train now so he can't break your bones. You decide that this solution is fine even at the expense of your attendance and grades.

Still he whispers against your neck, reminds you that you're screwing yourself over, that it'll come back to bite you in the back soon.

Turn up your music.

You're late to school; you decide to skip the rest of the class. Your insecurities drip out of his mouth, an acid that drops onto your shoulder and runs down your arm, burning and dissolving all the skin in its path. (Your bones truly are visible now.) Besides, even if you went to that class, it's hard to focus and take notes when you are expending all of your energy on trying to silently battle off the poison he's trying to kill you with. He'll say it isn't worth the energy. You'll agree with him. It's not.

You dread lunch; you dread seeing your friends. You shouldn't dread something like that, but you do because he is with you, and he is like a territorial dog in the way he wraps his arms around your torso and snarls at anyone who approaches you. You're his, and they can't have you. Crap, your friend spotted you. Smile at her like you weren't just having a conversation with your chronic illness about running and hiding in the stairwell so you wouldn't have to face anyone except for your own thoughts, no matter how scary the situation would be.

You have no way of knowing this, but she has the demon Inferiority tormenting her. You don't know but Depression does. He spotted Inferiority on her shoulder and under her skin. Demons like that have a way of finding each other. And she, like you, is doing her best to hide her insecurities from everyone. You're both very good at it; neither of you can recognize the other as one of your own, but maybe if you two paid a bit more attention she would be able to see the smoke fogging up your eyes, and you would see the Inferiority under her fingernails and in the wounds that she could never stop scratching.

(It's almost like she's trying to scratch Inferiority out of her, even at her own expense.)

You go home. You haven't done your homework in about a month; it's a wonder that you're passing any of your classes at all. But school is for work, and home is for a three-hour nap because the nine hours you get every night does nothing to satiate the tiredness that sleep cannot cure. Your parents get home late, and you go online. That's where you can truly be, where you have friends who know you and Depression personally. Where you have friends who suffer too. A friend with Abuse in the shape of their father always getting them to jump to the worst possible conclusion, a friend who wears Shame like gloves stopping him from reaching out because of his fear of his sexuality, friends with Loss, Anxiety, Fear, Hate, Hate, Hate.

These are the people you are at home with.

Depression doesn't want you talking to them. Depression hates the support you get from them. Depression wants to find a way to stop you from leaving him, no matter what the cost.

Depression speaks impulsively, says whatever comes to his mind without thought or care. Depression is apathetic. He says the things you've tried to stop yourself from thinking. Drown yourself in the bathtub. Try not to. Rush out of the bath, only checking that you're clean enough because you're scared of his words. You're scared of your thoughts.

(Your mom has a Depression following her too. Her Depression says it's her fault that his brother has taken to you. Your Depression says it's your fault that you can't help her.)

Sleep, now. You're tired and upset. Don't bother entertaining the hope that you won't wake up in the morning. It's never worked before, and you know it won't work now. Sleep is when you're free, where he doesn't follow you and torment you. Where you can exist without his corrosive hands touching you. You think that sleep is bliss. On the outside, Depression runs his hand along your side. He could go into your dreams, he could torment you if he wanted to.

But at night he lets you be happy so that the next waking day you turn back to page one, where this story started really getting gory. Breaking the miracles down into shards and pieces plenty.

Tomorrow is another day.

Bethpage

by CAMREN HERNANDEZ

My childhood was superb. I remember always being super excited to go to school everyday because it was so close to my house. It was down the block from my house, less than a five minute walk. I enjoyed school. I enjoyed my town, Bethpage. I enjoyed every single thing. Everyone went to the same supermarket, the same park, and the same shopping center.

Every day after school, my grandma would take me to this local toy store, and I would feel so special. She would allow me to get three items, and sometimes even more. I would end up buying a Webkinz plush toy, and then the next day all of my friends and I would compare stuffed animals. I remember always being picked up after school and walking with my grandma to my cute local store and buying junk food just because. My childhood was the best thing ever because I would come home to a full house, cooked food, and a cute toy poodle greeting me at the door.

During my elementary years, I joined Girl Scouts, made a bunch of friends, and looked forward to all of our meetings. My favorite one of all was when we went to Benihana Restaurant and learned how to do all the cool tricks that the hibachi workers do. This made me so happy. However, one time at one of our meets, we were making bird nests, and I thought I was invincible and could touch peanut butter without getting an allergic reaction. That's a lie. I broke out in hives and was rushed home. Obviously, I'm still alive.

My neighborhood made me so happy because everyone knew everyone and I never felt discriminated against, living in a highly populated white area (although my mom is white) amongst a million other things. I enjoyed taking bike rides, walking my little sister in her stroller, or even walking my two toy poodles, Mevo and Marley. I loved my private school. There were always bake sales and swim meets, and it was so welcoming. We had a chef come in all the time to make us healthy meals. Nothing was ever wrong during my childhood.

One interesting thing that occurred in Bethpage happened before I joined my county's track team. I was in kindergarten, and we had a sign on the bathroom door that said "Stop" and "Go," like a traffic symbol. So, like usual, I went to use the bathroom. There was only one stall, and I turned the sign to "Stop" because I didn't want anyone disrupting me while I was in the bathroom. Then my crush walked in on me using the bathroom and I was so embarrassed. My teacher called the principal, and it turned out this girl who didn't like me was the one who turned the sign to "Go" so that my crush would walk in on me.

My childhood was like a movie, and I loved it. However, it was the end of third grade and I tragically found out I was moving out of Bethpage to Fresh Meadows. As a child in the third grade, getting news like that was equivalent to receiving news about your favorite teen boy band breaking up. I was so distraught. I now had to make new friends and go to a new school. But, it turns out the change was for the better. I went to the best middle school in the district and met a bunch of cool friends that I am still friends with today.

I do miss Bethpage, though. I really do, and it's sad that we didn't have social media back then so I couldn't get my childhood friends' contact information. I loved the greenery in my neighborhood; all the colors were so vibrant and bold. My neighborhood was my neighborhood. My childhood was the happiest time in my life. So far, I had no worries, and I lived in a picture-perfect town. I don't regret moving to the town I live in now because they're sort of the same. The only difference is that social media is around now, so no one embraces their surroundings as much. I miss Bethpage and the juvenile Camren.

I Am Home

by SUSANA DELOSSANTOS

I remember the walls of her room, filled with portraits of us. I remember the sound of her TV playing football and hearing her cheer every time the Jets scored. I remember how alive the house was. Quiet but alive. Independent but together.

But most of all, I remember how happy she was. The way she made everyone feel. The joy on her face when she made people laugh. I remember how nothing was impossible, just hidden and it was my job to find the answer. I remember trying to understand. I remember crying, screaming, stomping, and grieving. I remember her consoling me when it was she who was supposed to be consoled. I remember when it happened.

I remember hating her for hating me, because if she didn't, she wouldn't have left. I remember shutting down and then suddenly, like a switch, powering back on. I finally understood, and with understanding comes feeling and emotion. Emotions that were coming so rapidly that I couldn't decipher them.

I remember no longer hating her, but hating myself. I remember starting to resent her once again for letting me hate her. Then I remember loathing myself for allowing myself to hate her in the first place. She was home. She is home. I couldn't allow myself to hate my home, because she did everything for me. She did it for me. For me. She laughed for me. She was happy for me. She tried for me. She consoled me. Actually, no, she consoled me for herself and for me. I needed the strength, and she needed the reassurance.

I remember figuring it all out, and really understanding. Understanding that she left when she did to help me, to make sure I was ready to be without her. I remember knowing I wasn't. But I wasn't going to have to. Staring at the bed she once slept in, I remember saying that I got her message, because she never really left. She's always been on the left side of my chest, pumping blood through my veins, where she will remain forever. Because she is home. I am home.

Hurt

by ABIGAIL PEREZ

It was the place where it started--all the love, hurt, confusion, and anger. Though I am much older than I was before it happened, I now understand that such an event occurred, and I no longer feel the love a daughter should feel for her father or the confusion as to why this happened. Hurt and anger are present now. Those emotions are the only thing I know I will feel for him. Every time someone talks about him or puts in their two cents about how I feel (I really hate when someone thinks they know me well enough to think or say how I feel), it angers me that he is coming out of their mouth when they don't know a thing. It's not a touchy subject, so to speak, but in my opinion nothing is going to change, so why continue to talk about it? It's not going to make the situation better or make it disappear like it never happened. It did.

My stepsister looks at me with an inscrutable expression when I tell her that I won't forgive him, but she insists on continuing to butt in and tell me what to do. But I won't listen. I feel how I feel; no one can change that no matter how hard they try.

Waking up to only my brother and sister while my "dad" was nowhere to be found, I knew then that something was off. That I was a daddy's girl at the time when he left us hurt. I can't lie to you and say I had a feeling he was going to do something like that, but I can tell you that I remember him checking out a girl when we were in front of our house in the car just playing around. He was in the driver's seat, and I was in the passenger seat. He had the nerve to look back at her just because she had a body. Like, dude come on. In front of your kids? But I guess not everyone has a brain; clearly he didn't.

My mother encouraged us to write a letter so we could send it to him. I let all my feelings out, all the foreign emotions I once felt for him poured out onto the paper like a river flowing. I put my pen to the paper a few weeks after we moved back to New York from Florida and kept writing nonstop to tell him how I felt. I don't remember the note, but I remember a specific moment where my tears stained the paper expressing all that I felt, hoping to make sure he knew not only from words but from the dried up tears how he affected me. Blaming myself for my father's departure angered my mom, even though she tried not to show it, because I was young and couldn't possibly be the cause for this. As I grew up, I knew better than to blame myself, because all I could ever do as a child was love him, and indeed I did. It didn't help that I was depressed, partly because of him leaving, but for other personal things as well.

Therapy never happened, even though my doctor said I should go for the depression and anger issues he insisted I had. I'm not exactly sure if I am depressed, though I used to think I was. But, how is it that during the day I can laugh and have fun, even though sometimes it might be fake, but when at night or any time I'm alone

I forget how to feel happy? Should I even be here? Suicide was an option too many times, but going through with it? Not likely.

Once about one or two years ago I came close. Holding a razor blade against my wrist can do the trick of bleeding a lot, but subconsciously I knew I wouldn't fully go ahead with it. It's funny because I'm surrounded by people who can or who already did, and I always reply to them saying "lucky." But are they really lucky? I guess knowing that a close relative was indeed in the same boat as I was is completely shocking because I could tell he was sad at certain moments but never would I have ever thought he was suicidal. I would like to say I'm not completely sure how I was before, but there is that part of me lurking in the shadows of my soul, ready to pop out whenever necessary to take control of all my other emotions, making me forget how to live.

Dark and Light

by DARK AND LIGHT

The spot next to me was empty. The sun was streaming down with strong beams of light, bringing down the heat like a sauna to where I sat in solitude. I watched as the glistening sun danced over the ledge on the clear blue water of the East River. This big space was my escape from my problems, but this time I couldn't escape. For the first time, the East River didn't make my problems seem small in comparison. The river had been moving slowly. Everything around me had been moving in slow motion. Moving on, but I was against the current. Not moving on. Not flowing. Stuck in one place, as if I were drowning.

To my left was the very long bridge. A bridge where someone could start in one place and end in another, but as they went on the view changed and the climb got harder. The heat from the weather was making it harder to breathe as the water built up then was set free, like a rushing waterfall, from my eyes. The clear, bright blue sky contradicting the gray silence, the thundering emptiness, the lightening of sorrow, and the gray fog of confusion that was hidden underneath the surface of my trembling. I held myself tightly, trying not to fall apart from the internal screaming of pain and loss.

The loss of the person who meant the world to me. My grandmother. Not being able to hear her singing her songs, her wisdom filled stories from her life, and embracing her small self tightly, never wanting to let go. She and I had a bond like no other. She was my inspiration to live a better life. I closed my eyes, concentrating on the dark, remembering the promise I made her, and praying to see the light and for another support, because I knew even before it happened that I couldn't do this alone. The tension in my muscles started to release, and I took a deep breath, almost letting the misery consume me.

Then I felt it, a large hand resting on my shoulder. I took a deep breath after the initial scare and slowly opened my eyes. It wasn't dark anymore. There he was, standing bright in front of the sun—tall and strong was my light in the dark, always popping up at the right moment. Who in this world would have guessed that he'd mean everything to me in the end? The last person in this world that I would have thought would be there for me was the only person who showed up, stood with me through it all, and is still there for me now. Little did I know that past emotions were flooding in; I just wasn't aware of it. He was a hand to hold and a shoulder to cry on. Then I knew that the beautiful, clear, sunny day was a secret message from her, my lost world, letting me know that I was going to be alright. It took losing her to make the change in me that needed to be made.

WE CRAVE
THE MAYHEM

Limitless

by ALEXIS BAEZ

New York City is my city, it is where I was born and raised. A city that works during the day and parties all night and is so filled with life that it doesn't get a wink of sleep. Being bored here is nearly impossible, unless I'm at home or school. I'm able to explore and discover new places every day. My city is never the same, it's always changing and evolving over time, like me. People are everywhere you go, crawling on the city's face. But recently, I've started to think there are too many people here. In certain places, there are several homeless people on a single block. It's a sad thing to see nearly everywhere you go. My city is a light that attracts every single bug. Because it's a place of prosperity, filled with opportunities … But dance with the city demons and you'll get beaten down to your knees, and the city will take everything except the clothes on your back. I can't imagine what that's like. Trash on the streets, spit, gum, who knows what else. There are more germs infesting this place than people.

I could be chilling in a subway car or packed in tight like a new box of crayons. I'm not gonna lie, though, it beats having to drive. My city of lights—partying all night seduces kids like me, making us want to grow up fast. In the seventeen years I've lived here, I've sprouted from a bud into a fully bloomed flower. You see, when you live in the city, you must see the beauty … You may see broken glass covering the streets, but I see a street covered in crystal sheets. Nice to view from afar but I always walk around it. You see smoke polluting the air, but in such a beautiful way, dancing along with the winds. In my city—so filled with life—inspiration is everywhere you go; arts thrive in the veins of these city streets, including my favorite … fashion. The wave of style starts here and expands to everywhere else. Styles from different decades—some original, some with a modern twist. I watch and learn, put on *my* own twist. I feel I learn more from my city than I do in school.

New York City is my city, where heaven and hell live together and the sky's your limit … I'm limitless here.

Knockout

by ERICA JOHNSON

Like any other day, we wrestled in grandma's room when of course we weren't supposed to. That queen-size bed was the perfect place to do it. Throwing, kicking, body slamming—it was the usual. I was hyper and ready to brawl at all times. Next thing you know, "Slam!" That was the sound of my face hitting a hard, solid surface. It was the dresser that happened to be directly behind the bed. I opened my eyes to see blood and teeth in my hand. "Mikey, what did you do?!" I said, but the words didn't come out.

"I'm sorry, Erica. I'm so sorry. Oh my God, I'm so sorry!" Over and over. He started to sound like a broken record. I couldn't muster a response. The shock was slowly fading, replaced with pain. Then the tears ensued. Hysterical crying. "Oh God, Erica! Please don't cry!" I held my head in pain and and dropped my teeth.

For some odd and inexplicable reason, he picked them up and left the room to confront my mom. I followed. "Um … yee." She freaked out.

"Oh my God! What happened?" He opened his hand with my two front teeth in it. Mom hit the floor in shock with a loud thud. Being five and having never seen anyone faint, I assumed my mom was hurt or dying. I immediately stopped crying to shake her and see if she was alive.

"M-m-mommy?" After what felt like an eternity of waiting, she finally woke up. The trip to the emergency room was full of crying and lots of questions from the doctor. By some miracle, I didn't get a concussion. The wrestling between my uncle and I stopped after that stressful day eleven years ago, and then so did the hanging out. Now we barely talk. The love is still there, but the attachment isn't, and I like it better this way, considering I have all my teeth. So much mayhem has happened in grandma's place, especially the bedroom, and no matter how many times I leave, I always come back. Guess I crave the mayhem.

Little Shop of Treasures

by JAH CHINA DELEON

For it is only this place that I can call another home
One that
Resembles all that I am
And all that I will be
A mismatched heart
Made of a perfectly imperfect blend of old and new
Yet always full of treasures

The shop
You will never know what this place beholds
The place no enters
The place no one goes
The trade
The exchange
The exchange of a memory for a buck
And a wish of good luck
A memory left behind

Now an item left for me to find
bought for a nickel and a dime
An enchanting world hidden behind closed doors with an open
sign
Hidden trophies covered gleaming with need through glass
Under the cheap buzzing rectangular lights
Saying "add me to your list of confidants
We won't be bad"

The shop where my mother bought
the earrings that I hold near and dear
That dangle the sun, the moon, and the stars from both ears
And make me feel as though I am floating in the air
The earrings that sing in the sun
playing the most upbeat tune you could ever hear
and dance in the night
casting the faintest of glimmers in the darkest shadows
And cast away the demons that dwell on the insecurities that I fight

The place where she bought the camera
That opened the world of possibilities
Exhilarating images with a pixilated presence
That have given me new purpose
And found me a new perspective to turn to

This place
This shop
has defined me
And made me more
Of what I am

And what I will be
Forever and always
A mismatched heart
Made of a perfectly imperfect blend of old and new
Yet always full of treasures
And always

me

Cardboard Chronicles

by BRANDY SARABIA

The cardboard building really does make a first impression on you; every floor has its own identity.

The first floor consists of desperate women who try to make a living off easy money. "*Las vagas*," we would say, because they sell themselves instead of working. The young and beautiful daughter of the lady trying to make ends meet. The young and beautiful daughter who won't make it far. Usually, when you walk inside the building, you can see either a group of guys walking to the woman's house or the woman waiting outside her apartment, smoking. I always greet the younger woman when I see her, since she is really nice and her fluffy dog always sits with her. I feel very bad for her; her whole life is a wreck. She and her mother spend countless hours sniffing cocaine and smoking, waiting for another man to come their way.

The second floor is unheard of. No one speaks about them. Rumor has it that it is a no-man's-land. When you finally see them (which is super rare), be prepared for an annoying elevator ride because they are too lazy to actually walk up from the first floor. I remember that one time in the summer when it was so hot my family and I had just came back from a walk, there was a group of people who smelled so bad. They lived on the second floor and would always dye their hair and wear dark colors. Now let me remind you again; it was a hot summer day. They reeked of spoiled fish. Imagine how they smelled. I'm not going to say they weren't nice people; they were. But they just were too lazy to take the stairs, and then the elevator smelled like ten stink bombs exploded in that small, compact room.

The third floor is the floor of the forgotten. Elders whom no one seems to care for, but everyone knew about them too well. Funny how the ones who gave everything to their families are the ones to be forgotten by said families. No wonder they are the grumpiest and saddest people of the cardboard building. There's this old couple, and they are everyone's *abuelo* and *abuela*. Not going to lie, they irritate the life out of me because they are always so mean. My parents bring them food or some other things, and they are sometimes so ungrateful. It's no wonder why their son and daughter-in-law don't go visit them.

The fourth floor is designed for families of six or eight people. These families are so sad because generations upon generations finished high school and decided that it was perfectly fine to give up their education. The grandmother takes care of her granddaughter while the mother goes out with friends. I guess they have become accustomed to the idea of just staying with family, creating a chain that can at one point become unbreakable. My mom talks to a woman who lives with her four kids, her mother and father, her twin sister, and the sister's child. I can't picture what that place must be like. It's no wonder that we Mexicans have a stereotype that we live with our extended family. Funny how no one believes that I only live with my parents and my siblings.

If you ever need a little reminder of the city life, welcome to the fifth floor! You can find yourself lucky enough to converse with a drug dealer or teenagers smoking away the last bits of brain cells they have left, and you'll still have enough time to get into an argument with the fellow from the other side of the building. In a perfect world, you wouldn't go to a family friend's party because it's pretty lame. But in our imperfect world, parties that consist of family friends can never go wrong. Then again, like I said, this is an imperfect world. Once stepping into the scene of the party, forget about the innocence. Forget the fact that you and your siblings look washed up in Forever 21 dresses. *Rule number one of surviving a Bronx party: this isn't Midtown Manhattan; you should have dressed more comfortably.* Your family friends don't mind the fact that you dressed up for the party, but everyone else seems to think otherwise. I mean, everyone else in this party is dressed is in tight, short dresses or crop tops and skinny jeans. Well, this will be fun.

You sit in the nearest chair in sight, you flip through your phone and try to make conversation with your best friend only to be interrupted by the closest person who can resemble a friend here.

"Hey!" he says. "Yo, you wanna go smoke some weed in the stairway?"

Now, let me remind you that this kid is seventeen, turning eighteen soon, and your mother is staring at you from the other side of the room. *Rule number two of surviving a Bronx party: when dealing with an uncomfortable situation, run to the bathroom and stay there 'til your sister comes looking for you.* This will most likely make you look stupid, but it helps you avoid a conflict, and you can also rethink why you even came to this party. Around midnight there will be an argument with the drunk guys and the gossiping of the drunken women. The "cool" kids will be in a room smoking or dancing. Tell your mom you're going home, grab the keys, and run like hell upstairs.

The sixth floor is a constant war between sleep and bachata music. If you're lucky, you may even wake up to the nostalgic sounds of broken glass, doors banging, and people fighting. Of course, there's the welcoming smell of smoke slipping through cracks underneath the door during the nighttime, and get ready for all the women in the apartment next to yours to break their necks when you step out of the elevator after school. Try not to get mad at the fact that they cannot stop listening to the old Romeo Santos album on repeat as if they ran out of other music to listen to. Or that there are always dumb kids playing around in the hallway, making noise while you try to do your homework over the weekend. The most important thing to remember is to never sit right next to the doorway or you will be gifted with the stench of smoke. Do not, under any circumstances, tell your mom it smells of pot. You do not want her to go downstairs and have an argument with the nineteen-year-old high school dropout and then have your dad start yelling.

It will not be a happy ending.

Away

by JAH MEEKA TAYLOR

It's wintertime, January if I remember correctly. Right before my eighteenth birthday I found out my father would be going to prison. We're best friends, two peas in a pod, and, most of all, father and daughter. These next couple of years will be the hardest and, because of that, life won't be the easiest. I hold no emotion as I have flashbacks of our best memories. Like my eighth birthday, when you bought me the prettiest pink motor scooter, or just our random talks about life. What is life without you here? Best friends and our bond. The day my brother and I walked you into that pine-smelling prison facility is when reality really hit me. When it was time to tell you goodbye it broke me; I felt like I lost my other half. When you walked through that gate and looked at me one last time for a long time you looked lost. I promise to make you proud; hard work is all that matters. Never really thought you would leave, but just because the gate to the prison is closed doesn't mean you're gone; I'll put in hard work and I've got the inspiration, but I need more motivation because since you've been gone I haven't felt like myself lately. When you come home, just remember and know that you'll still be king.

Home

by ANDREA AVILES

Home is the place where I can somewhat rest in peace. It's where I will always fight and scream with my siblings, knowing that at some point our mother will yell, "*Me los voy a chingar a los dos, si no paran!*" all the way from her room. Home is where I can come to after a long day of school, go to everyone in the family, and give them a kiss and say hello. Home is where I can call out my sister's name, "Angie, Angie, Angie, Angie," several times just to annoy her, all while knowing that she's sitting right next to me. Home is where I can laugh, cry, sing, and dance without worrying if I look silly. Home is where I can find my dad sitting on the couch, watching TV and saying, "I'm not tired," although we all know he is. Where I see my mom in the kitchen, cooking us food while watching the news on Noticiero 47. Where I find my brother Benjamin in his room, saying that he's doing his homework when he's actually playing his Legos. Where I find little Gonzalito sleeping, with his musical bear by his side, all covered up. Where

I find my sister sleeping on the couch, though I'll know that she has already slept all day. Home is my special place. Home is my happiness.

Home Is Where the Heart Is

by DIANA GARCIA MARTINEZ

When you come from a very culturally diverse family, it can be a little intimidating to show off your best side.

Mexico was where I learned that speaking Spanish wasn't an option, but a necessity, and that you can't just have your sister be your own personal translator. However, regardless of the fact that I was a senseless mule, I have come to love the country.

The food, the colors, and the ancient pyramids are probably the best part. I like how close everyone is with nature and the kind interactions between the folks. I never got used to that environment, but it is a good feeling. I remember how the waterfall was within walking distance from home. The thrill of adventure rushed through me as my source of adrenaline.

Growing up, my family has always found a way to fix problems using nature. "Oh, you're sick? Drink this tea." Or, "Let's run this egg all over your body to cast those bad vibes away." It always seemed kinda silly—scratch that, it's ridiculous—but of course those superstitions had to come from somewhere where they worked, which is why they continue to use them. Mexico is a place where I learned and experienced many wonderful things that have shaped and redefined my outlook on life. It seems pretty dramatic, but coming from a very famous city to a secluded and outdated village, the changes are drastic. Nevertheless, it inspires me to know that my parents have come from such harsh conditions and have been able to do so much more.

Hospital Run!

by HILARY LEON

Long night, a panic that nearly startled me. My mother's face full of fear and tears: "I need to go to the hospital. I can't lose this baby." Everything felt numb, like I was standing on a glacier. I had no idea what to do; like a ventriloquist dummy, I needed someone to control me and guide me to my next movements, feelings, and sayings. My mom was only seven months pregnant; her blood pressure was over the roof, and she was in what doctors call "critical condition." Nerves and fatigue were setting in because I needed sleep, but my mother's health was the priority. Hospitals are such a bore, but the anticipation from waiting was killing me; not knowing her condition made me nervous, palm-sweating nervous. Weeks later, a miracle happened: my sister, Alina Esther Clemente, was born. The hospital was so rapid and quick, but the excitement and thrill of meeting my sister was killing me. This little peanut in the incubator just put me to tears and made my whole world turn upside down on this day.

Pickle

by OLIVIA GIGANTE

It is a snowy Christmas Day in Brooklyn, New York. My whole family has come over my house to celebrate it, as they do every holiday. The men are in the dining room watching sports, while the women are in the kitchen talking about the latest gossip. This is all going on upstairs while the children's annual game, "pickle," is about to begin downstairs in the living room. The older boys set the living room up like a baseball diamond. This consists of using the square pillows as the bases, long pillows as the bats, and rolled up socks as our baseball. The girls put all valuables safely away.

The two oldest cousins, my brother Anthony and my cousin Nick, pick the teams. "Peter," "Marissa," "Olivia," "Dean," "Joe," "Gianna."

We are all finally called and placed on a team. It is now time to play ball.

We are all so small, and the living room seems so huge to us. We are even able to slide onto home plate, giving us rug burns going down our arms. The grown-ups have no idea of what is going on, and we do not want them to find out, afraid they will put an end to our fun. We're now on our second game and my team only needs one more home run to win.

Anthony's up to bat; we're all hoping he scores the home run we need. Dean pitches the ball to Anthony; he swings, and the bat flies out of his hand. It slams into the thin stained glass window, and it bursts into a kaleidoscope wonderland. How could we have not been more careful? All of our mouths drop open in awe.

The adults hear all the commotion and come downstairs to the living room. They find the once beautiful stained glass window now on the carpet. We explain to them what was going on but never reveal the guilty party.

That is the end of the "Holiday Pickle Games."

A Valuable Lesson from Growing up in a Nursing Home

by PATRICIA SANTANA

Trust me, it wasn't as depressing as it sounds. When people first think of nursing homes, they tend to think of IVs, disgruntled elderly people, and gelatinous foods—not the typical place a child would like to be. But to me, it was nothing like the stereotypes. I made some great memories there, and the images of the seniors I met have stuck with me to this day. Even though I said I didn't have any favorites, Ms. Iris held a special place in my heart. She was a spunky grandmother of two with an infectious smile. She used to always say, "You're like one of my grandbabies, Patty!" Sometimes I secretly wished I had been. I remember her birthday one year; I really wanted to do something special for her. Days went by, and I just couldn't think of the perfect gift. It was the day before her birthday, and I didn't have any more time to think of something. I didn't have much of a budget to work with since I was just in the third grade. I had to think of something, and I had to think of it quick.

My mom noticed my frustration and gave me some valuable advice: "Just do something from the heart. She'll like that more than anything you could buy her." Then it clicked: "I'll make her a card!" This wasn't just any card scribbled in pen and given without a second thought. There was glitter; there was a plethora of scented markers; there was everything you could think of on that jumbo-sized birthday card. I spent the night at home trying to perfect the picture inside the card. It was a drawing of us in a field of irises—her favorite flowers—holding hands, smiling, and surrounded by a bunch of multicolored hearts. I used up a ton of my art supplies as I tried to finish the whole thing in one day. Bet you could say I really loved this woman to sacrifice a few snapped crayons from my 64-pack along the way.

The next day, as I got on the train to the nursing home with my mother, all I could think of was whether she would like it or not. Was there not enough glitter? Was there too much? Did I draw her haircut right? Does it look too sloppy? All of these questions and not enough time to think of answers as the time was here! She was surrounded by her friends and looked ecstatic, at least from the outside. I didn't want to ruin her day with a terrible card, but I gave it to her anyway. She took a long pause, and I thought she hated it so much that she couldn't find the words to describe it. To my surprise, she said. "Aw … I love it, Patty!" and, without saying another word, hugged me for a very long time. When she finally let go, she was sobbing and I didn't really understand why.

I didn't understand some things about the seniors until I got older, like that the reason why Ms. Iris cried so much was because her own daughter didn't call her on her birthdays. Spending a large portion of my childhood in a nursing home taught me lots of things, one of them being that you never know what someone is going through in their life, so you should always treat them with respect and dignity.

That Valentine's Day

by FELICITY GOODMAN

It was Valentine's Day, a day normally full of love and happiness; it was a day my life changed forever. I sat in my room, excited because my dad was coming with my balloons and chocolates. I stared at my walls and my ceiling, noticing little cracks in the wall. I also noticed a small stain on the ceiling, wondering where it was from. Then I heard my dad's signature car honk, and I ran downstairs to open the door.

"Hey, Dad," I said and hugged him. He replied, "Hey, baby." He handed me my balloons and chocolates, and we walked upstairs. We talked and hung out for a few minutes, drinking fruit punch.

"Okay, baby, me and mommy are going to talk for a few, so hang out in your room for a few."

I walked to my room and opened my chocolates. I admired the horse imprinted on one and the heart shape on another. I heard quiet arguing, and I frowned. I heard the default AT&T ringtone. I heard my dad say, "Hello?" and then more quiet murmurs. Then I heard "What?" and a phone drop. Me being nosy, I walked into the kitchen. I saw my dad's face over the sink and I heard quiet sobbing. In all my life I had never seen my dad cry. Until then.

I asked, "Dad, are you okay?" I saw a flash of pain on his face, quickly replaced by no emotion. That was how I found out that my grandpa, in Honduras, had passed away. I felt my heart drop to the bottom of my chest.

Grilled Cheese Sandwich

by ELIZABETH VANDERHORST

Smoke filled the kitchen and began circulating the apartment like a black smog coming in before a storm. And, oh man, this was a bad storm.

"Elizabeth! Elizabeth!" My mother's screams echoed through the apartment. On my end, there was silence as I stared at the burnt grilled cheese sandwich. As I slowly raised my head, there stood a woman whose face was beet-red like a tomato, with steam coming out of her ears. My mind was saying, "Oh, boy."

"You could have burnt the entire building down," shouted my mom.

"I was hungry and just wanted to eat," I snapped back.

This would be the end of my days as a chef. And the beginning of my new career as a prisoner in my home. Confined for two weeks at home. Every time I pass the stove, it calls to me, "Elizabeth, where have you been? Elizabeth, cook on me?" However, I know I cannot or else I will be punished even longer. My room is dark as the night sky and tiny, and the bed is hard as a rock. The window shades barely let light into the room, making it a hell. This is enough for me not to touch the stove. I long for the days I can cook those grilled sandwiches again.

The Borderline

by ENYASHA HARRIS

I stood still, admiring the stained brown exterior of the dainty old building. I breathed in the slightly foul smell of Central Brooklyn air deeply and remembered all the family memories made on this very stoop, with a smile stretching from ear to ear, as though I were a mother who had just witnessed the incredible birth of a newborn baby.

Never in a million years would you think that a place could have so much meaning to a person, but for me, just a mere year and a half later, my smile was replaced with a frown. All the happy memories on that stoop would become memories that I only wish to forget. Lying down on the rough brown surface of the pull out sofa with my mother lying next to me, I remember a place in time when I didn't have to deal with this situation. It was somewhere back in the summer of 2013, when the hot sun hit my face, darkening my light-brown complexion as each minute passed. I could feel my heart falling into the pit of my stomach as I stood like a mime taking one last look at the lime-green walls that shaped my childhood. Moving was a constant factor in my life, but those lime green walls were the first walls to secure me with a solid home for more than two years.

However, as I stare at the white walls that now surround me, I think back to the lilac walls of Sumpter Avenue and I think of how my dark brown eyes lit up when those walls were presented. I knew in my heart this is where I belonged until further notice. What I didn't know was that further notice would come sooner than we expected. At the time, I didn't care about being ripped out of the streets of Central Brooklyn, but I did care about no longer being able to take walks in the park as the crisp air smacked me across the face; however, I would no longer have to endure the pain of older men staring at me as though I were some sort of a snack. I thought the biggest issue was that I would no longer be able to chase after Justin Bieber and get home in under thirty minutes. Everything became about the borderline and its depth. Whilst I struggled to find myself on the borderline, I was able to enjoy the subtle sounds of my tiny feet dancing around the house. I could blast the television as loud as I wanted to without having anyone tell me to turn it down. Gosh, and those lilac walls …. Those beautiful lilac walls. I could stare at them for hours as I lay my head across the headboard-length turquoise pillow for my after-school naps. But the lilac walls failed to mention that within a few months I would become prisoner to the white walls belonging to the Wicked Witch out West. The angelic feelings the white walls gave off became my orange jumpsuit, suffocating me as each day passed.

Nevertheless, those lilac walls watched me in the first few steps of finding myself and becoming a young woman. For some people, the struggle of finding yourself can be an never-ending cycle, but the best thing to know is that you'll always be all right and to understand that you are not the only one dealing with issues which can take a toll on you. The best thing to do is remember a place and time when life was simpler and you weren't expected to act like an adult. Whilst both places carry weight in my heart, nothing will ever compare to my love for the lilac walls of the borderline.

Cucina

by SEPHIRA BRYANT

The smell of mesquite and basil fills the air while the meat below soaks up the flavors as thoroughly as a plant would the sun; at the same time, sweet, velvety potatoes with freshly-scraped cinnamon and sprinkled brown sugar - like the morning dew upon glass - are mashed. The graham-cracker crust is like s'mores from the campfire, so warm and smooth that it eases the throat like fresh honey from a bee, yet still maintains its crunch. There's a five-cheese baked macaroni with such distinct flavors you can taste their mother countries. The cheddar and marble from England, muenster and pepper jack from the United States, and the swiss from Switzerland. However, we are done because we are forever busy, like the New York streets. Here, you can smell grandmama's homemade sugar cookies and hot, savory, sizzling bacon.

This place is where the grandest of feasts are made, and today is no different, except on a much smaller scale. It is a slow day, just like most of my vacation days, but today is the day where I put all of my research to the test. The ingredients laid out before me: the shiny white eggs catching the gleam of the lighting, the butter melting fast as ice cream, even the brown sugar playing hide and seek with me. I follow the recipe step-by-step, going from the dry to the wet ingredients and then combining them. Once completed, it feels like I am in a Rocky movie: as Rocky had his challenges, I have mine, and mine is the waiting game. It feels like centuries have passed and I am going to waste away like ash. Then I hear the *beep*! and the waiting game finally comes to an end. The dark clouds finally lift, and the aroma of rich velvet with light cream fills the air. They are finally done, the red velvet cookies with white chocolate chips. The path was long, but the destination is sweet and delicious.

This is only one of many stories that were created here, but the kitchen is not just a kitchen. It holds the sounds of laughter, pained yelps from the sharp knives or the popping of grease, the screams of frustration when we don't meet eye-to-eye, even the jump in our skin when one doesn't make a sound when entering. It's where culinary masterpieces are made and fond memories live. After all, there is no place like the kitchen.

Nirvana

by NADINE ROCA

Can you imagine everything you love in one place? Just picture it: every section and row filled with it all, you're so anxious, you just want to get your hands on every bit of it. Well, that's how I feel when I'm shopping for makeup. Every time I walk into a makeup store, it's like my eyes wander off into another place. It's basically love at first sight for me: I see something new and I just gaze into it, like "Yes, I need this!" (Meanwhile, we all know I don't really need it.) I pick up everything, not even thinking about the price: the glitter (oh yes!), the lipstick (can I just have every color?), the highlighters (will China be able to see me with this glow on?). This is like my home. I know exactly where everything is once I walk in, and it's a must that I have ten million of everything. I can't just have one; you know they don't all look same. And it is very true that one can be too pigmented or one too bright or one that is just right. Especially if you're freelance, of course, you are going to need it all. Makeup stores are a huge deal for me because you need to know the right place to go to to get the right products. Once I walk in there, there's no price tag on anything.

Eating At Restaurants Alone

by SAMANTHA DUER

Eating at restaurants, alone. I may go to different places, but I order the same foods from each. Eating at restaurants alone has given me a newfound independence, an independence I didn't find by being strong or by being lonely, but by knowing myself and being comfortable with myself. Just because you are alone doesn't mean you are lonely.

When I sit at restaurants alone, my eyes wander; admittedly they sometimes wander where they aren't wanted. My eyes wander from faces to food and sometimes to shoes. What I smell at restaurants alone is uninterrupted by awkward conversation in order to avoid awkward silence. What I smell is other people's food; I always think to myself, maybe I'll order that next time. I never do. I've grown accustomed to my food the same way I've grown accustomed to sitting quietly.

At restaurants, I sit alone with my coat and bag slouched over the chair across from me. At restaurants alone, I sit at cozy booths in the back, preferably with an outlet. What I hear at restaurants alone is soft-spoken chatter and low, hidden secrets. It's none of my business. However, there are the occasional outbursts of anger, usually from breakups. I notice a lot of couples at restaurants.

Sometimes when I am at restaurants alone, I take notice of the quiet ambience of the music. I notice when the volume changes; I notice when a song is over and when one begins. When I sit at restaurants alone, I appreciate that this is the only time in the day that I have all to myself, a time where I can change who I am because no one knows who I am here.

Experiences in 138

by ASATTA BRADFORD

When I got to middle school, it felt the same as elementary because I was in the same school. My school was P.S.138 located in Crown Heights, Brooklyn, New York.

My school was very big, with four floors and two sides—the north and the south. In school I was nice, cool, and fun to be around. I went on lots of trips in the sixth grade and had great teachers. I remember when I went to Central Park with my friends, and we had fun. We climbed rocks, played tag, and bought ice cream. Another time, my class had a food fight in the lunchroom with another class. It was funny. I was throwing food at everyone, and it was all fun and games. Sixth grade was a good year, and I shared so many memories with my friends.

Now, seventh grade was a little difficult because of my teachers. I remember one time when I was in math class, my friend put a book in the microwave and put it on for a minute. That was so funny; I was almost dying of laughter. But he then got in trouble and that was it for him. But another time we played manhunt in gym with all of the seventh grade classes. That was a fun day, and we planned this so everyone could play because we were always bored. Seventh grade was an amazing year, but there were fewer trips.

Well, eighth grade was slightly different. I had to think about prom, graduation, and high schools. Eighth grade was still a fun year, and I miss it a lot. I remember when I got accepted to HSFI, I wasn't really excited because I wanted to go to the High School of Art and Design, but I figured that they were probably the same. When I went on my senior trip to Six Flags in New Jersey, I had fun and went on all of those crazy roller coasters. That day was fun. I played games, ate food, relaxed, and had lots of snacks. I thought that I was going to die on some of the roller coasters, but I still had a good time. Prom and graduation were the best times; I felt like I accomplished a lot but it was still kind of sad because I missed my friends. Prom was so fun; all of the classes had a good time. The food tasted so good and we danced a lot. On the other hand, graduation was fun but kind of sad because we were like family, and we were all leaving each other.

I still see my friends from middle school because we meet up sometimes and go to visit my favorite sixth, seventh, and eighth grade teacher, Ms. Faulk. She really helped me become who I am today, and I really appreciate her. I had so many great experiences in P.S.138 in Crown Heights.

Advice to a Younger Me

by AMARIS LAROSE

Sixth Grade

It's the first day of school, and you will not want to go and rightly so. Your knee-high socks and hand full of band-aids will make you the "freak" and the "loser." You'll make some fake friends and some even faker ones, and people will start to dislike you. Why? Girl, I just don't know. But you've got your best friend, Tyrique.

Seventh Grade

It's the first day of school, and you will not want to go and rightly so. The hatred that was formed against you last year will only increase. This year, you must choose seats wisely; last year you sat next to A.C., a busty girl with eczema around her mouth, and she was the start of all your problems. This year you've got to be strong. You'll be alone when your best friend moves to New Jersey. People will spread rumors, want to jump you, and send death threats. Stay strong. This year's problem is K.M. Rekindle with Maqusi.

Eighth Grade

It's the first day of school, and you will not want to go and rightly so. Middle school has taught you to keep a serious face and show no emotion. Taught you that you have no friends. Kindness is a foreign word, tears kept inside. Do what you have to do because, girl, you're at the end and these people and their bullying will be behind you. You will only need two. Tyrique and Maqusi, they'll be the only ones who know how to read you, since you've seemed to master a face of equilibrium and eyes that show emptiness when you're crying inside. Get through with a brave face, young me. It's only a phase.

Speak Up! Let Your Thoughts Flow

by ARIANNA ALCIDE

My room is my comfort zone. Without it, I wouldn't know where to let all my emotions loose. When you're in a room alone, with practically no sound, you're able to hear all your thoughts. Speak up! There's no good reason why nobody is ever around when I need them the most. Sometimes I hate my personality, but sometimes I'm thankful for it. It's easy to feel uncared for when people aren't able to communicate and connect with you in the way you need them to. Yes, it can be hard not being able to realize that silence is a reflection on your worth.

Most people are so caught up in their own responsibilities, struggles, and anxieties that the thought of asking someone else how they're doing doesn't even cross their mind. They aren't inherently bad or uncaring; they're just busy and self-focused. Speaking for myself, I am always around when others need me. I am supportive and caring. But nobody's ever asked me if I'm okay or how I feel about certain things. Sometimes I think that it would be better if

I would just stop being present for everybody and worry about myself, which should be something that I should always do anyway.

I don't want to have a negative vibe, so therefore I will continue being there for others, but I will just focus on being more myself. In addition, I know that even though I can be down at times, my room is my comfort zone where I can write little Post-it notes about how I'm feeling, whether it's negative or positive. My room is my special place.

To Give Time to Animals and Get Annoyance Back

by DAVID MORALES

My days are not always the best. Well, what I mean is that it will start off good, but, someway, somehow, it will just end up to be the worst day of the week. You probably think I am overreacting, bringing up minor problems and blowing them up, but just hang on, because you'll see—well, read, you know what I mean.

Hmmmmm … Let's see. How about I start off by telling you about my morning?

It's Saturday morning. Sun is barely up, which gives the sky a murky blue tint with gray swirls; birds are chirping to signify the morning has come. I'm also woken up by the loud, obnoxious garbage truck making its morning route. Anyway, I get up and head straight to the bathroom, you know, for obvious reasons. A cold, crisp shower to get me up properly is probably not that bad, but come on, do you really wanna be woken up that way? The kitchen is the next stop. I drink a glass of orange juice, then I'm off to complete the busy day I have waiting ahead.

Okay, so you see my morning so far has not been too bad. But this is where it begins, right when I step out the door. Walking outside into the cold February weather isn't the best, especially since all I have on is a sweater. But I have to deal with it because I'm already late.

First, before I get into anything about today, let me fill you in on my situation a bit. I work as a volunteer at three animal shelters, two in Brooklyn and one in Manhattan, and I've been at those three for approximately three months. Honestly, it's been a good time, at least some of the time. The whole point, though, is that this day, this one very cold, dark, gloomy, and very annoying day, is the last day I'm with all of them, which, in my opinion, is God's little bit of fun.

Once I get to the train station, I'm all tired again, but I get my wallet out, swipe my MetroCard, and go through this ridiculous turnstile that gets stuck halfway through the turning motion while I'm in the middle. I'm fidgeting with it so I can get free and get to the train before I miss it, but nooo. The MTA helper is yelling, "Hey, kid! What are you doing?" And so I have to stop to explain myself and say, "I'm stuck! What does it look like?" So I spend about ten minutes there, goodbye to being on time.

Flash forward to the shelter. Honestly, I'll just go straight to the facts because it's better if I do and not give you the very minuscule details.

The first shelter I go to is the one in the city, so I step in, smell the newly mopped floor and a very, very strong disinfectant. I head to the back and so far so good. I look at the stained calendar on the wall and see that it's the day we give the cats a bath. So I get started and all I hear is ear-ringing screeches from the cats, and claws are flying everywhere. When I'm done, I look like I just got out of amateur surgery. Every part of my body that was not covered is cut very badly, but I deal with it. Now here's the punch line to the first part of God's joke: I walk up to person in charge of the whole business there and she says, "Go home. We don't need you here anymore. I just wanted you to wash the cats, and then I was going to let you go." I'm so mad that I curse at her as I leave.

Now, off to the two other shelters, both in Brooklyn. Back on the train. I offer my seat to an elderly lady and she gives me the dirtiest look before starting to converse about me to her friend, probably about my hair or something, seeing how it's blue right now because I recently dyed it. I get off and I'm at the other shelter now. I've worked here for about three months straight, but I've helped on and off for about a year total. Anyway, I step in and they tell me I'm not allowed there any more. I ask why, and their response is, "The other employees say that you're not doing anything." At that moment I am just mad, like, "What? I've done more work than those idiots have ever done here. I've taken care of all the animals and I've even done some of their jobs sometimes." All they say is that the others "voted" and now I am done there.

Now the last shelter, that one got to me. I walk there because it isn't far, and when I get there, I see that they are getting in a new shipment of supplies, so they ask for my help. So I help, trying to forget the day I've had so far. Then when I bring the last box inside, the guy in charge, the guy who actually got me the gig, tells me to go home and that I am basically fired. All I have to say is, "You jerk, this day has been the worst. I've lost three volunteer jobs and I even did the work. What am I supposed to do now?!" All he says is, "I don't know." I go home and go to bed; I just want to get this day over already.

See, what did I tell you? I said it was gonna be a bad a day— and guess what, it was! To be very honest, that's just how it is with me. It really is. But hey, at least I got the other days to not be too bad and I kind of look forward to them. I have my teachers, my friends, and, most importantly, my girlfriend.

Grace Beauty Salon Transformation

by SHAIMELYS MARCANO SANTOS

Train stops. Walk up the stairs. Turn around the corner where Dunkin Donuts is. Grace's Beauty Salon is where you want to go, located on 125th street.

I arrive. I walk in and look around. Women everywhere look at me as I step in. I stand upright, push my chest out, lift my chin, and walk towards the counter. I know once I leave this place that I'll look my best.

I'm taken to the washers. As I let my long hair fall down my back, I notice the cold looks and envious stares—the ones that make me feel uncomfortable yet are the source of my confidence.

After being assigned to a lady, I take a seat. As I sit there, I begin to prepare myself to be tortured. Like always, the lady with the long nails is assigned to me. "Come here, mami," she says. I lean back and begin to feel the cold, relaxing water running through my hair. She begins to "massage" my head but in reality it feels as if a hawk was carving out my brain, pulling my hair and scratching my scalp. Soap gets stuck in my ear. The lady doesn't notice until I speak up and tell her. If I hadn't, the soap would have stayed stuck in my ear. When she's finished, she walks me over to the next station.

Someone is assigned to me. As the lady begins to brush my hair and put it in rollers, once again all eyes are on me: cold, envious, desiring stares. I begin to feel uncomfortable again, but I remind myself that the reason why they look at me the way they do is because they're jealous that I have something they can't have. They are the source of my confidence. She finishes putting my hair in rollers, walks over, and, pointing to a dryer, she says, "Sit there, mami." As I walk over to the dryer, I think of the torturing, skull-crushing, thought-burning dryer. The machine is capable of burning my scalp, of erasing all important thought or emotions. All I can feel is pain. As I sit there, my mother's lecturing words repeat in my mind, "*Para ser bella hay que ver las estrellas.*" In order to be beautiful you must see the stars, meaning that you must go through pain in order to look and feel beautiful. I sit there for an hour and a half. Repeating my mother's words in my head, giving me the strength to endure it all.

Dryer stops. I step out of the dryer. I feel as if a weight has been lifted from my head. In pain and nearly asleep, I make my way to my final destination—the lady with the blow dryer. "Come here, mami" she says. I sit down and catch a small glance at the mirror. I'm almost there; I'm nearly transformed. She begins to take off the rollers. A heavy tension begins crawling on my back. I look around and notice different women all around staring at my hair. Cold, envious, desiring, desperate looks add fumes to my confidence.

When she's finally done, I begin to put my jacket on. As I look at my reflection, I see a strong and beautiful young lady. She's looking back at me. I give her a smile, as if not believing she is me. My hair silky and shiny. Full of life. As I walk out, I feel ready. One look back, and I see those women again. I give them all a smile and say, "Goodnight. Enjoy the rest of your day, ladies." With confidence I step out. I'm ready to ignore those who mean harm to me. I am ready to take negativity and turn it into something positive. The envious looks and stares are my source of confidence. I raise my head high, push my chest out, and walk with confidence. I am transformed. I am ready to be discovered by the world.

Tell the Heavens I Am Done Waiting

by FATHA ALMA

The scariest thing about aging has been acknowledging the inevitable and abandoning the naiveté we naturally possess as children. As we move through the stages of childhood, we not only realize the lack of simplicity in life, but we also conjure up countless distractions and excuses that help us believe that it is.

I grew up in a fairly religious household and was always taught to fear God; it was internalized, but it is useless when you are a disbeliever of creationism and like to live without limitations. There are always undermining scientific explanations to every phenomenon, which is a concept I live by; however, this never failed to contradict my family's philosophies of life.

White Noise

by ASIA REDDISH

White noise (noun)—The term "white noise" is sometimes used as slang to describe a meaningless commotion or chatter that masks or obliterates underlying information.

White tile floors, white cabinets, white walls, white everything. The ticking and the tocking from the broken clock drown out the sound of my tears, but I turn on the water just in case anyone can hear. I sit in the pearly white tub, and the sound of the neighbor's television seeps through the paper-thin wall. The smell of the birthday cake scented Yankee Candle fills the air, and I sink deeper into the warm water. I close my eyes and envision myself eleven years ago.

I am sitting on the faded green futon wearing my favorite ankle-length satin dress with my fresh wash-and-set. I'm next to a woman with the smoothest chocolate skin, as if she drowned herself in cocoa butter. She is wearing a tiara and a sash that reads "Barbie," and even though I know she isn't the "real" Barbie, just for a second I believe she is and I am mesmerized. My living room is filled with smiling faces of relatives and family friends. Everyone is coming over to congratulate me on my graduating from kindergarten and handing me thick cards filled with money. Like a routine I've done over again a million times, I smile, say "thank you" politely, and take the card. I scan the room and finally spot my mom. Her red hair is wrapped with a million visible bobby pins keeping it up; she is wearing a white T-shirt and sweatpants, running around like a chicken with its head cut off. She is making sure everything remains perfect, that no one breaks anything, and most importantly, that no one goes inside her kitchen.

I get up from the faded futon and walk through the crowds of people, and since I don't have my own room, I decide to go to the only quiet place in the house: the bathroom. I get on the cold bathroom floor and crawl into a ball. I close my eyes and picture the events going on the opposite side of the bathroom door, tiny feet jumping around and running, adults laughing and drinking (despite it being one in the afternoon), "Barbie" reading stories to the starstruck younger girls, and even my mom finally taking a breather. Everyone is just enjoying being in each other's company. And before I know it, I am drifting off into a deep sleep with a smile on my face.

Eleven years later, at the age of seventeen, I can still find comfort in the middle of this white wonderland. I still love the white tile floors, white cabinets, white walls, the white everything. My bathroom is my sanctuary where I can sit back and wipe my tears, remember the good times, and feel at peace.

Middle School

by **SHIRLEY ROSEMOND**

I was like an unsteady boat running down a rocky stream. Unable to dodge the rocks that thrashed and hit me, causing me to slowly sink. On the first and second day around, I wasn't welcome, there were no open arms, no "Hey there, welcome, my name is …"
None of that …
I was an outcast
Pushed away and forgotten
Concealed in loneliness, hidden in the shadows, grabbing on to the little hope I had left in me.
I just wanted to fit in, but it was never possible.
I was never understood
I just stood out … innocent, weak, and highly sensitive
They saw how broken I was but only on the outside, inside I was crumbling, almost giving up.
But they just kept hitting me
To them I was a toy to play with

Something to break and enjoy breaking, without feeling one piece
of guilt.

To them, I wasn't normal

I didn't know many things

I didn't understand many things

Always in the back corner silent … hiding my presence.

I just wanted to run away, like a rabbit running for its life from a
pack of foxes.

It wasn't until one day, someone actually noticed me, actually
cared and saw what I was going through. I ended up befriending
him and his other friends, who soon became mine. And soon
enough I wasn't so weak and tortured. I ended up being happy.

An American in America

by SUKARI WEBB

Conversations usually start like this: *Hey, what's your name?*

Su

Oh, cool, where are you from?

America

No, like where are you from from?

America

Ok, so where are your grandparents from?

America, I'm American

Then they say *"oh,"* with a sigh of disappointment in their voice and disgust scribbled all over their face. This is a common transfer of dialogue for me when I first meet people. I could understand if we were in another country, but I'm in America. Why is it so shocking to have an American living in America?

Growing up, I was always the only African American surrounded by Caribbean Americans. As a child, I saw no differences between us, but as I got older, the bridge between the cultures seemed to expand. Soon it became if you weren't foreign you were boring and guess who wasn't foreign? The "Yankees," they called us (and I sure am not boring). A lot of Caribbean people think that African Americans lack culture and customs, as if it's my fault that the ship I was brought here on didn't allow me to pack a carryon. The little bit that did survive the journey was left in cotton fields. Yet we have rebuilt our culture. African American culture is presented in the way we speak, dress, and even in our mannerisms. Stereotypes such as us being "uncultured" are just made to continue to tear apart a race of people that are really the same. We may not speak the same or have the same traditions, but we all stem from Africa.

I think one would be interested to know that yes, I'm from America, but I haven't been to a single Yankee game.

Yes, I can dance, and when I don't, it's not because of my incapability; it is because of my desire not to. At family events, my family does not wine their waist (well, occasionally for a turn up) but most times we do the electric slide. Yes, I've had jerk chicken, Ackee, and saltfish, and oxtails before but those are not things I eat every day. A classic dish for me is barbecue chicken, candy yams, collard greens, and catfish. Yes I've heard of Mavado and Popcaan, but I prefer to listen to J. Cole, Nas, Lauryn Hill, and Erykah Badu. I say this to say yes, we have obvious differences but we are more alike than we realize. We can no longer allow the places we live to dictate how we feel about one another, because in reality our roots all stem from Africa. My flag is green, black, and red. Yes, I'm an American living in America, and I'm not ashamed of it.

Home Sweet Home

by JINET ALMANZAR

There is this girl that loves being home. She wakes up every morning wishing that she could stay in bed and just sleep all day. Home is where she thinks about life, cries when she has problems, and relaxes all day until her mother comes home and bothers her to do something. When she's in school, she thinks about going home and showering and eating. But when she gets out of school, she won't go straight home. She'll go chill with her friends. Then, when she's done having fun, she will go home and just relax. When she's lying down, she will wonder if she should do her homework or not, then she ends her day by falling asleep and doing the same routine tomorrow.

Shamari

by MARIAH AMADOR

Standing next to me, he was a whole foot taller than I was. Looking down at me, he watched me choose a movie to see while my best friend Analyssa and my other friend Nicole flirted with their dates a few feet away.

He grabbed my hand, leading me to the theater playing *Fantastic Four*; my big, chubby hand was in his even bigger, cold hand. We walked inside; the movie was already starting. We sat all the way in the last row, Shamari and I in the middle and my friends on the end. He started off sitting but then ended up sprawled out onto the chair next to him with his head on my shoulder. I caressed his face in my hands and admired him.

Around half an hour into the movie we started to get hungry, so we all got up to to get some snacks. I ordered my favorite: pretzels with nacho cheese.

My head rested on his chest as we waited. I saw a sign that said the movie Southpaw was playing at that moment. I suggested we movie-hop, so after we got our snacks, we snuck into the theater around the corner from the stand.

Again we sat in the back of the theater, he and I in the middle and my friends on the end. Even though the movie was already halfway through, he didn't complain about the idea. A few minutes after we got in, his head resting on mine, he looked at me; even in the dark the outline of his strong jaw made me weak at the knees. He smiled with his pearly white teeth, grabbed my cheeks, and gave me a kiss. I melted a little inside.

Raising me to my feet, he sat me in his lap and kissed me again. My heart was beating so hard and fast I thought he could hear it. He looked me in the eyes, and it felt like we were the only two in the theater.

"Am I your girlfriend?" I whispered shyly, remembering that earlier he said to Nicole, "Hands off my girl" when she gave me a hug.

"Yeah, finally," he replied, cocking his head up and flashing me that smile that I love.

In that moment, I felt like the happiest person in the world. Looking at him, I thought to myself that August 8, 2015, at around 2:00 AM was the best moment of my life. I knew that I found my forever, and that no guy could compare to him because, God, he's so rare.

Money Given

by AKIRA LEWIS

Today there was a guy on the train. The stale, recycled air filled my lungs while I read. Reading is something I almost always do on the train. Today was different though. His voice was cracking, his hair long and dark, wrinkled clothes covering his tall frame. He was asking for change.

He never gave his name. That was fine. He wanted McDonald's, cheap and fast food for those with a small amount. I gave him a dollar, losing some of what little money I had left. It was worth it. Someone else gave him some of what they had while others ignored him altogether. He said his thanks and I couldn't help but think about how he looked like Ezra Miller. The guy was cute, and yet I was kind because of his awkward stance and cracking voice, watching his body slowly shuffling forward. I know how that feels, being embarrassed to ask for something. I am glad I gave him some of what I had. His smile was enough to make me happy.

Lunch

by SOPHIA MOHAMMED

Life is hard, and it doesn't take a genius to figure this out. For instance, it's hard for me, but I'm getting used to it. I've also had to deal with the cafeteria's rancorous stenches throughout my years of school with rotten food and the grade-F meat. I've also had to submit to a struggling community, which has brought about a maturity that has helped me develop into the lady that I am. The community I grew up in was poor and underprivileged. I know because we were very poor, and my family struggled because my mom had two kids. I wished to have a better education. When I was little, I would come home around lunchtime, and my great-grandmother would sit on a couch—and I remember to this day—she would say, "Dodo, how was school?" I used to just look at her and smile with my blueberry ice slush and say, "It was good" or "Okay." But I cherish those times because I knew that I could go to and finish school, unlike her, because she had had to raise ten kids and wasn't provided the same opportunities. She'll never have the chance now because of her untimely death on her favorite holiday, which was Christmas. Then the next Christmas followed with the murder of my cousin, whom I'll miss and who showed me that I could be myself and that I deserve love and respect. I also knew the experiences that my friends went through and that my grandmother had.

There was one day in middle school I will never forget, when my teachers helped encourage me to go to school. That day was a regular day; I woke up, showered, brushed my teeth, and walked to school. The security detectors were at my school for random inspection. I, of course, didn't wear the uniform and ended up in the holding room with all of the delinquents.

My female friends had boyfriends, and some had to even quit school before going to middle school because their parents said they had to become brides. In this day and age I feel that I need to get an education so I can be successful. I know from those experiences like being in a crowded cafeteria with chanting kids cheering on a girl who was picking on a seventeen-year-old because she had two kids in the sixth grade. The social stigma in the school was wrong, and I learned to stay away and to go to my teachers during lunch. To them I am what I am: Sophia Mohammed, and they knew no one could change who I am. I am Trinidadian tribally and also mixed with Venezuelan, Indian, and black. My Fashion teacher/supervisor and mentor took me to a UFT meeting, and a guy there told me, "Life isn't how many times you fall; it's about how many times you get back up." It's like when I'm in a wrestling match, and it's me or the person I am wrestling.

I am who I am, and I will not go down without a fight. I am who I am and I won't take no for an answer. I am who I am and will always get back up if I'm knocked down. I am who I am, and you can call me Sophia, Sophie, Sassy; it's all me. I am who I am, and you can't change my nose to a straight one. I am black, and I don't need some boy telling me I'm white. I'm clearly not when I wake up with my tangled afro; I'm not white just because I'm light-skinned. I'm a colored female and refuse to be oversexualized because I'm light skinned. I'm educated, and this doesn't mean that I'm "white."

I'm sick of all these guys hitting on me since I was in middle school. They make you feel dirty, and you want to take five showers. It's always the girl's fault. Her jeans were too tight; she's light-skinned; they say she's like that, or the famous, "You can't graduate and be a virgin, or you'll be made fun of." Well, I'll tell you, no, you stick your nose so far in a book and absorb all that information. This is because boyfriends and those friends aren't gonna be taking the test; you are. That's why I stayed close to my teachers, and every day at lunch I would go and talk with them. Their classrooms were empty, and they had the old heaters, and the room was filled with chalk and dust from the chalkboards that would soon be replaced by Smartboards.

Now, I learned from all of the rapes and tragic circumstances my friends had to go through in the hood, like the guys that would hide in bushes or flash you when going home. I remember a time I was walking home in broad daylight, and this guy asked me for the time. I turned to look at him, and I saw the thing my teacher showed us in sex ed. He was all out in the open. I didn't have my phone, and I knew that if I went to the cops I would get no help. So I bolted down to my house, thirteen and scared to death. My sandals flopped all the way home, like Pocahontas, till one flew off. I quickly went inside and grabbed my little sister. I didn't want what happened to me to happen to her. And I knew from then on and from my teachers that I needed to go to a high school that wasn't around any of this. That's why I came to the High School of Fashion Industries.

The shootouts at the end of the day with rival gangs have taught me a lot, that this was all caused by underdeveloped programs and that the community causes a repetitive cycle that doesn't help with the situations we have at home. That's why I wake up every day and I try to be a better person than I was yesterday. Because I know if I don't, I will waste the twenty-four hours I get in a day. You only get that amount of time, and you have to make the most of it. I repeat this mantra over and over. I've also learned from losing a lot of opportunities that procrastination is the enemy. Just do it, and let nothing and no one get in your way. You have to go above and beyond if you want to succeed. I saw change in myself due to the borough I was in. I'm glad I learned not to let all the negative energy and lies from all these haters make me feel bad.

I am what I am, and I am female and will not ever apologize for it. The boys in middle school tried to ridicule me and tease me and even did things I had to report, and none of it goes away. I will always remember. Also the terms that the girls and boys use, such as "loose" and "girly" are thrown around too lightly. Being a female doesn't make you weak; no, it makes you strong. I know this because days when I couldn't walk and had to be hospitalized made me stronger. Do boys go through periods? Do they birth humans out of them? No, they don't, and when a guy tells you you're weak, I'd say "A woman pushed you into the world, would you say that to her?" I looked at the quote my seventh grade science teacher, Ms. Dolce, put in her classroom. It was a quote by Lao Tzu that said:

Watch your thoughts for they become words.
Watch your words for they become actions.
Watch your actions for they become habits.
Watch your habits for the become your character.
Watch your character for it becomes your destiny.

My Life Was A Stage: Survival Guide

by AUDRA PRYCE

Have you ever been to a dance recital? No, not those tacky ones in the dance studio where parents sit on plastic chairs and observe the class. A real one, where the venue cost more than your tuition; with multiple quick changes, bright lights, huge stages; with blood, sweat, and tears. That was my life for ten years, dance. Dance at the studio was never about learning. It was about the journey to the top, and what you were willing to do, and who you were willing to step on to get there. It was about who was the best of the best and who was the replacement. Who was willing to replace you without even the tiniest remorse. Who was closest to the front and who was the lead. Who had a solo and whose solo you could take. Who was willing to leave their soul on the floor. I survived ten years, but when I turned thirteen, I really opened my eyes and saw what I was living in.

First day, you're prepared, ready to learn new things and see your friends; wrong, you're in for a surprise. First month, technique is out the window like summer air at the end of October. Who cares if you can't do a proper passé, make it look pretty, because if you don't, you will suffer in the back where your parents, who paid hundreds of dollars on classes and costumes, can't see you. Three-month mark, costumes. Hyperventilating in the changing room, praying that it fits. *The costume doesn't fit you; you fit the costume.* Make sure the boot covers are bobby pinned to your shoes and that headpiece is sewed to your head because if it falls off on stage, you're screwed. Six-month mark, picture day. One of the many days where you can't eat until it's all over. Everything you'd eat will make you bloat and stretch your costumes the wrong way. The sounds of fussing mothers who spent an hour in class trying to figure out how to do makeup and hair perfectly for the pictures and the girls who ignored the "no eating rule" trying to get rid of their previous meal mold together like a deafening and inescapable melody. Hours of positioning and changing hair-dos, makeup, and outfits move around you like the tilt-a-whirl, with you feeling trapped and unsure of its endpoint. A week before the show, dress rehearsal. The auditorium is beautiful when you first see it. But the lockdown makes it a prison. No one in, no one out, six hours of nonstop run-throughs of the recital. Once again, no meals until it's all over. Quick changes, bright lights, and six different cues in one act quickly overwhelm your brain. There're falls and sweat, blood, and tears between every crack in the wooden stage by the end of the night. Only the strong survive.

Five in the morning and I'm in hair and makeup, eating, but not too much so I don't have to lose it before stage time. This is what you've worked for all year long. Every fall is appreciated; every dance is perfection, second row and up for all dances, center; you've earned it. It's showtime. During the first show you get out all your jitters, any corrections can be made up in the night show because that is the important one: the show where scouts come to recruit dancers, the show your distant family comes to, but for me it was important because this was my last of the last. The final dance is done. Every cue is perfect, every solo executed beautifully. As I take my final bow, a tear rolls slowly down my face. This is the end of my life. I'm closing a chapter that is no longer healthy for me. I pack up my makeup box, costumes, and shoes for the final time, no one expecting my departure. When I walk away from that recital, I leave my younger soul on the stage and never look back.

Tranquility Calls

by RACHEL HOCHER

I have been to many places, but none of them evoke as many feelings in me as the beach. I don't get to go there very often, but when I do, I make sure to savor every sensation, every feeling, for as long as I can and hold on to it until the next time I come back. The drive in the car always seems to take forever but, getting close to the beach, there's always this field of cattails with lots of purple and green dragonflies buzzing about. I can look past the field and see a body of water that's connected to the sand. I can see people out on their boats—fishing, swimming, and having a good time. Then there's this big statue that looks like a giant needle; when we drive around it, it means we're tantalizingly close. Then I can hear the seagulls calling to me as I enter the sandy parking lot. As we finally get out of the car, I can hear the waves as they crash on the shore. Then I can smell a mix of seawater and french fries as I walk down the beach (the stores at the beach sell the best french fries) and see the waves crash on the shore in an explosion of white foam. I can see all the colorful kites whirling around in the sky and, above them, the airplanes with those colorful banners flying behind their tails. I can feel the hot sand on my feet and the sharp edges of broken shells as I get closer to the shore. Then, yes, I finally get to feel the crisp, cool water on my feet as I feel a piece of seaweed rub up against my foot. As I stand there, I realize again the reason why I love it here so much.

It makes me feel free just standing in the ocean. I look out over the horizon and it just looks as if the ocean goes on forever. To swim forever in the endless ocean would be amazing. To leave this world behind and see a totally new world within the same planet. To swim amongst the creatures that have yet to be discovered and to be free from everything that plagues the surface world: greed, hatred, responsibility, stress, anxiety. When people ask me what my greatest dream is I wish I could tell them I just want to disappear into the ocean to truly be free.

I don't know why but being in the ocean makes me happy—or being in any body of water, really. It just makes me feel calm and carefree like nothing is wrong and the world is at peace. I don't feel any stress in the water and sometimes I wish I could just lay there forever. (That's probably why I take such long showers; seriously, I'm in there for like two hours just thinking about life.)

I recommend going night swimming. I've only done it once, but it's really cool. I went night swimming down at Breezy Point, a few years back, before Hurricane Sandy hit. I was by myself in a quiet bay and I could see the lights from the city reflected in the water in all kinds of distorted shapes and colors. It was great being there by myself and just being free to do as I please. The water was the perfect temperature, and it was so peaceful, but then a crab pinched my toe, so I got out. I have never been able to go back to that beach, but I wish I could because I want to relive that moment of pure tranquility.

Some people don't like it, but I love to smell the salty sea air and the warm breeze because it makes me feel like that's what life is all about. I can be really depressed, but just feeling that breeze, I know that this is what life is supposed to be: savoring the small things and appreciating the beauty this world has to offer us. The breeze brings me back to a time in my life when things were simpler, less complicated, less sad.

I remember through the years going to the beach collecting shells and putting them in my special bucket. I would walk up and down the shore looking for a shell that would catch my eye. When I would find one I liked I would pick it up and inspect it carefully to see if it would be good enough for my collection. I would look for any cracks or broken pieces, no imperfections allowed, but sometimes I would make an exception. I would find all kinds of things: scallops, clams, snail shells, and oysters, and one time I found the molted shell of a crab that had what looked like a purple leopard print on it. However, as the years passed I noticed I would find fewer and fewer shells, until eventually I didn't find any. All I found were tiny broken pieces of shells, along with the occasional bottle cap. It made me sad, because it forced me to realize that time goes on and certain memories follow along with it, until all traces of that memory eventually fade away like the sunlight when it is eclipsed by a cloud. Now every year I have nothing new to add to the bucket, and I'm forced to watch as the bucket becomes lost in the flow of time and is pushed to the dark corners of my memory.

It's a tradition in my family now that we go to the beach at least once a year. I look forward to it every year. To go back to that place that can melt my stress like eating a piece of chocolate can.

The place that makes me feel safe and comforts me. To feel those sensations and those memories and to see that scenery. I used to remember each visit to the beach so vividly, as if I were just there yesterday. However, it eventually all just starts to feel like a dream as I realize each trip to the beach is less memorable and just not worth remembering. Time doesn't slow down—the sand dunes keep changing and the waves keep crashing and I keep growing farther and farther apart from the place I once loved.

I don't want to separate myself, but it seems like it just keeps getting harder to get there as life keeps pulling me away from the one place I felt happiness. Now it just feels like I'm stuck in a dark wasteland full of despair and unhappiness that I can't escape from as I search desperately for that tranquil place that brought me serenity. However, even when I find it, I don't feel the same happiness that I once did. My beach is becoming polluted with sadness that I don't want there but don't know how to get rid of. The bright light that once shone on my beautiful beach is now withering away. It won't be long until there's nothing there but complete darkness, and the worst part is, I can't stop it from happening. All I can do is watch and hope that one day the light will return to the shore. I hope that day comes soon because I don't like the dark, and I don't like not being able to find peace in anything anymore. But I won't lose hope, because I know after every storm there is a rainbow, and then I will be able to feel that breeze that will once again remind me why I'm here and why I chose to continue living my life instead of ending it amidst all the darkness. That breeze that reveals to me the secrets of this world, of this life. I want to feel that breeze again so I will keep hope that one day the sun will shine so bright it will melt away all the darkness from my beach and I'll be able to once again hear the seagulls call me, watch the dragonflies fly through the cattails, and see the colorful kites dance in the sky. A place that once had so much happiness can't just disappear, so I will wait for the day when that happiness returns because having that one place, that one serene, tranquil place to call my own—that's what life is all about. That's why we are all put on this earth, to find that one place amidst all the insanity that evokes feelings of joy within us, because being able to go to that one special place is what makes life worth living.

MEET THE AUTHORS

A

SEBASTIAN AGUILAR

VISUAL ARTIST

Creative, funny, and caring
Lover of food, movies, and hanging out
with friends
Who believed in feminism, aliens, and
that we shouldn't have gym class
Who wanted money, a job, and a car
Who used hats, a clear mind, and his
phone 24/7
Who gave food to friends, love, and
money to those in need
Who said, "Everybody should be
treated equal."

LISSETH AGUILAR

GRAMMAR ENTHUSIAST

Quirky, passionate, and hopeful
Lover of luxury, aesthetics, and words
Who believed in world peace, good
vibes, and that there's a reason for
everything
Who wanted freedom, money, and
happiness
Who used calligraphy, books, and
Pinterest
Who gave her all in school, at home,
and herself
Who said, "Well, that's something for
ya."

KAMILA AKABIROVA

A HELPER IN THE MAKING

Soft, cute, and short
Lover of reading, good music, and
math
Who believed in fact over fiction,
comfort over all, and comfort food
Who wanted to help people,
understand mankind, and be logical
Who used help from others, textbooks,
and advice found on the internet
Who gave food, love, and secrets
Who said, "Be kind to everyone
and everything, and never miss an
opportunity."

ARIANNA ALCIDE

THE CYCLE OF AN EVERYDAY GAIN OF FAITH

Caring, funny, and small
Lover of Minions, grapes, and buffalo
wings
Who believed fairytales exist, every day
is not a waste, and only the toughest
battles go out to the weak to toughen
them up
Who wanted to be successful, find what
makes her happy, and not give up on
her dreams
Who used music, paper and pen, and
food to release her feelings
Who gave her time, kindness, and
support to those who deserved it
Who said, "Everyday is a tough battle,
but a trophy is received every time."

FATHA ALMA

INDEPENDENT

Lover of music and art
Who believed in peace
Who wanted satisfaction and isolation
Who used to explore
Who said, "If it makes you unhappy
then let it go."

DAWELYS ALMONTE

PASSIONATE, SPONTANEOUS, AND WEIRD

Lover of serial killer facts,
extraterrestrial theories, and gender
equality
Who believed in aliens, ghosts, and
that serial killers are awesome
Who wanted food, an unlimited
amount of money, and love
Who used people, feelings, and
sarcastic comebacks
Who gave corny jokes, sarcasm, and
serial killer facts
Who said, "Perfection exists while
living in this imperfect little world."

JINET ALMANZAR

FUNNY, CARING, AND KIND

Lover of food, animals, and friends
Who believed in herself, her family,
and in others
Who wanted a job
Who gave love, respect, and kindness
Who said, "Nobody is perfect; just be
yourself."

SAMANTHA ALVARADO

CURIOUS, OUTGOING, AND SMART

Lover of urban exploring, adventure, and traveling
Who believed adventure, ambition, and the fact that Donald Trump is a pig
Who wanted happiness, fame, and peace
Who used a camera, social media, and her feet to get to places
Who gave her heart, her all, and her emotions into everything
Who said, "YOLO."

JARLYN ALVAREZ

AMBITIOUS AND SENSATIONAL YOUNGING

Ambitious, open-minded, and phenomenal
Lover of Mexican food, money, and the idea of living up to dreams coming true
Who believed that hard work pays off, that time is money, and in reality and future rather than being stuck in the moment
Who wanted to build a better world, to give everything and more to her mom, and nothing but food at her funeral
Who used critical thinking, big words when speaking, and her phone 24/7
Who gave to the less fortunate, gave love in abundance, and gave in exchange for nothing in return
Who said, "If money can't buy you happiness, you are shopping at the wrong store."

MARIAH AMADOR

OUTGOING, FUNNY, CONFUSING

Lover of pancakes, music, and piercings
Who believed everyone makes mistakes

MARYLOU ANDRADES

MULTITALENTED EXTRAORDINAIRE

Determined, athletic, and friendly
Lover of sports, writing, and drawing
Who believed that anything is possible,
that there are open doors all around,
and that she would do great things.
Who wanted pen, paper, and a chance
Who used every chance I got, my
notebook, and my friend's pencil
Who gave interesting stories, advice,
and memorable moments
Who said, "Only you can choose the
path you take and only you can change
that."

NICOLE APARICIO CRUZ

FRIENDLY AND SMALL

*Lover of drawing, kale smoothies, and
shopping
Who believed in mental health days
Who wanted to pass chemistry and trig
Who used healing stones and the
process of elimination
Who gave money to a less fortunate
Who said, "At least I got thirty minutes
of sleep."*

HALEI AVILES

CARING AND INDECISIVE

*Lover of helping children in the future,
writing, and music
Who believed in peace and love
Who wanted to travel all over the
world, become a teacher of children
with disabilities, and to make the
world a better place
Who used writing as an escape and art
as an expression
Who gave thoughtful conversations
Who said, "You have to reach out for
your dreams. They won't be handed to
you."*

ANDREA AVILES

LOVELESS HATER

*Unique, shy, caring
Lover of chocolate, beds, and fun
Who believed in always having a
reason
Who wanted a normal life*

SPENCER AYVAS

THE MOST ATTRACTIVE PERSON IN THIS BOOK

Artistic, tall, and great with cats
Lover of videogames, animation, and
his eyebrow tweezers
Who believed in multi-reality,
reincarnation, and hope
Who wanted money, many cats, and
fast Wi-Fi
Who used enthusiasm, inspiration, and
lots of 2AM cups of coffee
Who gave ideas, ambitions, and
dreams
Who said, "You come first."

B

OULIMATA BA

FABLO FRESHCOBAR

Funny, outgoing, and charismatic
Lover of money, clothes, and Fabolous
Who believed in karma, her gut, and
that everyone deserves a second chance
Who wanted a BMW and Fabolous
Who used her brain, her gut, and her
lurking skills
Who gave money to the homeless, so
many chances, and clothes to the needy
Who said, "Snakes in the grass keep it
short."

ELYSE BABOORAM

DETERMINED FASHIONISTA WITH HER OWN FLARE

*Petite, professional, but humble
Lover of cosmetics, dogs, and exotic
islands
Who believed in herself, the simple
beauty of nature, and seeing the good
in all bad
Who wanted world peace, an end to
the unjust things of the world, and an
unlimited supply of cash
Who gave a friendly smile, good
advice, and a helping hand
Who said, "Though she be little, she is
fierce."*

ALEXIS BAEZ

STYLISH PERSONALITY

*Rebellious, fun, and unapologetic
Lover of anything glam, fashion, and
food
Who believed in karma, that 11:11
wishes come true, and that school is
torture
Who wanted to do big things with her
fashion ideas, always be happy, and to
graduate high school already
Who used foul language, NYC slang
terms, and paper towels to curl her
hair like Farrah Fawcett
Who gave help to all those in need
Who said, "Life is just one big party."*

CLAUDIBEL BATISTA

THE CLA IN BEL

Outgoing, fun, and unique
Lover of me, myself, and I
Who believes things happen for a
reason
Who wants to be more than what
everyone predicted
Who uses the method of ignoring
everything negative or false
Who says, "The only person you should
try to be better than is the person you
were yesterday."

DIAVION BENN

PRINCESS OF OVERACHIEVING (THINKS PINK)

Lover of pink, sparkles, and fashion
Who believed in the tooth fairy,
Spongebob, and that she could be a
princess as an occupation
Who wanted fame, fortune, and fans
Who used her brains, beauty, and
talent
Who gave time, effort, and
commitment
Who said, "I'm going to take you to the
top of the world."

SAMANTHA BERGER

POP-PUNK PRINCESS

Sarcastic
Lover of All Time Low, cats, and Tim
Riggins
Who wanted world peace, Spotify
Premium, and good eyebrows
Who gave the world dark humor, a
knowledge of vertigo, and headaches
Who said, "The Staten Island Ferry is
my name."

AMENCIS BERQUIN

OPTIMISTIC ENTHUSIASTIC ASPIRING ARTIST

Caring, enthusiastic, and crazy
Lover of literature, having fun, and
trying new things
Who believed in achieving anything
you want, and fighting for what you
want
Who wanted to always be focused, and
better herself as well
Who used dedication, determination,
and hard work
Who gave respect, second chances, and
opportunity to anyone who deserved it
Who said, "You can be the prettiest
or the ugliest. People will always have
something to say, so ignore it and strive
to be better."

SHANIQUA BLACKWELL

OUTGOING AND SMART

Lover of reading, 80's classic movies, clothes, and fashion
Who believes in peace, love, and happiness
Who wants to create, bring joy, and have further knowledge of herself
Who uses her mind, spirit, and talent to create this book
Who gives her drawing skills, her favorite place, and her memories
Who says, "I want to show a little of myself to the world."

GLADYS BES

OPTIMIST FEMINIST

Liberal, kindhearted, but temperamental
Lover of places, people, and food
Who believed in vibes, the goodness of people, and herself
Who wanted to grow, find inner peace, and create outer peace
Who used retail therapy, comfort food, and art to heal
Who gave judgment-free advice
Who said, "Be the energy you want to attract."

SHAROYA BRACEY

MEMOIRIST/MUSICIAN

Over-analytical, supporting dreamer
Lover of music, food, and dreams
Who believed in herself, you, and your
friend
Who wanted to be understood better
and over-stand
Who used her heart, soul, and
experience to do so
Who gave hope, laughter, happiness,
and words of wisdom
Who said and believed, "Be yourself;
everyone else is taken."

ASATTA BRADFORD

FASHION

Funny, shy, and outgoing
Lover of ice cream, science, and
strawberries
Who wanted to explore the world
Who gave us trigonometry, chocolate
ice cream, and global history
Who said, "I have a dream..."

GELIA BRADOR

SARCASTIC DOG ENTHUSIAST

Blunt, overthinking, night owl
Lover of bands, animals, and eyebrows
Who believed in human and animal
rights
Who wanted endless peace and
happiness
Who used an open mind

KIANNI BRADSHAW

NOT MUCH TO KNOW ABOUT KIANNI

Weird and strange
Lover of chocolate, science, and sleep
Who believed that failure isn't an
option, feelings are a distraction, and
everyone deserves a chance
Who wanted to be a surgeon

ISIAH BRANCH-EL

NOT YOUR EVERYDAY, TYPICAL BOY

Lover of art, fashion, and basketball
Who believes everyone has a purpose,
your struggle makes you stronger, and
a smile can change the world
Who wants to prove everyone wrong
who doubted him, to build a career in
fashion, and to live life to the fullest
Who said, "My job is to make everyone
smile."

ANITA BRIGGS

TIRED ARTIST

Happy, inspired, and tired
Lover of chocolate, nature, and
hardcover books
Who believed in herself, the idea that
everyone has potential, and the idea
that you can achieve everything
Who wanted to create, discover, and
explore
Who used paint brushes, pencils, and
intellect
Who gave photographs, doodles, and
kindness
Who said, "Don't be afraid to be
yourself because someone out there will
appreciate you for you."

FIONA BRISEÑO MEYER

PRINCESS

Colorful and outgoing
Lover of vintage clothing and tattoos
Who believed in dressing up always,
and not letting age define you
Who used traveling and transportation
Who gave many forced years of
education

JASMINE BROOKS

WINTER VILLAGAS

Goofy, nice, and fun
Lover of monkeys, ice cream, and
Pharrell
Who believed that popcorn is life,
everyone is born an actor/actress, and
things happen for a reason
Who wanted to act, sing, and model
Who used her skills, her mind, and
her soul
Who gave her time, her effort, and
passion
Who said, "What God knows about
me is more important than what others
think about me."

SEPHIRA BRYANT

THE WALKING FULL-STOCK REFRIGERATOR

Calm, bright, and staying forever
hilarious
Lover of candy, Gatorade, and hats
Who believed in freedom, love, and
karma

KELFRI BUENO

DOMINICAN HAPPINESS AND JOY

Fun, sensitive, and happy
Lover of picnics and walks, adventures,
and discoveries
Who believed love is love, mermaids
are real, and that things happen for a
reason
Who wanted a dog, a car, and to live
outside of NYC
Who used phones every day, similes
to compare objects to people, and
happiness to make others smile
Who gave love to many people, hugs
to friends and family, and a smile to
brighten up people's days
Who said, "Nothing will stop me from
doing what I believe I can do."

C

ALEXIS CABAN

OUTGOING

Lover of ice cream, reading, and
dancing
Who believed in el raton (tooth fairy),
clouds are cotton candy, and the ocean
is a black hole
Who wanted to give back, teach dance,
and become successful
Who used common sense, past
experience, and fast thinking
Who gave sarcastic responses,
impulsive lies, and food to the hungry
Who said, "You can never have a
second chance for a first impression."

RUTH CABRERA

FUNNY AND ASSERTIVE

*Lover of food, fashion, and music
Who believed in loyalty and remaining
humble
Who wanted to create, design, and
express herself
Who minded her own business, stayed
away from gossip, and kept her hands
to herself
Who said, "Trust yourself because
that's all you truly have."*

NATALIE CANDELARIO HERRERA

NETFLIX ENTHUSIAST, FAIR-MINDED,
AND A FUTURE NURSE

*Lover of sleep, sleep, and more sleep
Who believed in feminism, growth,
and happiness
Who gave guidance, comfort, and tears
(of laughter of course!)
Who said, "A flower doesn't think of
competing with the flower next to it. It
just blooms."*

ELIZABETH CANELA

"BLANK" "WORDS" "MIND"

Funny, nice, and unique
Lover of the fashion world, creativity,
and animals
Who believed in unicorns, aliens, and
that wishes come true
Who wanted happiness, fairness, and
trust
Who used skills, creativity, and
knowledge
Who gave smartness, love, and
patience
Who said, "People will stare so make it
worth their while."

AALIYAH CASTILLO

QUEEN OF LAUGHTER

Fun, free-spirited, and loving
Lover of art, animals, and attention
Who believed in true love, happy
endings, and endless laughter
Who wanted to make everyone
happy, everything fun, and everlasting
happiness
Who used laughter, jokes, and art
Who gave fun, a remedy for sadness,
and laughter
Who said, "Come on, you can't be mad
forever," or "I see you smiling, you can't
hold it back."

TENNILLE BRIENNA CHONG

THE IN-DEPTH GIRL

Indecisive, blunt, and deep
Lover of poetry, world's view, and peace
Who believed that she can say what
she wants, in strong beliefs, and in best
choices
Who wanted love, wealth, and fun
experiences
Who used inner thoughts
Who gave deep conversation
Who said smart things

MUSHFIKA CHOWDHURY

CREATIVE SPONTANEOUS EXPLORER

Funny, hopeless romantic, and
adrenaline junkie
Lover of good style, dedication, and
food
Who believed regrets shouldn't exist,
and music heals everything
Who wanted to travel the world with
her closest friends
Who used Urban Decay setting spray,
Black Pilot G-2 07 pen, and Instagram
as a flirting tactic
Who gave perfect eye rolls, makeovers,
and advice to younger family members
Who said, "If you want to go fast, go
alone. If you want to go far, go with
others."

LIZET CIELO VELAZQUEZ

NERD

*Intellectual, curious, and independent
Lover of math, science and detail
Who believed in fundamental
theorems, God, and family first
Who wanted to live life, enjoy life, and
have fun
Who used a pencil, a notebook, and a
brain
Who gave criticism, advice, and
solutions
Who said, "School is fun."*

AMAYA CONTRERAS

ARTIST IN THE MAKING

*Creative, distracted, and sarcastic
Lover of books, music, and art
Who believed that humans (no matter
race, gender, etc.) should be treated as
equals no matter what, that the world
can get better, and that just because
something has been done a certain way
doesn't mean that that's the only way.
Who wanted to travel, to give art her
all, and to live to see a better world
Who used words, art, and references
Who gave the pizza sandwich, the
bucket speaker, and certain art pieces
Who said, "That really steams my
clams" and "Diddily darn." I really
don't say many remarkable things.*

JUSTINE COOPER

FUTURE COSTUME DESIGNER

Intelligent, talented, and funny
Lover of bowling, wrestling, and
fashion design
Who believed that if you keep
something in your closet long enough it
will eventually come back in style
Who wanted to win a Tony Award for
her designs in a critically acclaimed
Broadway play
Who used wit and her will to become
successful
Who said, "I won't start a problem, but
if you bring it to me, I'll finish it."

ANYELA CORONADO

TIRED, HUNGRY, AND A REBEL

Lover of food, books, and Netflix
Who believed in friendship, courage,
and equality
Who wanted to be surrounded by
happy people and things, make sure
her voice was heard, and make the
world better
Who used her life experience, her
voice, and her memories
Who gave advice from life experience,
happiness, and courage
Who said, "Don't be afraid to show
who you are. The people that love and
care for you will always be there."

DANIEL CRUZ

THE MYSTERIOUS, TALL BOY

Lover of food, science, and the mind
Who believed in aliens, enlightenment,
and peace
Who wanted food, peace, and to feel
loved
Who used a clear and open mind to
accept all things and everybody
Who gave his time, patience, and food
to others
Who said, "We're just an ant farm of
something bigger than us."

D

ALEJANDRA DELEON

YOUTUBER

Crazy, shy, and caring
Lover of cellphones, cameras, and
computers
Who wanted to make others happy,
express her thoughts, and be relatable
Who used life, Internet, and the people
around her
Who gave her thoughts, her voice, and
her story
Who said, "Don't listen to others and
stay true to yourself."

JAH CHINA DELEON

BUBBLY, ARTISTIC, AND OPEN-MINDED

*Lover of food, the idea that you are
what you make, and art
Who believes that throwing pebbles at
your window in the night means they
care, that crying is a godsend, and
smiling means hope
Who wants a larger life in a smaller
world, a gift, and a dream
Who used smiles to define her, hope to
rely on, and family to rise with
Who gave a laugh to the world, and
a smile to the damned, and a shine in
the night
Who said, "There's a light at the end of
the tunnel, but no trains coming."*

MAYA DELLA

SARCASTIC, QUIET, HILARIOUS

*Lover of anything that revolves
around shoes, nice people, and solving
problems
Who believed that there is some good
to rude people
Who wanted to achieve any goal that
was in sight, build up a business that
would benefit people, and start an
amazing family
Who used connections with others and
communication to achieve goals
Who said, "No one else's opinion
matters but mine."*

SUSANA DELOSSANTOS

ANNOYING LITTLE MOUSE

*Short, strange, and open-minded
Lover of food, books, and movies
Who believed in options, diversity, and
defying society
Who wanted equality, fun, and a whole
lot of pizza
Who used her voice for those who
couldn't, makeup to transform herself,
and words to fight her battles
Who gave up her thoughts to share
with others*

SAMANTHA DUER

AN APPROACHABLE, WELCOMING PERSON

*Lover of making things happen
Who believed in change, but never
expected it
Who wanted to help, and to be helped
Who used the world to her advantage
Who gave comfort and consolation
Who said, "A lot of things, but nothing
quotable."*

ANNIE DONG

LOVER OF BOOKS, CHOCOLATE, AND TRAVEL

F

ICIS FELDMAN

ARTISTIC, CREATIVE, AND FUN

Lover of animals, art, and food
Who believed in feminism and that
aliens are real
Who wanted money
Who used an open mind
Who said, "Everybody is beautiful so
don't care what people say."

AALIYAH FAIRWEATHER

SHOPPING ENTHUSIASTIC

Dramatic, awkward, and corny
Lover of shoes, Netflix series, and Vine.
Who believed in the tooth fairy, herself,
and that sarcasm is the only way to
communicate
Who wanted to stay out past 7, more
than 16GB of space, and Starbucks gift
cards
Who used memes, emojis, and subs on
Snapchat
Who gave all her money to
McDonald's, song suggestions, and
cheap laughs
Who said, "Fake it to make it."

PAULA FERREIRA

ADVENTUROUS, OUTGOING, AND OPEN-MINDED

*Lover of softball, food, and ice cream
Who believed that chasing after the ice
cream truck in the summer is one of
the best feelings
Who wanted to be successful and have
ambition
Who used a wise mind, smart
decision-making, and hustling
Who gave others a helping hand and a
shoulder to cry on*

TAMMY FONG

LORD OF THE SLOTHS AND KEEPER OF SECRETS

*Introverted, intelligent, and clumsy
Lover of books, video games, and food
Who believed in hard work,
determination, and dreams
Who wanted 1,000 cats, dogs, and
cookies
Who said, "Money can't buy happiness,
but it can buy ice cream, which is
pretty much the same thing."*

G

DIANA GARCIA MARTINEZ

THE SILLY CUPCAKE LOVER

Way too sarcastic for her own good, random, yet tame
Lover of sour things, blue things, and CHEESE!
Who believed that your zodiac sign reflects you personally, that Santa Claus was real until age 10, and that candy is good for your health
Who wanted to travel and see the whole world
Who said, "Be yourself regardless of any circumstance."

YAILIN GACHUZ

HUMBLE, KIND, SHY

Lover of makeup, animals, and the gym
Who believed in superstition, karma, and creativity
Who wanted to better herself, work hard, and graduate high school
Who used kindness, creativity, and intelligence
Who gave good advice and a helping hand
Who said, "Do what you want."

NATALIE GAY

SLEEPING DRAGON

Creative and hardworking
Lover of food, Fire Emblem, and sleep
Who believed in a better future,
support from friends, and sriracha
sauce
Who wanted time, energy, and sleep
Who used patience, analysis, and
efforts
Who gave advice, pens, and food
Who said, "Somehow, I wonder if
the monster under my bed is getting
claustrophobic."

OLIVIA GIGANTE

VISUAL EXTRAORDINAIRE

Funny, blunt, and smart
Lover of art, music, and fashion
Who wanted to travel the world, be
peaceful, and happy
Who used procrastination, social
media, and her phone
Who gave laughter, positive vibes, and
fashion advice

CHASTITY GLASBY

DAYDREAMER

Creative, funny, and ambitious
Lover of music, food, and sparkly/shiny
things
Who believed that everything that
glitters is gold and everything happens
for a reason
Who wanted success, money, and a
good life
Who used her imagination, her
dreams, and her hope
Who gave good vibes, corny jokes, and
dreams to last a lifetime
Who said, "It's okay to dream, but you
also have to work for what you want."

FELICITY GOODMAN

THE FASHION MAJOR WHO DOESN'T WANT TO WORK IN FASHION

Bubbly, yet shy and innocent
Lover of food, her phone, and music
Who believed that money DOES grow
on trees 'cause it's paper, that you
should always be yourself, and forget
the haters
Who wanted a Prince Charming and a
castle made of food

EZRI GOROSTIZA

A GIRL WITH A PEN

Funny, easily amused
Lover of books, movies, and music
Who believed in the paranormal, in
the impossible, and in Karma
Who wanted to not procrastinate, pass
her classes, and graduate
Who used her mind, a pen, and books
Who gave thought, time, and effort
into her writings
Who said, "We were born to be real,
not to be perfect."

MARIA PAZ GUERRON

CRAZY ON THE INSIDE, BUT QUIET ON THE OUTSIDE

Quiet, short, and loyal
Lover of dogs, food, and music
Who believed in not giving up, trying
your hardest, and not caring about the
haters
Who wanted a good life, a good job,
and lots of money
Who used her phone, her computer,
and ideas
Who gave money, advice, and opinions
to her friends
Who said, "I am hungry."

JESSENIA GUZMAN

PASSIONATE ENVIRONMENTALIST

*Supportive, caring, and an
environmentalist
Lover of nature, dark chocolate, and
oneself
Who believed in unicorns, humanity,
and that it wasn't too late
Who wanted to dream, believe, and to
make the world a better place
Who used every space on the paper,
used to eat meat, and used creativity
on everything
Who gave away love, hope, and
support
Who said, "Stop killing the trees."*

JUAN GUZMAN

ALWAYS IN TROUBLE

*Cool, funny, nice
Lover of music, sports, and video
games
Who believed in karma, religion, and
honesty
Who wanted to go outside, to watch
TV, and to play video games
Who used a clear mind, relaxation,
and quietness
Who gave time, location, and life
Who said, "Word of advice: Don't ever
steal or else you might find yourself in
prison like I did."*

H

ALEXANDRIA HAUGHTON

FUNNY, SHY, AND FASHIONABLE

*Lover of food, fashion, and traveling
Who believed in the change of features,
fashion, and technology
Who wanted to create garments, sell
them, and become a name brand
Who used simple sewing skills,
determination, and ambition*

ENYASHA HARRIS

AMAZING STUDENT

*Hardworking, spicy, and beautiful
Lover of things that help her grow into
a better person
Who believed that all good things
must come to an end, but if you work
together the good things will never end
Who wanted to be an early childhood
educator because uniqueness must
start from the place children spend all
their time
Who used to be an obnoxious young
lady that was extremely rude
Who gave up that bad attitude because
it would get her nowhere
Who said, "Times are rough only when
you make them, but surround yourself
with great people and you'll live a life
of happiness."*

CAMREN HERNANDEZ

FUTURE FASHION STYLIST, CONSULTANT, AND BUYER

Stylish, intelligent, and strong
Lover of fashion, Drake, food, and food
Who wanted to marry Jesse
McCartney, be on Disney Channel,
and influence the youth
Who used positive ideas, stern tones,
and never giving up
Who said, "Everything happens for a
reason."

KASSANDRA HERNANDEZ

QUEEN OF ALL THINGS DISNEY

Smart, loyal, and a perfectionist
Lover of fairytales, roses, and
Shakespeare
Who believed in true love, fairies, and
the imaginary
Who wanted to create, write, and
design a new world
Who used intelligence, skill, and the
love of those around me
Who gave advice, love, and funny
stories to ease your sorrow
Who said, "Our small, stupid
conversations mean more to me than
you'll ever know."

RACHEL HOCHER

CREATIVE BUTTERFLY

Creative and crazy
Who believes in aliens, destiny, and
karma
Who wants to draw, create, and design
Who used her mind and her
unbreakable determination
Who gave a new philosophy and a
different outlook on life
Who said, "Don't let people tell you
that you can't do it. If you want it, do
it."

MADISON HORNBROOK

CREATIVE, IMAGINATIVE, AND OPEN-MINDED

Lover of cats, art, expression, and
curiosity of life
Who believed in kindness, character,
and peace for all mankind
Who wanted success, happiness, and
fulfillment
Who used strength, family, and
experience
Who gave much love, effort, and
everything she had to get where she is
Who said, "Be the rich, eccentric
relative you wish you had."

KIARA HUSBANDS

CALL ME K

Nonchalant, quiet, and goofy
Lover of music, food, and life
Who wanted to love, live, and be happy
Who used independence, self
determination, and self motivation
Who said, "There is only room for one
in a casket, so strive for yourself."

BRITTNEY IDEHEN

PERSON

Quiet, silent, miniscule
Lover of bake and saltfish, cats, and
peace
Who believed that people are originally
nice unless otherwise influenced,
education is the key to success, and
strength in silence
Who wanted peace, equality, and
happiness
Who used an open mind, deep
thinking, and a dictionary
Who gave the world her best effort
Who said, "I don't understand why
people can't just be nice to each other."

ZUAIRAH ISLAM

BELIEVER IN FATE

Independent, quirky, and real
Lover of the quiet, her bed, and her
phone
Who wanted all the makeup she could
have and to live on a beach

J

BIANCA JACKSON

TROPICAL MEMORIES

Appreciative, adventurous, and caring
Lover of positivity, food, and sweets
Who believed in equality, grace, beauty
in everything, and happily-ever-afters
Who wanted perfection, unity, and
good vibes
Who used a clear vision, made an
effort to help things change for good,
and used school as the tool to help
make change
Who gave us a different view on things,
made us realize that everyone is going
to need help and that education is a
seed to success
Who said, "It will all be good in the
end. If it isn't good yet...it isn't the end
yet."

CHELSEA JAMES

DEBATEABLE "KNOW-IT-ALL"

*Sarcastic, intelligent, and innovative
Lover of investigation discovery,
English buildings, and food
Who believed you can never have too
much to be happy about, twins are evil,
and math is the worst subject to ever
have to do
Who wanted to travel the world, learn
seven language fluently, and live in
Sweden
Who used to rock climb as a kid, hike
in the mountains, and pretend the bed
was a trampoline
Who gave knowledge to others, attitude
to those around her, and money to
many
Who said, "You are a sponge soaking
up my knowledge and returning it."*

SHANIA JAMES

FUNNY, ENERGETIC, AND INTERESTING

*Lover of music, positivity, and food
Who believed in second chances, bad
luck, and mermaids
Who wanted to create, express, and
end world violence
Who used common sense, good
decisions, and creativity
Who gave advice, attitude, and
friendship
Who said, "You just can't live in
that negative way...make way for the
positive Day."*

ISIS JANNIERRE BATES

STUDENT

Can of worms
Lover of books, art, and man's trash
Who believed little things, big things,
and medium things
Who wanted big things, small things,
and little things

ASHLEY JAVIER

ASPIRING OPTIMIST

Dog lover, feminist, and self-diagnosed
narcoleptic
Lover of Dominoes, makeup tutorials,
and Nicholas Sparks' novels
Who believed that beauty is pain,
everything is temporary, and koalas
should be considered bears
Who wanted world peace, better
eyebrows, and a puppy farm
Who used procrastination, lost of Edge
Control, and eyeshadow
Who gave great advice, lots of laughs,
and lots of attitude

DANIELLE JEAN-LOUIS

ZOE QUEEN/PORT-AU-PRINCESS

*Chill, friendly, and difficult
Lover of individuality, creativity, and
food
Who believed in God, true love, and
education
Who wanted success, love and
happiness
Who used goal setting, inspirational
quotes, and jokes
Who gave advice, hope for a better
future, and trust
Who said, "Tomorrow is another day."*

PARIS JEROME

BRIGHT SOULFUL DREAMER

*Assertive, but shy and expressive
Lover of literature with unique
characters, music that makes me feel,
and art (controversial or character
work) that's colorful and pops
Who believed that there are certain
energies that affect our mood, you
can only get what you want if you're
determined, and witches are real
Who wanted the world, free will, and
happiness
Who used her phone every single
second, all of her patience, and the
knowledge and skills she admires in
others
Who gave straightforward advice,
sarcasm, and rambling speeches of
nothingness
Who said, "I like Nutella"*

HENNESSY JIMENEZ

ASPIRING PUBLIC FIGURE

*Tall, enthusiastic, educated, and
beautiful
Lover of fitness, traveling, food, and
friends and family
Who believed in dancing as art, singing
as peace, and beauty for desires
Who wanted to be known for her
variety of talents
Who used close supporters/motivators,
love, and a healthy mind
Who gave herself hope in pursuing all
of her dreams no matter the challenges
Who said, "Don't let anyone tell you
no just because they were told no or
couldn't."*

ERICA JOHNSON

QUEEN BEE

*Bubbly, social, and weird
Lover of chocolate, pizza, and foooood
Who believed in reaching for the stars
and in unicorns
Who wanted to feel full of life and no
limitations
Who gave all her heart to the people
she cared about
Who said, "You can't spell America
without Erica."*

K

ARIA FAZIHA KHANDAKER

ANALYTICAL PHILANTHROPIST

*Versatile, independent, and stubborn
Lover of my mother, babies less than
two years old, and adventures to any
new place
Who wanted less stress, more fun,
and Belgium dark chocolate brownie
sundaes
Who gave the world a makeover
through her own business, a makeover
in style, and a makeover in ideologies
Who said, "Of all that we take into the
world, there is nothing more powerful
than your mind."*

FANTA KANTE

THE CLUELESS GENIUS

*Unique, optimistic, and corny
Lover of corny jokes, laughter, and
FOOD
Who believed in karma, true love, and
that laughter is the best medicine
Who wanted to make people happy
and tell her stories
Who used her brain, creativity, and
slight humor
Who gave a story none can relate to,
and a chuckle
Who said, "No, I was not named after
the soda on purpose, but it is unique."*

L

ASHLEY LAIRD

STRIVING STUDENT

Positive, optimistic, and outgoing
Lover of food, Disney, and fashion
Who believed in peace in our time, that
everyone has some kind of talent, and
being adventurous
Who wanted to influence everyone in
a positive way, continually invest in
her human capital, and make herself
happy
Who used love, words, and an open
mind
Who gave great fashion tips, money to
charity, and good advice
Who said, "Give everything you do
100% or nothing at all."

SHAZIAH LA VAN-SMALL

KIND-HEARTED FASHIONISTA

Intellectual, creative, and sensitive
Lover of shopping and music
Who believed that you should never
not be yourself

KADEEM AARON LAMORELL

AN ARTIST IN DISCOVERY

*Creative, and cautious, yet petty
Lover of fashion design, social justice,
and Tumblr
Who believed in the beauty in all
things, in treasuring the past, and in
looking towards the future
Who wanted design, structure, and to
beautify
Who used a creative eye, a skilled
hand, and a detailed mind
Who gave a perspective, a story, and
a style
Who said, "Bad taste is better than no
taste."*

AMARIS LAROSE

OBSERVER OF ALL THINGS

*Model, fashionista, and entrepreneur
Lover of food, sleep, and exercise
Who believed that loyalty, observance,
and food are the keys to life
Who wanted to build an empire based
on dreams
Who used a face, a dream, and a big
brother to get started
Who gave realism, understanding, and
the brutal truth
Who said, "If it's not organized, I'm as
good as gone."*

JADA LEBELL

ADVENTUROUS FLOWER SEARCHING FOR SUCCESS

Adventurous, funny, but quiet
Lover of ideas, fashion, and science
Who believed in being unique, loving
yourself, and sleeping
Who wanted to discover, investigate,
and create
Who used a good eye, fashion, and
experimentation
Who gave us the guide to fashion
Who said, "If you can't love yourself,
how are you going to love somebody
else?"

HILARY LEON

BUSINESS MARKETING STUDENT MULTITASKER

Kind, crazy, but sneaky
Lover of dogs, video games, and
anything having to do with the mind
Who believed in unicorns, world peace,
and aliens
Who wanted to have equality for all
races and genders, make the world
a better place, and change people's
perspective
Who used life as a lesson, an open
mind, and intelligence
Who gave questions, clues, and
mystery
Who said, "Who really knows what
normal is?"

IYNN LEE

THOUGHTFUL, INTELLECTUAL, AND GULLIBLE

TAMMY LEONG

ALWAYS TRYING TO KEEP POSITIVE

Kind, shy, and open-minded
Lover of art, fashion, and life
Who believed anything is possible, that
life is worth living, and that a positive
mind is the best
Who wanted to explore the world and
learn about everything
Who used her heart, spirit, and
happiness
Who gave happiness, a smile, and
creativity
Who said, "Life is too short to waste."

AKIRA LEWIS

THE QUIET ONE

Short, sarcastic, and observant
Lover of books, bonds, and Tumblr
Who believed that she could do
anything she put her mind to, and that
having a big brain was better than a
sharp tongue
Who wanted the world to be a better
place, for her book collection to grow,
and to be a published author
Who used her brain, wit, and creativity
to make a difference although most
don't see it
Who gave everything and anything to
help others when she could
Who said, "My books are a part of me.
They have pieces of me scattered within
the characters of novels."

YING LIU

CRAZY

Wild, but deep
Lover of uniqueness, poetry, and
nature
Who believed in astronauts, mystery,
and reality
Who wanted peace, to create, and to
explore the Universe
Who used humor and figurative
language
Who gave confusion
Who said, "Never judge. There's always
a hidden message."

ASHLEY LOPEZ

BOLD, EXPRESSIVE, AND GOOFY

Lover of baseball, pizza, and clothes
Who believed getting this new house
was impossible, karma, and in herself
Who wanted her own room, to meet
Future, and to be rich
Who used her brain, ideas, and her gut
Who gave people second chances when
needed, money to the homeless, and
her clothes to poor kids in D.R.
Who said, "Fitting in isn't fun for a
person who wants to be extraordinary."

ANGELICA LORA

MEMOIRIST

Short, funny, and annoying
Lover of Thomas Hobbes, money, and
herself
Who believed in lies, laughs, and
stories
Who wanted money, a broken ATM,
and more money
Who used her phone 24/7, sometimes
people, and everything else
Who gave corny jokes, food, and a
bum Chipotle
Who said, "Although beauty may be
in the eye of the beholder, the feeling of
being beautiful exists solely in the mind
of the beheld."

BONNIE LYNCH

EVERYONE'S FAVORITE KNOW-IT-ALL

Quirky, clever, perfectionist
Lover of fiction, music, and
strawberries
Who believed in evolution, the big
bang, and science
Who wanted a good book, success, and
some alone time
Who used the Internet, the library
card, and a $50 Amazon gift card
Who gave advice, complaints, and
random trivia
Who said, "Hello."

M

KIMBERLY MARQUEZ

THE QUEEN OF ME

Gregarious, feisty, and emotional
Lover of ideas, thoughts, and mankind
Who believed in love, in crying, and in
everyone's thoughts
Who wanted intelligence, to make
change, and to become better
Who used Siri, the mind, and ideas
Who gave life a new meaning, advice,
and attitude
Who said stuff that shouldn't be said to
make a point

SHAIMELYS MARCANO SANTOS

LOST GIRL IN A REALLY BIG WORLD

Crazy, awkward, and silly
Lover of nature, hamburgers with fries,
and overly dramatic movies
Who gave love, respect, and honesty to
the world
Who said, "It's better to die young than
old and wrinkly."

EMILY MARTINEZ

EMYY BALLA

Mean and crazy
Lover of blue fish
Who wanted positivity in the world
and a lot of money
Who used a phone
Who said, "Never fear a man if he
bleed too."

SHANIYA MARTINEZ

QUEEN OF GLITTER UNICORNS

Shady, mean, and a fangirl
Lover of money, concert tickets, and Bo
Who believed Justin Bieber, One
Direction, and Halsey need more
credit, that money makes the world go
round, and that Crocs are great
Who wanted Melanie Martinez and
Marina to collaborate, to see the 1975
again, and to go to Coachella
Who used manipulation, money
and her father's weaknesses to go to
concerts last year
Who gave zero cares about people's
opinions, Nicolas a few bruises, and
her all to her best friend
Who said, "Okay, but I legit don't care
if I drink coffee from a Sprite can, I'm
not gonna stop because you think it's
weird."

KEILYN MERCADO

COOLEST DOCTOR YOU'LL EVER MEET

*Chill, cool, yet a hopeless romantic
Lover of medicine, the beach, and love
itself
Who believed in ghosts, the afterlife
(reincarnation), and finding your other
half
Who wanted to travel the world,
become a surgeon, and find her true
love
Who used books, movies, and
experience to do the things she wanted
to find and do
Who gave kindness, loyalty, and respect
to people
Who said, "Always follow your dreams
and don't let anyone come in your way
no matter who they are!"*

SOPHIA MOHAMMED

PHILANTHROPIST / ENTREPRENEUR

*Ambitious, effervescent, and proud/
confident
Lover of Reese's chocolate, malta, crazy
shows, and yaoi manga
Who believed in logic and
understanding the world around us,
in the feminist movement and racial
rights, and in giving back.
Who wanted to step up in life
and prove that she is worth it and
intelligent
Who used her hair and personality
to get what she wants, who pushed
through troubling situations and got
back up, and who turned negative
energy into positive energy
Who gave trust and understanding to
others, gave time to those she loves,
and gave to people who are in need
Who said, "Watch your thoughts."*

DAVID MORALES

ANIMAL LOVER

Energetic, nerd, and hungry
Lover of culinary, veterinary, and
comics
Who believed in ideas, in deserving
what you get, and in never being mean
Who wanted to travel, to always have
an opportunity to take photos, and to
take care of animals
Who used happiness to get by,
laughter to blend in, and an energetic
personality to make friends
Who gave ideas to people who needed
them, care for people, and work to
grow
Who said, "Give up."

TIARA MORENE

ARTISTIC INTROVERT WITH CHILL AND NERDY

Funny, creative, and sporty
Lover of books, chocolate, and aliens
Who believed in candy for breakfast,
creative freedom, and trying new
things
Who wanted to travel the world, look
at the world in a different light, and try
out-of-the-world, eccentric things
Who used dope memes, a high spirited
personality, and a sketchbook
Who gave us a different way to look at
things, and random alien drawings

CINDY MOROCHO

LIVING HUMAN BEING

Silly, weird, and thoughtful
Lover of anime, K-pop, and Kdramas
Who believed in love, change, and
compassion
Who wanted to see Japan, China, and
Korea
Who used pens and pencils to write
down her thoughts
Who gave it her all
Who said, "Shikata ga nai."

MILEIDYS MOSQUERA

A STUDENT OF MANY STRUGGLES

Creative, misunderstood, and funny
Lover of books, different personalities,
and music
Who believed in creating her own
reality in a small amount of space
away from society's ideas
Who wanted to be a good friend and
lover towards all people
Who used to think that not everyone
had a special someone
Who had the ability to stand out even
when not spoken to
Who said, "I would always be secluded
if there are people around."

N

JASIRAH NUR

AMAZING

Emotional, outspoken, and positive
Lover of love, food, and music
Who believed in love, Santa Claus, and
love at first sight
Who wanted happiness, peace, and
long lasting love
Who used giving things time, always
seeing the good in people, and going
with her heart
Who gave love, positivity, and hope
Who said, "Love is the only real thing
in life."

KAYLA NELSON

FASHION MODEL

Humble, confident, cool
Lover of ice cream, fashion, and old
school music
Who believed that all things good come
to people who wait
Who wanted her own clothing line,
to be an actress, and to get married
unlike most women in her family
Who used intelligence, beauty, and
fashion
Who gave her energy and time into
everything
Who said, "Patience is the key to life."

P

ABIGAIL PEREZ

ANTISOCIAL, QUIET, AND WEIRD

*Lover of food, candy, and going outside
to explore new areas
Who believed that we can one day fly
Who wanted to travel, bake, and to be
successful*

JULLY PATEL

LEONARDO DA VINCI IN THE MAKING

*Artistic, fun-loving, and adorkable
Lover of chocolate, pizza, and freedom
Who believed that not every princess
needs a prince to save her, that you
could never get bored of pizza, and
reading is a way to escape reality
Who wanted to explore the world,
learn new things, and enjoy life
Who used her adorable smile, weird
thinking, and curiosity
Who gave friends a reason to stick
together, accept one another, and live
life to the fullest
Who said, "I am awesome sauce."*

CHEVANIE PETER CUNNINGHAM

OVERTHINKER

Intelligent, alexithymian
Lover of singing, dancing, and writing
poetry
Who believed that everything happens
for a reason
Who wanted to be a dermatologist,
model, and photographer
Who used her amazing mindset
Who gave her creativity to the world
Who said, "Follow your dreams."

CELINE PICHARDO

TEEN GENIUS

Intellectual, funny, but mature
Lover of food and music
Who used life lessons, perseverance,
and personal goals to guide her
Who gave laughter, and those around
her a friend to confide in
Who said, "I want to be successful."

TENIA POOLE

INDEPENDENT, CREATIVE, AND LOVING

*Lover of food, music, and family
Who believed in giving people another
chance, that failure isn't an option, and
in living your life to the fullest
Who wanted to be happy all the time,
for things to go back to how they were,
and to live carefree
Who used music and sleep to calm her
down
Who said, "If I don't have a watch I
have no time."*

AUDRA PRYCE

THE REALIST

*Blunt, fashionable, and striving
Lover of manolos, shopping, and coffee
Who believed in late nights, crazy
adventures, and never thinking twice
Who wanted success, happiness, and a
fabulous collection of shoes
Who used her mind, soul, and intellect
to make it to the top
Who gave laughs, reality, and gossip
Who said, "Either you're in with me or
you're in my way."*

STEPHANIE PUJOLS

GROWING FLOWER

Fun, adventurous, and outgoing
Lover of animals, outdoors, and life
Who believed in exploring, living life
to the fullest, and being unique in your
own ways
Who wanted to think outside the box,
build new memories, and enjoy life
Who used imagination, passion, and
the outdoors
Who gave a new outlook on life, a new
hobby, and a good place to clear your
mind of the negatives
Who said, "Stop trying to rush into
things, forgetting how to live and have
fun. Take small courageous steps and
be proud to be living in a beautiful
world."

Q

NICOLE QUACH

EVERYONE'S FAVORITE ASIAN

Funny, savage, rad
Lover of bands, money, and nice
weather
Who believed in conspiracy theories
Who wanted fame, money, and world
domination
Who used lots of makeup, Snapchat,
and the solution book for my Calculus
homework
Who gave sass, and money to starving
friends
Who said, "I can't do it and I won't
try it!"

R

ONJALIK RASUUL

ONJALIK ALTER EGO ALISSA JOHNSON

*Funny, exciting, and aspirational
Lover of trap music, creativity, and
food
Who believed in God, her mother, and
in herself
Who wanted an iPhone 6s, a successful
future, and a calmer personality
Who used deodorant constantly,
perfume regularly, and soap daily
Who gave gum, mascara, and
deodorant to the needy
Who said, "LOL." (a lot)*

ASIA REDDISH

THE MELANIN GODDESS

*Caring, determined, and soulful
Lover of makeup, crockpot lasagna,
and RuPaul's Drag Race
Who believed that everything happens
for a reason, you should never change
for anyone to fit society's standards,
and you should always be yourself
Who wanted to be happy, successful,
and to never change
Who gave people confidence to be
themselves, great advice, and a "beat"
face
Who said, "People stare at me like they
never seen a walking goddess" -Kim
Kardashian*

EMMANUELLA REINA

STRIVING FOR GREATNESS

*Witty, humorous, outgoing, and
determined
Lover of bike riding, cookies, and
making money
Who believed in karma, equality, and
herself
Who wanted to be happy, positive, and
work on herself and strive
Who used hope, optimism, and self
love
Who gave determination, strength, and
grace
Who said, "Wolves don't lose sleep over
the opinion of sheep."*

TYLER ROARTY

MOTHER OF TWO DOGS

*Pop-Punk Activist
Lover of music, books, and stress
Who believed in the power of making
friends with strangers, the power of
music, and the power of dogs
Who wanted dogs, food, and unlimited
attention
Who used record players, flashcards,
and planners
Who gave us sarcasm, annoyance, and
faith in people*

TREYSHA ROBINSON

GIRL WITH BIG DREAMS

Spiritual, believer, and mildly insane
Lover of our planet, the unexplained,
and the weird
Who believed that any and everything
is possible, everyone has the potential
for greatness, and the weird are the best
Who wanted to give back to her planet,
achieve what she dreams of, and learn
to love
Who used books to escape reality, math
to clear her mind, and music when
words failed
Who gave inspiration when she could,
love when she wanted to, and kindness
when she had to
Who said, "The word 'impossible' does
not exist in my vocabulary."

NADINE ROCA

SPANISH MAMI

Funny, outgoing, and intelligent
Lover of makeup, dogs, and money
Who believed in love and karma
Who wanted to be a makeup artist and
to travel

NEFTALIN RODRIGUEZ

LOVER OF PASSION

Outgoing, loyal, and trustworthy
Lover of writing, self expression, and
trying new things
Who believed in going for what she
wanted, trying again, and making good
observations of the things and people
around her
Who wanted to create, inspire, and live
happily
Who used a strong mind, hope, and
hard work

DEREK RONDA

FUNNY, ACTIVE, AND FRIENDLY

Lover of playing sports, video games,
and girls
Who believed in following your dreams
and goals in life

NATHALIE ROSARIO

HUMOR

Creative, drama/actress, and active
Lover of animals, movies, and family
and friends
Who believed that life has a meaning,
in understanding others, and also that
everything counts
Who wanted to be an actress, an
author who inspires others, and help
my neighborhood
Who used books and movies to help
her in understanding history
Who gave her friends her thoughts,
and who gave questions about life,
society, and history
Who said, "Anything is possible. Think
outside the box."

SHIRLEY ROSEMOND

HAITIAN FURY

Funny, crazy, and creative
Lover of food, fashion, and horses
Who believed that beauty comes from
pain, there's always an opportunity,
and something comes from nothing
Who wanted to create her own
business, one day have her own home,
and to be able to travel the world
Who used a creative and positive
mindset, and who experimented
Who gave happiness to everyone and
who always made each day brighter
Who said, "Don't give up until you try."

JARAI ROSS-MACKEY

AU NATURALÉ QUEEN

Free-spirited, strong, and confident
Lover of fashion, music, and art
Who believed in love, family, and
happiness
Who wanted to become a fashion
designer, an entrepreneur, and a good
daughter
Who used her brain
Who gave four years of her life to
track and field, love, and her mother
unconditionally
Who said, "No, I've never straightened
my hair."

S

CARMEN SALAS

QUIET AND SILLY

Lover of food, John Mayer, and The
Legend of Zelda
Who wanted to learn to speak Korean,
French, and Russian
Who gave her brother a book bag
Who said, "I want to be a laser eye
surgeon when I grow up."

JAILENE SALAZAR

REGULAR HAPPY GIRL

Outgoing, happy, and understanding
Lover of pizza, pasta, and salad
Who believed in Santa Claus, karma,
and love
Who wanted revenge, freedom, and
peace
Who used jewelry, heels, and lipstick
Who gave hugs, comfort, and love
Who said, "Everything happens for a
reason."

ANA SANCHEZ

ENERGETIC AND CURIOUS

Lover of Polaroid pictures, lattes, and
road trips
Who believed that home is not a
physical place, but rather feeling
comfort around the ones you care for
Who wanted to get out of NYC for
good, find new places, and go to as
many coffee shops as she could
Who used positive thinking, a creative
mind, and a whole lot of energy to
move around
Who said, "When you want something,
you go for it like fire."

PATRICIA SANTANA

CALM, COOL, AND COLLECTED

Who believed in seeing both sides of a story, being rational, and thinking for herself
Who wanted to be happy, successful, and comfortable in her own place in this world
Who used practicality, procrastination, and peace

NATASHA SANTIAGO

OUTGOING, GOOFY, AND SENSITIVE

Lover of cats, art, and food
Who believed in the creativity of animation and the free spirits of people
Who wanted tacos
Who used Sharpies and computer graphics

BRANDY SARABIA

BUSINESS QUEER EXTRAORDINAIRE

Shy, smart, and outspoken
Lover of cats, cartoons, and positive
vibes
Who believed in science, art, and
Mitchell Davis
Who wanted to search for happiness,
food, and be free
Who used art, procrastination, and
Instagram
Who gave positive vibes, awesome
photography, and dope art
Who said, "Screw the government and
politics. Be yourself."

YOSELIN SARITA

STUDENT

Intelligent, comical, and quirky
Lover of food, tea, and makeup
Who believed in science, people, and
perfection
Who wanted to become an
anesthesiologist, model, and lowkey
artist
Who used chemistry to annoy people
who said it will never be used in reality
Who gave love, compassion, and
laughter to the people
Who said, "You'll never be done with
your work; it will always improve."

RASHAIL SHAKIL

INDECISIVE, ADVENTUROUS, CARING

*Honest, courageous, strong
Lover of humor, movies, and family
Who believed in change, creation, and
myself
Who wanted to be free, to travel, and
to have fun
Who used knowledge, heart, and
creativity
Who said, "Happiness begins with a
change in your mindset."*

KEYANNA SPANN

UNDEFINED

*Strong, independent, and creative
Lover of fashion, family, and fun
Who believed in God and chances
Who wanted to dream, experience, and
achieve
Who used life, large bags, and time
Who gave perspective, voice, and art
Who said, "I don't want to just exist, I
want to live!"*

ALICE SUNGUROV

WONDERLAND CHILD

*Curious, spiritual, and enthusiastic
Lover of thought-provoking ideas,
cultures, and experiences
Who believed nothing "just happens,"
you have to dance to your own drum,
and in cliché quotes
Who wanted to escape into the
unknown, live in the unknown, and
explore the unknown
Who used a camera, a tripod, and
patience to capture those sweet things
Who gave love, her trust to others, and
nothing up unless it was love
Who said, "It's not all in my head, I
swear!"*

JENNA SURIEL

WEIRD IN A CUTE WAY

*Shy, emotional, and friendly
Lover of her family, food, and her
future
Who believed in her childhood, love,
and friendship
Who wanted a good life, good friends,
and a big future
Who used her words to make things
better, her grades to get farther in life,
and her sister's death as a learning step
stone.
Who gave money to the poor, love
back, and her all in school
Who said, "Money won't buy you love
or happiness. People who you care
about will give you love for free."*

T

SAGINE TEERATH

SHY, HELPFUL, AND UNIQUE

Lover of food, family, and friends
Who believed in trying your best to
accomplish your goals, that family is
forever, and in having fun
Who wanted to live life to the fullest,
have interesting experiences, and do
well in school
Who used hope, independence, and
bravery
Who gave advice

JAH MEEKA TAYLOR

JAH #1

Intelligent, humorous, and petty
Lover of Chris Brown, Jordans, and
reading
Who believed in herself, God, and her
mother
Who wanted the best in life, love, and
her father home
Who used her beauty, her brains, and
her heart
Who gave chances and a very stubborn
attitude, and maybe gratitude
Who said, "Everything is a major key
in life."

AKACIA THOMAS

THE EPIPHANY

Funny and loving
Lover of Drake, Netflix, and books
Who believed sleep is important, God
is real, and life is what you make it
Who wanted endless wealth, success,
and happiness
Who gave great advice and funny
remarks
Who said, "Don't show feelings because
then you get hurt."

MERCEDEZ TIBURCIO

BELIEVER OF REALISM

Intelligent, outspoken, and impatient
Lover of nature, family, and friends
Who believed in all things perceived
unbelievable, in herself, and in the
friends she chose
Who wanted nothing more than peace,
good vibes, and to experience every
feeling known to man
Who used her mind to hold memories,
her eyes to view beauty, and her heart
to store secrets
Who gave inspiration, advice, and
trust to those she saw fit
Who said, "We don't have choices, we
have chances and if by chance we have
a choice, choose the choice that gave
you that chance."

CHARLIZE TORRES

CREATIVE, ADVENTUROUS, AND POLITE

*Lover of nature, people, and places
Who believed things happen for a
reason, and that you are free to create
your own fate and be who you want
Who wanted to travel the world, have
a name in the hall of fame, and for
people to be nice
Who used kindness, small bits of
confidence, and curiosity to understand
ways of life around the world
Who said, "Be nice to nice."*

U

NATALIE ULLOA

19 GOING ON 60... OR MAYBE 6

*Imaginative, independent, and
energetic
Lover of world peace, the number 13,
and Justin Bieber
Who believed that dogs are better than
people, feminism will save the world,
and aliens are real
Who wanted to be sincere, confident,
and always optimistic
Who used positive thinking, creativity,
and personal experiences to tell a story
Who gave the world someone to laugh
at, a relatable story, and way too much
time and energy
to celebrities
Who said, "Yikes."*

V

ELIZABETH VANDERHORST

RAINBOW DASH

Fun, crazy, and nuts
Lover of animals, food, and X-Men
superheroes and villains
Who believed in Jesus, in spirits, and
in change
Who wanted to create a loving world
with 5 emotions and world happiness
Who used a clear mind, an open mind,
and kindness
Who gave away clothes, shoes, and
games
Who said, "People that have been in
prison can get a second chance at life."

LAURYN VINCENT

CURIOUS

Independent, distant, and
communicative
Lover of researching anything,
pomeranians, and large apartments
Who believed aliens existed, anything
can happen, and that J.Cole is king
Who wanted to be successful, be happy,
and be content
Who used chocolate as a soother, ice
cream as a treat, and Kit Kats as an
energy booster
Who gave love, food, and advice
Who said, "The past is not a product of
the future, but the future is a product
of the past."

W

SUKARI WEBB

PINK LEATHER JACKET

Smart, loyal, and fun
Lover of shopping, YouTube, and
decorating
Who believed in saving the
environment, that you walk with more
confidence when your toes are painted
(even in the winter), and that Sephora
is perfect when you want to change
your nail polish color
Who wanted a peaceful world, and
endless happiness
Who gave money to people that didn't
need it and gave tips to people who
didn't deserve it

SHANYA WEATHERS

ADORABLE PRINCESS

Outspoken, friendly, and funny
Lover of animals, babies, and going out
and meeting new people
Who believed you should enjoy your
life while living
Who used patience, understanding,
and confidence
Who gave good advice, confidence
boosters, and a different, creative
mindset for living

IYANNA WEBSTER

YANNA

Sweet, memorable, and distinguished
Lover of ideas, cartoons, and food
Who believed in peace and greatness
Who wanted sleep and peace of mind
Who used her mind, herself, and peace
Who gave nothing to the world yet, but
plans to do so soon
Who said nothing at all

Acknowledgements

First of all, a huge thank you to the following 826NYC volunteers and interns for taking the time to work with us on our pieces every week in the classroom: Alexis Collazo, Leah Falk, Eben Fenton, Sam Greenhoe, Lindsay Griffiths, Genevieve Little, Alex Stein, and Kyra Sturgill. Thank you to 826NYC's Director of Education, Rebecca Darugar, for organizing this project and working with us during our editorial board meetings after-school.

We are also grateful to our teacher, Ms. Eisenberg, for helping us to be better writers and learners, and for bringing the 826NYC project into our classroom. Also, thanks to our Columbia Artists and Teachers for supporting us on this endeavor.

We are honored that Ms. Sheri Booker was able to write the foreword to this book, and we thank her for her words of wisdom and encouragement.

We'd also like to thank Sarah Azpeitia and Anne Hiatt for considering our design suggestions when creating this book and the accompanying website. A special shout-out to all of the volunteers who helped copy edit and proof this book. That means Alli Dunn, Jill Fitterling, Erin Furlong, Lindsay Griffiths, Caroline Knecht, Nora Pelizzari, Lauren Rogers, and Rachel Spurrier.

We would also like to thank our classmates, who were brave enough to share their stories and memories here. Your stories are inspiring and we are thrilled to be able to learn from you.

Lastly, thank you to *AT&T, Amazon, the New York City Department of Cultural Affairs* and the *New York State Council on the Arts* for funding this project. We are grateful for your support and for giving us this opportunity to shine.

826NYC LOCATION AND LEADERSHIP

826NYC AND THE BROOKLYN SUPERHERO SUPPLY CO.

372 FIFTH AVE
BROOKLYN, NY 11215
718.799.9884
WWW.826NYC.ORG

Joshua Mandelbaum, *Executive Director*
Rebecca Darugar, *Director of Education*
Liz Levine, *Volunteer and Programs Associate*
Sabrina Alli, *Writers' Room Coordinator*
Genevieve Little, *Programs Associate*
Miles Portek, *Programs Associate*
Kyra Sturgill, *Volunteer Associate*
Erin Cass, *Development Coordinator*
John Anspach, *Development Associate*
Chris Eckert, *Store Manager*

826NYC Programs

AFTER-SCHOOL TUTORING

We offer free tutoring five days per week for ages six-eighteen. Students work in small groups with volunteer tutors to finish homework assignments, complete twenty minutes of independent writing, and engage with various topics in our creative mini-workshops. We serve students of all skill level and interests, and work with parents and teachers to create independent learning objectives and support plans for struggling students.

EVENING AND WEEKEND WORKSHOPS

We offer free, writing-based workshops that provide in-depth instruction in a variety of subjects that schools often cannot include in their curriculum. These workshops cover topics such as college entrance essays, creating comic books, creative writing, journalism, writing poetry about the city, and filmmaking. All workshops are taught by working professionals from our volunteer base and are limited in size to ensure that students receive plenty of individual attention.

IN-SCHOOL SUPPORT FOR TEACHERS

The strength of our volunteer base allows us to provide in-school support to work with students in New York City classrooms. We recognize that large class sizes make it increasingly difficult for teachers to provide individualized feedback and guidance on research and writing. To that end, we send volunteers to the classroom to assist teachers with providing this essential one-on-one support.

HOSTED FIELD TRIPS

826NYC welcomes classes from public schools for mornings of high-energy storytelling activities. Our most popular field trip is our Storytelling and Bookmaking project, in which elementary school students write, illustrate, publish, and bind their own books in a two-hour session. At the conclusion of this trip, each student leaves with his or her own copy of the book and a newfound excitement for writing. Our other field trips cover topics such as memoir writing, screenwriting, and more.

STUDENT PUBLICATIONS

Through our writing workshops and after-school tutoring program, our volunteers work with students to help them create stories , poems, and 'zines. Because we believe that the quality of students work is greatly enhanced when they are given the chance to share it with an authentic audience, we are committed to publishing student works. By encouraging their work and by guiding them through the process of publication, we make it abundantly clear that their ideas are valued.